PRAISE FOR *GOOD SAM*

"Meserve's narrative has a . . . dry wit and well-conceived dialogue throughout. Kate's relatable qualities of self-reliance tinged with vulnerability drive this gratifying mystery-romance about finding the good guys—and knowing when to recognize them."

—*Publishers Weekly*

"In her debut novel,  good romance sparked with mystery.

—*Kirkus Reviews*

"If you are a Nicholas S̲ ̲ ̲ ̲ ̲ ̲ ̲ ̲ ̲ ̲ Evans ran, I'm betting you will like author Meserve's book *Good Sam*. Uplifting, heart wrenching, and a two-hankie read, this story is a winner."

—Cheryl Stout, Amazon Top Reviewer and Vine Voice

"This story had everything from suspense to drama. And the heartfelt ending had us smiling for days."

—*First for Women* magazine

PRAISE FOR *PERFECTLY GOOD CRIME*

"A first rate and undaunted protagonist easily carries this brisk tale. Kate is intuitive and professional, but it's her steadfast compassion that makes her truly remarkable."

—*Kirkus Reviews*

"Dete Meserve delivers a novel that is simultaneously mysterious, fascinating, and inspiring."

—BuzzFeed.com

THE
SPACE
BETWEEN

ALSO BY DETE MESERVE

Good Sam
Perfectly Good Crime

THE

SPACE

BETWEEN

DETE MESERVE

WITHDRAWN

Text copyright © 2018 Dete Meserve
All rights reserved.

Published by Lake Union, Seattle

www.apub.com

Amazon, the Amazon logo, and Lake Union are trademarks of Amazon.com, Inc., or its affiliates.

ISBN-13: 9781503901407
ISBN-10: 1503901408

Cover design by Rachel Adam Rogers

Printed in the United States of America

Silently one by one,
In the infinite meadows of heaven,
Blossomed the lovely stars,
The forget-me-nots of the angels

—Henry Wadsworth Longfellow

PART ONE

PART ONE

PROLOGUE

"What's wrong?" I asked.

Ben sat on the leather couch, his blue eyes planet-sized. Serious.

I closed the cabin door behind me, shutting out the cold wind that whipped the trees outside, and dumped an armful of firewood on the hearth.

"Everything okay?" I asked again. The wind and the hike up the hill deep in the Anza-Borrego Desert had stolen my breath.

I warmed my tingling hands by the roaring fire and turned to face him, foggy with fatigue. I'd been hoping our return to what we dubbed the Summer Triangle Haven would recharge my batteries after completing my master's thesis. But on the drive up and ever since we'd arrived, Ben seemed lost in thought. After two years together, was he having second thoughts about us?

"Sarah, there's something I want to talk about—" His voice was thick and low.

"Are you breaking up with me?" A shiver ran up my spine, but I wasn't sure if it was caused by the draft from the window or because I was afraid of what he was going to say.

He stood and crossed the room. "Actually . . . I'm asking you to marry me."

He pulled a ring box from his pocket.

"No," I whispered.

His warm smile pulled me to him. "No, as in . . . that's your answer?"

I covered my mouth with my hands. "No. As in, I can't believe you're asking me. You seemed so serious, I thought—"

"Of course I'm serious. This is the most important decision I've ever made."

It didn't sink in. "You're not breaking up with me?"

"I hope this is the beginning of our life together." He opened the box, displaying a ring with two diamonds encased in a golden infinity symbol. "Sarah Elisabeth, will you marry me?"

My breath hitched. I gazed at the ring and then at him. Then back at the ring.

"This is the part where you say yes," he whispered.

"I can't."

He blinked as though he wasn't sure he heard me. "You can't say yes?"

"How can I? I'm about to start my PhD at Caltech in a few months. Are you asking now because you don't want me to move to LA?"

He took my hands in his. "I'm asking because I can't imagine living my life without you."

"I'd be a terrible wife. I can't cook, I can't—"

"I don't want a cook. I want you."

"I would never be home, I'd be—"

"I don't care if you have to spend every waking moment peering through a telescope or writing important papers about the comparative albedo of asteroids—"

I smiled through my tears. "Albedo . . . you're actually throwing out astronomy terms like albedo at a time like this?"

"When I'm your husband, I have a feeling I'll be talking a lot about albedo and infrared and quasars and—"

I looked into his deep-blue eyes, framed by wavy brown hair—and the words rushed out. "Would you ask me again?"

He was silent for a long moment. Then he cupped my face in his hands and gently pressed his lips to mine. "Will you . . . marry me?"

"Yes," I answered, then he slipped the ring on my finger.

A day later, the ring disappeared. Somewhere in the miles of mountains and wilderness we'd traversed in the desert, it slipped from my finger and tumbled to the ground. We scoured every inch of where we'd been, scaling ridges and climbing boulders, squeezing through stands of prickly cholla, and searching in wide stretches of pale-yellow desert dandelion, wondering at first if the ring's disappearance was a sign we shouldn't get married. But as twilight fell and we stood beneath a vault of glittering stars deep in the desert, our worries fell away and we started our lives together.

CHAPTER ONE

FIFTEEN YEARS LATER

"Infinity is not a term we astronomers generally use," I say to a room full of scientists and administrators at NASA Headquarters in Washington, DC. "That's because infinity is not directly observable, and we have no evidence of its existence. But today I use the term because the major discovery we are about to unveil will give us *seemingly infinite* new insights into the birth of our planet."

My presentation, held in a sun-drenched conference room to a standing-room-only crowd of high-level NASA decision makers, is mostly a celebration. Rich blue hydrangea centerpieces cover the tables, and a sumptuous menu is planned for the lunch right after.

I tuck a strand of light-brown hair behind my ear. "And, since I've been on this quest for over a decade, it *seems* like I've spent an *infinite* amount of time seeking out this discovery," I say, which elicits scattered laughter from the scientists, who know how long it takes to make breakthroughs like this.

"I've scanned the entire sky in four infrared wavelengths, snapping pictures of three-quarters of a billion galaxies and stars throughout our universe, but, for me, finding an asteroid in Earth's orbit—a scrap of our primordial solar system—would be the greatest discovery of them all."

As I look out at their faces filled with anticipation, I feel my chest swell with shining pride. My voice catches. "And today I'm privileged to announce . . . we have found Earth's Trojan asteroid."

I glance up at the jumbo screen above my head and click the slide to a brilliant image of a sunlit planet Earth.

"Unseen by us, this Trojan asteroid has been leading us in Earth's orbit around the sun for over ten *thousand* years. Our sun shines so bright that it has been invisible to every living thing on Earth since before recorded time. But, on a hot summer night last August, our team at the Carnegie Institute of Technology used an infrared space telescope to spot our rocky escort, hidden in blinding sunlight."

Though I work to sound calm, I cannot contain the unstoppable joy in my voice. "Ladies and gentlemen, may I present to you, Earth's Trojan asteroid, 2010 TK7."

I switch the slide to an artist's rendering of the spiraling path of 2010 TK7, and the entire room erupts in applause. Several administrators leap to their feet, which prompts a room-wide standing ovation.

As I glance up at our discovery—the genesis rock that dates back to the birth of our solar system—tears gather in my eyes.

In this simplest of moments, I'm flooded with such an extravagant sense of joy and meaning that the only way to describe the feeling is to call it . . . infinite.

———

On the flight home from Washington, DC, to Los Angeles, I'm still buzzing from the NASA presentation. I have several reports to review for a new space telescope proposal that will allow us to search for planets orbiting nearby stars, but I'm so distracted by our Trojan asteroid discovery that I find myself reading the same paragraphs over and over.

That joy—that lightness—stays with me as I ride home. It's only fifteen miles from the airport, but even at one in the morning, it still takes nearly forty minutes to reach Brentwood, a neighborhood of midcentury homes and manicured lawns on the west side of LA. It's an area my husband, Ben, fell in love with last year, but I'm still getting used to its driveways lined with Land Rovers and Maseratis and the stream of pool guys, housekeepers, and nannies who make their daily pilgrimages up our tree-lined streets.

I step through my front door, drop my purse on the entryway table, and catch a glimpse of my reflection in the mirror above it. My cheeks are glowing pink as if I'd just come off the ski slopes or had been sailing. Or fallen in love.

"Ben?" I call out. No answer.

I head to the family room to find my son, Zack, on the couch, his face lit by the blue-white glow of his laptop.

"I'm going to bed in a minute," he grumbles.

"How was your class trip to Lake Hughes?"

He replies with all the sullenness of his fourteen years. "It rained almost the entire weekend."

"Is Dad home?"

"No."

"Did he say he was going to be late?"

"No," he says. "Why do you have to know where he is every second?"

I start to reply, then stop. Zack has been grounded for nearly two weeks. Right now, he thinks I overreact about everything.

I try to remember if Ben told me he was going work late. But we hadn't talked or even exchanged texts for three days while I was on my trip to and from NASA Headquarters.

I glance in the garage to see if his car is there. Empty.

I call his cell. It rings then goes to voice mail.

When are you coming home? I text.

Ben owns and runs Aurora, a top LA restaurant, so his workdays sometimes run late into the night. But it's not like him to be at work past eleven on a weekday.

?? I text.

I kick off my heels and head to the living room, where the Christmas tree lights twinkle in the dark. I breathe in the scent of fresh pine, surprised that Ben bought a tree this year. When Zack was little, we'd spend hours choosing the right one from a lot near our house, then trim it together over several nights. But it'd been a long time since we'd had a real tree, opting instead for a prelit Fraser fir look-alike. And it had been a while since Zack had shown any interest in decorating it.

I tap one of the vintage lights on the tree to induce the heat from the bulb to produce a stream of bubbles in the glass tube. The tree is a living archive of our life as a family. Baby's first ornament. Handprints in plaster. Tinfoil ornaments made by chubby five-year-old hands. Santa ornaments that Ben had collected: Biker Santa. Snorkeling Santa. Santa on the Toilet.

I'm puzzled to see a present, wrapped in silver paper, waiting beneath the tree. Addressed to me from "Santa." Ben always waits until Christmas Eve to buy and wrap presents and yet a gift is here, two weeks early. We'd had a painful discussion before I left. Was this his response?

I head back into the family room. "Dad didn't say *anything* about being late?" I ask Zack.

"What? No."

I dial his office at Aurora, but I'm not surprised when the call goes straight to voice mail. They rarely answer the phone after eleven.

I grab a small glass bottle of mineral water from the fridge and gulp it down. The water helps me think.

Maybe his phone died. Or maybe he didn't have cell phone coverage. In West Los Angeles, there are plenty of dead spots.

"Finish up and get to bed soon," I say, ruffling Zack's hair, then head upstairs to the bedroom.

———

The sound of a gunshot jolts me awake. Was it outside or in my dreams?

My heart pounds as I reach for my glasses on the nightstand and glance at the clock: 4:07 in the morning. The bed beside me is empty. *Where is Ben?*

Outside my window, I hear laughter and voices—men and women—talking loudly. I push the curtains aside and scan the front lawn and the street below. In the orange-sodium glow of the streetlights, I can make out a group of four twentysomethings stumbling down the sidewalk, holding each other up.

A boy with a mop of brown hair is kicking over the trash bins that have been set out against the curb. When they hit the asphalt, they sound like a gunshot blast, eliciting roars of laughter from the group.

I close the curtains and try calling Ben again. Voice mail. *Where is he?*

I drink more water to quell my rising fear, but it doesn't help. I wonder if he's deliberately staying out late. Is this his reaction to our discussion? Or is the present under the tree a truer sign of his feelings?

I pace the floor and consider what to do. Too soon to file a missing person's report. Call the hospitals? Where would I even start with that? I call Ben's assistant, Will. Voice mail.

I'm about to put my phone down when I notice the red voice-mail notification on my phone. How had I missed it before? The notification indicates that the call came in at 9:08 last night, but there's no caller ID.

I press the play button. The recording is eighteen seconds long and mostly intermittent white noise. I think I can hear a human voice breaking up in the background, but when I play it again, I have no idea what they're saying. Could this be from Ben?

I draw deep breaths like I remember from a yoga class taken a year ago and try to imagine Ben walking in the door as though nothing had happened, frustrated by his cell phone's lousy coverage or drained battery.

I need a distraction until Ben comes home, so I reach for a book I'd been reading about the early history of spaceflight. I know I won't be able to focus, but I hope the act of holding the book and following the words on the page will have a calming effect.

I pull on the nightstand handle, and in the dim light I can see the drawer is cluttered with a dozen or so of my books and magazines, as it always is. Except for one new item. A gun.

I switch on the light above the bed and peer into the drawer, blinking a few times in the futile hope that I imagined it.

In the corner is a black pistol. New. I shine the light from my cell phone into the drawer. Etched into the side of the gun is a large letter G and the word "lock" inside it. *Glock.* Sweat breaks out on the back of my neck. We'd never owned a gun. I'd never even held one.

I lift the gun out of the drawer. It feels cold, and heavy in my hands. I turn it over and flush with anger. It's loaded. What was Ben thinking leaving a loaded gun in the house with Zack at home? He knew the problems we'd been having with him.

Ben isn't careless like that. The gun's presence could only mean that he—or we—were in danger.

As I place it back into the drawer, I hear a loud thump outside, as though someone or something has fallen against the house in the narrow strip that runs alongside it from the front lawn to the backyard. For a brief flash, I think it's a sign that Ben is home. Maybe he's running the neighbor's annoying dog out of our yard again. Or maybe it's one of the intoxicated twentysomethings, bumbling onto our property.

I hear it again, heavier this time.

From the second floor there isn't a good view of the side yard, so I rush to my office in the next room and wake up the computer screen, clicking on the security icon to view the camera feeds outside and inside the house.

Ten views of our house pop up on the screen, but there is nothing—and no one—moving on any of them. The camera in the side yard shows bare dirt and a couple of bags of potting soil. I exhale sharply. Probably a possum. This side of LA, they're big and fat, feasting on all the citrus that falls from our trees and the expensive leftovers in our trash cans.

Then on the camera that surveys the front steps and yard, I glimpse someone in dark pants zipping across the frame. The action happens so fast I can't tell if it's a man or woman or child. I'm not even entirely sure I saw it.

I run to my bedroom window and slowly pull back the corner of the curtains a fraction of an inch. From the high vantage point on the second floor, I have a full view of the front yard and street. Completely empty. I stand there for a long moment, watching for signs of movement, afraid to make any sound that might alert anyone below to my presence at the window. Suddenly a man darts out from behind the sprawling oak tree, exits the yard, and sprints down the sidewalk. One of the young partyers trying to rejoin the group?

I return to the computer to play back what the cameras saw over the last five minutes and see that "Record" is not checked. Had Zack unchecked the box so that the system wouldn't capture anything?

We had installed the security system two weeks ago after coming home and finding Zack passed out in the backyard. Eventually, we got him to confess that he and two friends had regularly got together at our house after school—while Ben and I were still at work—to drink and smoke pot.

That explained the grades that had plummeted from always-on-the-dean's-list to Cs and Ds, why tens and twenties had been missing from my purse, and why liquor bottles disappeared from the cabinet in my office.

Zack swore it wouldn't happen again, but two days after that solemn promise, a neighbor informed us that his group of friends had expanded to five or six, and several of them were drunk and diving in our pool.

Our home-security firm offered us a package of ten cameras with microphones installed throughout the property, which we could also monitor from our phones or laptops. The system recorded round-the-clock so we could play back the feed from any camera any-time, and I regularly logged in from work to check on Zack after school.

Curious to see what the cameras *had* captured, I click on the data archive and discover the entire file has been deleted. FILE EMPTY.

After years working with data at the Carnegie Institute of Technology, I know my way around recovering erased or missing digital data. I get to work on the one-terabyte digital video recorder, running several utilities to recover the lost data. Nothing works.

I try one more utility, and after a few minutes, it turns up a seven-teen-second segment. I click on it. The clip is from the camera perched near the ceiling in the foyer and shows an image of the front door from the inside. The time stamp reads 11:30 a.m. Tuesday. Yesterday.

I watch as Ben approaches the front door and opens it. A blonde woman dressed in a stylish dark suit stands on the doorstep. "Simone," Ben says, then they embrace. The clip shuts off.

Ben had never mentioned anyone named Simone. And what was she doing at our house at 11:30 on a weekday morning?

I watch the clip several times, locking in on details. The way she hugs him seems to start collegial enough, but the hug apparently went on past the end of the clip. Had it morphed into something else? The audio is faint, so it's impossible to read if Ben is saying her name with any particular feeling. He doesn't seem surprised, though. It looks as if he had been expecting her.

I'm not one of those women who worries that her husband is cheat-ing. His restaurant business has him surrounded by beautiful, young women every day, so it didn't take me long to figure out that Ben's fidel-ity is something completely out of my control.

Still, I have a sick feeling in the pit of my stomach as I watch this clip for the fourth time.

Is Ben having an affair? Is that why he isn't home?

———

A few minutes later, I try Will's cell again, and this time he answers on the third ring. "Sarah, everything okay?" I hear people talking in the background as if he's at a party. At 4:30 in the morning.

"Have you seen Ben?" I say, trying to steady my voice.

"He's not home?"

"No. Not answering his phone, either. Or text."

"He didn't come into the restaurant—worked from home all day today . . . well, yesterday. Called me about nine yesterday morning and said he had to prep for the trial."

I'm confused. Ben had filed a lawsuit against his Aurora partners and was set to testify in January. "Isn't the trial scheduled for *after* Christmas?"

"We just found out his legal team was able to get it moved up. Ben goes on the stand *next week,* so he's supposed to be meeting nonstop with lawyers the rest of this week."

The new trial date catches me by surprise. "You think he could be meeting with the lawyers now?"

The noise around him quiets. It sounds like he's gone into another room. "Not this late. But, just in case, I can call the lead attorney to find out."

I grip the phone. "I know that Ben had a meeting with some-one named Simone here at the house yesterday. Is she part of the legal team?"

"I know everyone on Ben's legal team and there isn't—" His voice shakes a little as he realizes what I might be asking. "It's late and my memory's not so hot. Ben works with a lot of people and I can't keep track of all of them. Let me check in with the attorney and see what's going on."

He hangs up, leaving me sitting in the dark.

The silence in the room is deafening as next week's trial date sinks in.

A few months ago, Ben had filed suit against his Aurora partners claiming they stole millions in profits from the restaurant he started, which had quickly ascended to LA's top ten—lauded by critics for its modern American cuisine with a multicultural flair, its top-shelf American whiskey selection, and lavish VIP booths that often cater to a celebrity crowd, some of whom are so famous they are only known by their first names. With the trial date being moved up, I'm sure he'll be in long meetings with his lawyers. But at this hour?

I rise and head to Zack's room. His lanky frame is sprawled across his bed, face down, his feet dangling off the edge. At fourteen, he's already taller than I am, taking after Ben's side of the family. He's still dressed in jeans and a T-shirt and is sleeping on top of the rumpled comforter.

"Zack, did you talk to your dad—did you see your dad—anytime yesterday?"

He doesn't move. "Can you ask me in the morning?"

"This is important or I wouldn't be asking you. When did you see him?"

His eyes flutter open now, but his body remains inert. "After school. We hung out for a little bit, then he said he had to take off."

"He didn't say where?"

"No. Why would he?"

"Did you do the Christmas tree with him?"

"*Mom,* why do you ask stuff like that?"

I sigh. "I'm just trying to figure out what happened yesterday."

"He did the tree while I was at school. I guess. I don't *know.*" His tone is rude, as though I'd asked him to calculate the foci of a hyperbola while he's sleeping.

"Did you . . . did you do anything to the computer in my office? The cameras aren't recording."

His brown eyes spring open. "*No, Mom.* Why are you asking me that?"

"Zack—"

"No, it doesn't matter what I say. You're never going to trust me."

"I'm just trying to understand why the cameras aren't recording and the drive has been erased."

He buries his head in his pillow. "*How would I know?* You think I would break into your computer to do that?"

My cell phone rings. It's Will, so I grab it before it finishes the first ring.

"Stuart doesn't like the sound of what's going on, so he'd like to meet with you this morning, around nine."

"Stuart?"

"The lead attorney on Ben's case."

Ben rarely talked about his legal team, so I'm not surprised I don't know any of the players.

"And we've called the police."

"He's only been missing a few hours, I thought police—"

"A guy in Ben's position disappears just days before a high-profile trial? They'll probably be at your house before we even hang up."

CHAPTER TWO

DAY ONE

Detective James Dawson from the Los Angeles Police Department's Missing Persons Unit appears on my doorstep three hours later. His wavy reddish-brown hair is carefully clipped to department standards, and he has the lean, strong build and posture of someone who works out religiously.

"Dr. Mayfield?" he says, shaking my hand with a firm grip that jams my wedding ring into my palm.

"Call me Sarah," I say, letting him in.

He heads straight for the living room even though I had hoped we could sit in the kitchen where it's warmer. He looks around the room and seems to be seeing what I see. A perfect Christmas tree nestled in the corner, a wood-burning fireplace, and classic slate-gray furniture accented with rich walnut that my designer friend, Annette, had selected.

"Nice tree," he says casually, his eyes examining every ornament, every detail. "You do this?"

I pull my hair into a low ponytail. "No. My husband's creation."

He settles himself on the couch but doesn't take his eyes off the tree. "Look, Sarah, most—over seventy percent—of the missing adults we investigate come back within seventy-two hours. How long has it been since you saw your husband?"

"My son was with him yesterday afternoon. But his car is missing, and he doesn't answer his phone."

He writes in his notebook. "And when did *you* last see your husband?"

"Four days ago, actually. I left for DC to make a presentation at NASA Headquarters."

"You work for NASA?"

"I'm an astronomer at the Carnegie Institute of Technology. CIT. Working on a space telescope for NASA."

He smiles, clearly surprised. "What were you in DC for?"

"We've discovered an asteroid that has been hiding undetected in Earth's orbit for thousands of years."

The news doesn't register. I've just shared information about one of the most profound recent discoveries in our solar system, and he acts as though I just told him about my favorite laundry detergent.

"Is anything missing or out of place? Broken?"

I wonder if I should tell him about the gun. If I do, I have the feeling—right or wrong—that he'd take it away as some kind of evidence. But if Ben bought a gun and hid it in my nightstand, he must have had a reason to think we needed it. Even though I have no idea why—or for that matter, how to use it—I decide to keep quiet about it for now.

"Nothing is missing, as far as I can tell."

"I understand your husband was set to testify in a trial on Monday? What's that about?"

"Ben had filed a lawsuit against his partners claiming they stole millions from the restaurant he owns with them."

"Aurora, right? Your husband owns it with actor Michael Hayden?"

"Yes, and two other partners."

17

He holds up a photo on his iPad. "This your husband?" It's a photo of Ben on the red carpet at the grand opening for Aurora. He looks especially attractive here, with a two-day beard and his hair perfectly mussed to look like he barely did anything, even if it took twenty minutes to achieve.

I nod.

"He looks familiar. Have I seen him in the movies?"

I'm not surprised he asks that. My husband is handsome, even by Hollywood standards. The years have improved his looks, and now his thick brown hair and blue eyes have many likening him to an older version of Chris Hemsworth.

"He's not an actor."

He doesn't take his eyes off the photo. "Do you think it's possible he spent the night with . . . with a friend or—"

I feel the heat rise in my cheeks. "Are you asking if he's having an affair? That's the obvious question, right? Someone who looks like he does. Married to a scientist wife. That's clearly what's going on here. It certainly couldn't be connected to the upcoming trial where he's testifying against some very powerful men about millions—"

He squares his shoulders. "We've got to cover all the bases here, Sarah. And to do that, some of my questions are going to be uncomfortable. Did you hear from him during your trip?"

"No."

"Is that unusual?"

"Not really. The NASA presentations are especially intense . . . there's not much time for anything else . . ."

His eyes take me in. I think he sees my delicate features—high cheekbones, light-brown hair, and fair skin—and assumes my work is lightweight enough that I should be able to call my husband a few times daily while I'm in DC. He can't imagine that I was the one making the NASA presentation or that I'm the person directing the work of the three-hundred-fifty-million-dollar space telescope that spotted the Trojan asteroid.

"He didn't leave a note or anything?"

"Nothing."

"So you came home last night at . . . ?"

I rub my neck. "One. Or around that time. I had a late flight from DC."

He's silent as he writes a few things in his notebook. "I see security cameras everywhere. We're going to assume he'll return, but if he doesn't, can you give us access to the footage?"

"We just got the system. I checked it early this morning and apparently didn't set it up to record correctly."

He shakes his head. Writes something down. "Depending on what happens, we may want whatever you got."

Zack comes scrambling down the stairs then, slinging a backpack over his shoulder. He skids to a stop when he sees Detective Dawson.

"This is my son, Zack," I say. "Dad still hasn't come home."

His face falls. It's clear he thought I'd been overreacting last night.

"When did you last see your dad?" James asks.

"Yesterday. Afternoon."

"What time?"

Zack makes eye contact with him. "He was here when I got home from school. Around three thirty? He took off later. Around five thirty, I think."

"Did he say where he was headed?"

Zack looks troubled. "I don't remember, exactly. Maybe he was going to work?"

"I talked with his assistant," I say. "And he said Ben didn't come into the office all day. He worked from home."

Zack glances at his phone. "I'm going to be late for the bus. Should I go?"

"You can be late to school," James answers. "Have a seat."

The color drains from Zack's face, and he slowly drops his backpack to the floor. He enters the living room and sits beside me. I place my hand on his shoulder and feel the tension beneath my fingertips.

"What did your dad talk to you about?" James asks.

"Just, you know, guy stuff."

"Did he seem nervous about anything? Anything seem wrong?"

Zack shakes his head, his thickly lashed brown eyes trying to eke out the meaning behind the question. "No. Nothing."

"And he left in his car?"

"I guess so, but I didn't see. I mean, how else would he leave?"

James writes in his notebook. "And what did you do after he left?"

He shrugs. "Homework."

"And after that?"

"I went to karate class."

"What time did you get back?"

Zack looks at me before he answers. Except for his twice-a-week karate practice, Zack is grounded. After class, he's supposed to come straight home.

"Around nine."

"And no sign of your dad when you came home?"

Zack shakes his head.

"Did your dad say anything to you before he left?"

Zack thinks about this for a moment. "Yeah, it was kind of strange. He told me to keep the doors locked and set the alarm."

"Does he always tell you to do that?"

Zack looks at me again. "No. Never."

———

Despite its reputation as the place where O. J. Simpson lived and where his ex-wife was murdered, our Brentwood neighborhood otherwise is known as one of the safest in LA. Its wide streets lined with expensive cars and sprawling Spanish mansions make it one of the most sought-after places to live—it's not somewhere where you keep your doors locked and set the alarm while you're home.

Ben's instructions to Zack put me on edge. Were we in danger?

The detective doesn't seem fazed, however, because at that moment our home, with its coffered ceilings, towering Christmas tree, and living room with a view of the sparking pool, looks like a peaceful, safe haven. He doesn't seem overly concerned about the person I saw on the security cameras running through the front yard early this morning, either. "I'll take a look around before I go."

After the detective leaves, I switch on the alarm then head to the kitchen, where Zack is finishing a bagel and scrolling through his phone.

"I think you should stay home. Just for today," I tell him, although I'm not sure how long it will be before I feel safe again.

His voice is low, but not as deep as Ben's. "I have to turn in my history paper, and I have a big test in algebra."

"I'll call the school and let them know . . . what's happening," I say gently. "You can email your paper, and I'm sure they'll let you take the test another day."

He exhales a shaky breath. Except for the very few times he's been sick, he's never missed an entire day of school. Staying home makes this all the more real. "When do you think Dad will be back?"

I look into his brown eyes and struggle to find words that might reassure him. "I hope soon. Maybe his car broke down. Maybe that's all this is . . ."

After Zack heads upstairs to his room, I scour Ben's home office, hoping to find some clues to what happened. I'm not surprised that his laptop is missing because he usually shuttles it back and forth to the office. On his desk, alongside a rusty can of WD-40 and a flashlight, is a neat pile of papers. I review each document but see nothing but the usual bills, a request for donations to Zack's school's annual fundraiser, and a couple of receipts for coffee.

I lean back in his chair and text my sister, Rachel: *Ben didn't come home last night. Police are looking for him.*

Ten seconds later she types back: *Oh no! Tell me what I can do to help.*

Not sure yet.

I can be there in a couple of hours.

My sister lives in San Francisco, a few hours away by plane, but in recent years we haven't been particularly close. She's three years older than I am and can be overdramatic in tense situations. And bossy. Not what Zack and I need right now.

Not yet. I'll keep you posted. Call you soon.

OK will check in with you later, she texts and signs off with a double heart emoji.

I set my phone down and close my eyes, my anxiety soaring. And not just because Ben is missing.

I had lied to police. Told the detective I came straight home from the airport and then realized Ben was missing. I left out the part about drinking with my CIT colleague at the airport bar. Celebrating with four . . . or maybe it was five . . . shots of tequila. We were happy about our asteroid discovery, the two of us, and the liquor helped us laugh in a way we didn't—we couldn't—at work.

Aaron hadn't been invited to attend the NASA meeting. That privilege was given to me and CIT's Director of Astrophysics and Space Research, Steven Webster. So when I arrived back in LA, I was surprised to see Aaron walking a few feet ahead of me in the American Airlines terminal. He had been visiting family in Atlanta and his plane arrived just five minutes before mine. He wanted to know every detail about the NASA presentation, so we caught up over a quick drink. Which turned into five. And three hundred missing minutes between the time I landed and the time the driver dropped me off at my house.

I was stupid not to tell police the truth. Especially when they were eventually going to find out anyway. But I knew what they'd think. They'd assume any woman who's getting drunk in a bar late at night with a man who's not her husband is unstable. Unreliable.

Maybe responsible for her husband's disappearance.

CHAPTER THREE

With a name like Stuart Baxter, I expect Ben's attorney to be British. And because he's the lead attorney, I also expect him to be older—in his fifties or sixties. But Stuart Baxter is forty-two years old, according to his bio on the firm's website. Just three years older than I am.

"Sorry to be meeting you for the first time under these circumstances. I came as quickly as I could," he says.

"When did you last see Ben?" I ask, ushering him into the living room.

He threads his fingers through surprisingly glossy blond hair, then drops himself onto the same sofa where Detective Dawson had been sitting twenty minutes earlier. He sheds a cobalt-blue sport coat.

"Not since last Wednesday. We were successful at getting the trial date moved up, but Ben had said he was dealing with some big stuff, and so we'd planned to meet all day today."

"Big stuff?"

"He didn't really elaborate."

I walk him through the details of everything that's happened over the last twelve hours but leave out the part about the DVR. He raises an eyebrow when I tell him about the gun.

"That's strange. Have there been any recent robberies or break-ins around here that might have prompted that?"

I shake my head.

"Maybe he went someplace to get a little R&R before the trial. Do you guys have a second home, maybe a beach house or a cabin in the mountains?"

"No, this is our entire real-estate empire," I say, but my sarcasm is lost on him.

"What about his parents? Any chance he could've gone to visit them?"

"Not without telling me. His mother lives in Chicago. His dad has passed away."

"He has a sister, right?"

I nod.

"Okay, I'd like you to get started by calling his sister, his mom, and any close friends. Check in. Will is doing the same for his work contacts. I'm going to want a list of everyone with phone numbers and contact info."

I'd begun a list of friends and family, but held off doing anything with it, not wanting to worry anyone needlessly. Between our family, work contacts, neighbors, friends from Zack's school, and other friends, the list was enormous. I imagine dialing all their numbers—can you break such troubling news by email or social media? Where would I even start?

"In the meantime, we're monitoring his credit cards. So far, there's been zero activity since Tuesday when he spent something like fifteen dollars at the drug store around the corner. We're working on getting access to his cell phone records. When did you last see him?"

"Four days ago. I've been in DC making a presentation to NASA. But our son says Ben left here around five thirty yesterday and was heading to Aurora."

"He never made it there," he says without even trying to soften the blow. "Something happened to him in the five miles between here and the restaurant."

My voice is breathy. "*What* could've happened?"

"Look," he says, leaning forward. "We have a lot of evidence in this trial. It looks like Ben would prevail. And the other side knew it. I don't want to alarm you . . . but let me put it this way: at least two of his partners are highly motivated to make this trial go away."

I feel my heart hammering in my throat. "You mean to make Ben 'disappear'?"

He looks down and studies the pattern on the carpet. "If Ben prevailed in this trial, which it looked like he would, they had a lot to lose. A lot. What I'm saying is that the stakes are very high, and in situations like this, you never know what people are capable of."

"Mom, you've got to see this," Zack says, rushing into the living room. "Dad's on Channel Eleven." He hands me his phone with a video that's playing. "Well, not Dad himself, but they're talking about him being missing."

I'm surprised at how the media picked up on the story so fast. Standing on my front lawn, a dark-haired reporter named Kate Bradley is saying, "Ben Mayfield is the co-owner of Aurora, one of LA's top restaurants, and was scheduled to testify against his partners, including movie star Michael Hayden, about the disappearance of several million dollars in Aurora revenues. Sources say that Mayfield was to present tremendous evidence that would favor his case."

"We're going to need more help," Stuart says. And for the first time, I hear fear in his voice.

———

I have a bigger fear. If Ben stays missing for very much longer, I know that police are going to ask again for the security-system DVR. Even though the drive may be erased and only seventeen seconds is currently recoverable, they've got sophisticated technology to recover the data on that hard drive. All of it.

But Ben erased that DVR for some reason. Was there something he didn't want anyone—even me—to see? I consider the possibility that he accidentally erased it, but that seems unlikely, because he also went into a separate part of the program to stop the cameras from recording, too. That's not a casual mistake. It seems deliberate. And if Ben had a reason to delete the footage, I need to recover that data and figure out what it is before handing the DVR over to police.

And there's something else I don't want them to see. Something I don't want anyone to see. The clip with Simone is not the problem. The problem is what I said to Ben the day I left to make the NASA presentation. What I said in the office where the camera and microphone were recording every word.

I think we're broken.

Whenever I hear about a woman being unhappy in her marriage, it's almost always assumed to be the man's fault. He was cheating or ignoring her or abusive. But Ben hadn't done any of those things.

I had loved him deeply and was happy—joyful—in the life we built together. Until the strain of our everyday, complicated lives of working and raising a teenage son brought out the worst in each of us. Until the life we lived together no longer bore any resemblance to the blissful place where we'd started.

I know that sounds unquantifiable. Shouldn't I have a list of what drove me to feeling our marriage had reached a place of hopelessness? Isn't that what we always hear when a friend complains about her spouse: He is rude. He is never home. He is . . .

But this wasn't about what he *does*. This was about what he saw. With each passing day, I'd become invisible to him. Like the Trojan asteroid, I was dancing in his orbit day after day, but was completely unnoticed by him.

For months, maybe longer, we had barely exchanged a single word that wasn't about house repairs, the cars, Zack's problems, the schedules we were juggling, or the lack of groceries in the fridge.

And when I talked about the discoveries we were making about 2010 TK7, he was always distracted, eyes glued to the blue-light glow of his phone, scrolling through something that was clearly more important to him. "That's good," he'd say absently.

How could this discovery, which was so important—no, essential—to me, mean so little to him?

Once, we played. We geeked out looking at the stars or watching sci-fi shows on TV, then snuck back to bed after breakfast waffles. I adored him like crazy. I longed to be with him, to touch him. And yet even though he was still very attractive by all measurable standards, I no longer saw the man I married.

We were broken. And with each passing day, I found myself disappearing from him, visible within plain sight but completely unseen by him. He seemed to have forgotten me as his playful, funny geek, but instead I'd become a kind of generic person who shared responsibility for Zack and the house and spent too much time being paid to look at the stars.

I can't remember the last time we laughed together. Although I'm sure he probably laughs when he's at work. When I'm not around.

———

Richard Jenkins has a voice like a fine single-malt whisky, smoky with a smooth finish. He shapes every word so that it feels like it's meant for you alone, and he speaks as though he understands you better than anyone in the world.

Some people find that skill mesmerizing. I'm not one of them. Last year he was slapped with multimillion-dollar fines for unpaid back taxes and bragged about evading them.

He is also one of the three partners named in Ben's lawsuit.

"Sarah," he says to me on the phone. His voice drips with concern and care. "I just heard about Ben on the news."

It's early afternoon, and outside my kitchen window, the sun streams through the stand of tall palm trees that line my backyard. For a moment, I imagine this all has a logical answer. Ben's car broke down, so he waited for repairs. He's going to walk in the front door any second.

My voice is unsteady. "When did you see him last?"

"Well, you can imagine it's been a few weeks."

I settle into a chair. "What can you tell me that might help us figure out where he is?"

"The media are making it sound like we, his partners, have something nefarious to do with his disappearance." His voice is gritty now. On edge. "But we all know that's not true. And if you're the source of that lie, Sarah, you need to stop."

I feel a chill run up my spine. In person, Richard is 240 pounds with slicked-back hair and a swollen face that's perpetually red, which makes him look he's always primed for a fistfight. "I'm not your employee or your partner, Richard. And I'm not here to take instructions from you. I'm hoping you can help me find my husband."

"His lawsuit is bullshit." The whisky tones are gone, replaced by pure vinegar. "Your husband was stealing from *us*. At least one million. Likely more."

It feels like he just slapped me. "That's insane," I say, louder than I intend. "Ben wouldn't steal from anyone."

"I've always liked you, Sarah. Admired you, actually. You're highly accomplished. Smart. But Ben isn't the saint they're portraying in the media. Ben was stealing from us."

"I think you're telling me a lie, Richard. Because if you had any such evidence, *you'd* be filing the lawsuit instead of the other way around.

29

But your flimsy accusations are not the point. Ben is missing. Do you know where he is?"

There's a long silence on the phone. "No idea."

"Call me when you do," I say, then hang up.

I wander through the house, trying to shake off his accusations. I can't imagine Ben stole millions from his partners. Yet, for a brief moment, I wonder if that's what's been financing this house, our expensive cars, and Zack's private-school education. Is that why Ben has been preoccupied lately?

How much do I really know about how Ben does business?

I step into our bedroom and everything seems frozen in time—as though Ben could walk through the door any minute. Yet all that once seemed familiar and ordinary seems strange now, imbued with new significance.

I touch my hand to Ben's denim shirt at the foot of our bed. It smells like him. Old Spice, his favorite for as long as I'd known him. I hold the shirt up to my nose and remember him wearing it smudged with dirt a few summers ago when things were better between us. He had a flat tire and the towing company had said it'd be forty-five minutes before they could get here, but Ben was sure he could change it in less time than that. Except he couldn't. Ben had many talents, but fixing things wasn't one of them, so he didn't get past trying to get the flat tire off the wheel. He'd stormed into the house frustrated, tossed his tools onto the kitchen counter, and marched upstairs.

I'd followed him to our bedroom. "You okay?"

He wrapped me in his arms, his scent swirling around me, then pressed a lingering kiss to my lips. "I am now."

As I place the shirt back on the bed, I realize it's been months since we touched like that, and I can't remember what it feels like to kiss him. And have him kiss me back.

I head back downstairs and notice that his keys, cell phone, and wallet are missing from the green ceramic bowl where they usually sit on the entryway table. Then I glance through the trash in the kitchen—a frozen pizza box and empty milk carton—in blind hope that he'd written me a note and that it had fallen into the trash somehow. Nothing.

In the hushed stillness of the afternoon, I feel as though the house is holding a secret.

CHAPTER FOUR

It would be easy to jump to the conclusion that Ben's disappearance is because of his lawsuit against his Aurora partners. But our brains are masters at self-deception. Long ago when our ancestors roamed the plains searching for food, jumping to conclusions about the location of a predator helped us survive. In today's world, our tendency to do the same thing makes us lean toward what appears to be the most obvious, but perhaps wrong, answers.

As I head to the shower, I wonder if presuming Ben's disappearance is linked to the lawsuit might have us ignoring alternate explanations, ones that might actually lead us to where he is. I'm in the shower for all of three minutes when I hear the doorbell buzz.

Whoever it is leans on the bell for an entire five seconds without break.

I feel a jolt of relief, imagining what it could mean: *Ben is home.*

I throw on a terrycloth robe, scramble downstairs, then peer through the peephole. Standing on the doorstep is a man dressed in a black tweed suit.

"How can I help you?" I call out.

"Jeff Rosen. I'm the attorney Ben Mayfield called."

Attorney? I hesitate a moment then take in his appearance. His slicked-back brown hair says he's someone in finance, but his leather briefcase definitely reads attorney.

I open the door.

"Sorry I'm thirty minutes late. Is Ben still here?"

"Why are you looking for him here?"

He pulls a business card from his suit pocket and hands it to me. "He asked me to meet him here this morning."

I glance at the card: Jeff Rosen, Criminal Defense Attorney.

My first thought is that Ben called him to defend himself against his partners' claims that he was stealing from them. But considering his partners hadn't actually filed a lawsuit to that effect, and Ben already had a raft of attorneys representing him on the Aurora trial, that didn't make sense. Then I notice the address on his card: Fifth Avenue in Manhattan.

"You're based in Manhattan?"

He nods. "I was already out here on business," he says, rocking on his heels. "So I offered to meet him in person this morning. Where can I find him?"

The words are stalled in my throat. "My husband is missing. He didn't come home last night."

His smile fades. "I'm sorry, I—"

"It's been all over the news here."

"I haven't been paying attention to—"

"Can you tell me why he needed your services? I mean, you don't call a defense attorney unless you've been charged with some kind of criminal activity, right?"

He clears his throat. "Unfortunately, because of attorney-client privilege, I can't discuss your husband's situation."

I glance at his business card then back at him. "You can imagine that's not the answer I need to be hearing right now."

His expression softens. "I don't mean to be insensitive. I can say in all honesty that your husband didn't tell me any details of his situation except to say that he needed an urgent in-person consultation."

"But why did he call you when he's already working with a law firm here in LA?"

He hesitates a moment before answering. "He said he needed an attorney with experience in Manhattan."

———

There are a hundred things I know I should do, including getting started on calling Ben's family, but instead, I wrap the one-terabyte security-system DVR in a beach towel and stuff it in my black tote bag.

I'm certain that the clues to the hours and minutes before Ben's disappearance have been captured by our cameras at home and are recorded on the drive. If I can recover the data, I hope it will help me understand why there's a gun in my nightstand, why Ben erased the DVR, and why he asked for a meeting with a New York criminal defense attorney. And I know exactly who can help me unlock it.

Aaron.

I'd watched him do it before when one of our computers crashed at CIT. The engineers were unable to recover the data from the complicated architecture of the array and were about to resort to restoring the backup when Aaron, our lead programmer, came up with an unconventional approach. And it worked.

I sling the tote bag on my shoulder and head out the front door. Although I'd seen the TV news report earlier, I'm surprised at how many reporters and cameramen are camped out on the parkway in front of my house. There are nearly two dozen, and when they see me, they rush forward, pushing cameras and microphones in my direction.

"What can you tell us about your husband's disappearance?" asks a tall blonde reporter from one of the local TV stations.

I have no idea what to say. "I'm . . . overwhelmed with what's happened to our family," I begin. "I appreciate all of your attention and concern for helping Ben. But I'm in no frame of mind to talk to anyone about it right now. I hope you understand."

The next few minutes are a surreal blur as I slip into the car and slowly maneuver it through a street crawling with reporters and crowded with news vans. I have a sense that the media could help us find Ben, but I have no idea yet how to make that happen.

On the drive to CIT, I call Ben's mother and tell her the news. Silence meets my words, and I worry that I've traumatized her. She had a stroke last month and hasn't fully recovered. "Oh no," she says, and I hear her soft Texas accent even though she's lived in Chicago for forty years.

"Have you talked to him lately?" I say, trying to sound calm.

"Not since Sunday. He talked a lot about the trial. He seemed worried about that . . . and a lot of things."

I wonder if Ben had confided in his mother about our discussion. He'd often shared things with her that I hadn't even thought to discuss with my mother when she was alive.

"You may get a call from detectives or other people on Ben's legal team." I draw a deep breath. "But don't worry. We're going to find him. This is all a big misunderstanding."

"Oh Sarah. I wish that would be true," she says, then breaks down crying. They're a mother's tears. Deep. Raw.

I listen, knowing there are no words that will make this easier for either of us.

Her voice is barely above a whisper. "Please give him a chance, Sarah."

———

Energy shoots through the soles of my feet as I take the DVR straight to Aaron's office in Building 18, a sprawling, block-long laboratory on CIT's 168-acre campus that not only houses the Space Systems Laboratory, where Aaron and I work, but also a wind tunnel and a massive indoor flight facility.

I find Aaron sitting behind two large monitors in his office on the top floor. He's sporting four-day stubble and scanning a screen full of Python code in a program he and his team have been developing. I close the door behind me.

He looks up, puzzled, but then a slow smile slips across his face, remembering last night. "My head hurts. You?"

"Everything hurts."

I sit in the chair across from him but don't know where to start. How to explain what has happened in the less than twelve hours since we left together from the airport bar.

I pull the DVR out of my tote bag, unwrap it. "My husband is missing."

His eyes are gentle. "What? What happened?"

I ramble on about the lawsuit, the gun, the security-system cameras, and the erased DVR, aware that I sound like someone in shock. Last night we were drinking tequila and celebrating a major discovery. Now I must sound like someone who can't grasp that this is what my life has suddenly become.

He fixes a pair of dark-blue eyes on me. "Let me help. What can I do?"

I lay the DVR on the desk and take a moment to organize my thoughts. "I think the answers to what happened in the hours before Ben disappeared might be on this drive. But I've only been able to recover one seventeen-second clip."

I explain all the utilities I've run, what I've already tried that didn't work.

"Do you want me to see what else I can recover?"

"Yeah." I draw a deep breath and feel the constriction in my chest. "There's no one better at this kind of data recovery than you. But, it's probably best if you don't look at anything you recover."

He shifts in his chair. "What am I getting myself into?"

I glance down at my hands and see they are clenched into tight fists. "Look, it appears to have been erased by a fairly high-powered scrub utility, which makes me think it was deliberate. Did Ben erase it? I don't know. But if he did, he must have had a reason. And I need to find out what that was."

He leans forward and doesn't say anything for a moment. I look at him then, and that is my mistake.

Sometimes when I look at him, I completely forget I'm a nearly forty-year-old married woman with a teenage son.

It's not simply that he is attractive, with eyes the color of the night sky. He is enormously talented. He can develop anything in any programming language. Can instantly spot an error in chunks of code and fix it. I write Python fluently, but the other languages didn't come as easily for me. Aaron is like a universal translator. He can interpret whatever we need to happen and think through the complex steps to do it in whatever program language we are dealing with.

And he shares my obsession with discovery, especially with the search for the Trojan asteroid. The night we confirmed the asteroid with optical telescopes around the globe, he hugged me, and the room spun around as if we had stepped into a kaleidoscope.

I suspect he found me attractive, even though he had never once said anything to give me that impression. So maybe it had been my imagination that his gaze met mine and held it for longer than it should. Or that he smiled at me when I was talking. Scientists and programmers aren't always known for being the best at social cues. Maybe what I thought was attraction was simply some kind of social tic.

But attraction is purposeful. We are in control over it. Never surprised by it.

So was I choosing to be attracted to Aaron? Or was it how it felt? Inevitable.

"I'll do it," he says. "But the results could be messy. The files may have been recorded chronologically, but there's no telling in what order we'll be able to recover the data or whether we'll be able to stitch it together in the way you want."

"Understood. The data is highly sensitive so—"

"I'll use my private encrypted server and send you an invitation to sign in, then deliver data dumps if I can retrieve anything."

I suddenly feel like I have a low-grade fever and decide it's because I've looked at him too long. "Thank you."

I stand. He's dressed casually, wearing a black fleece jacket and a white T-shirt. I shouldn't be distracted by that, but I am. I move my gaze to a diagram on the bulletin board by his desk instead of looking at him.

He picks up the DVR. "Last night was . . . confusing and amazing," he says in a low voice.

"Yes, to both."

Then I make the mistake of looking at him again. And now it's my turn to smile slowly.

It's all your fault, I think. *It's all your fault that I like you too much.*

———

What is wrong with me? My husband is missing and I'm thinking about another man. It's as if an illness—a madness?—has taken over my brain and body, squelching reason.

I've rarely been confronted with a situation I couldn't handle, and this is the first time that I feel powerless to control my own thoughts. My feelings. I've run through all the rational theories—midlife crisis, too much estrogen, too little estrogen, or complacency with my marriage—and rejected them all.

I resolve—no, promise—that I will not think about Aaron again. I won't let my mind linger back to our time together last night. I will wipe my brain free of him, just like the erased hard drive.

I actually believe I have that kind of willpower.

In the hot sunlight, I head to my boss's office in Building 37. Steven Webster is a no-nonsense guy with self-professed OCD about organization, and his office reflects that. He has a small stack of reports on his desk, but otherwise every other surface is immaculate and clutter-free. There's not even a sign that he has a wife and three kids—not a photograph or a crayon drawing anywhere to disturb the minimalist quality of his office setting.

I tell him that Ben is missing, and he immediately encourages me to take whatever time I need to sort it out. The deadline is looming on our twelve-hundred-page presentation to NASA—a proposal for a brand-new two-hundred-million-dollar space telescope that will look for planets orbiting the brightest stars in our galaxy. Even though he talks as though it's all going to work out, I can see he's already developing a plan for someone else to take over for me if Ben isn't found soon.

I don't tell him that police think this is related to Ben's upcoming trial against his partners, which include movie star Michael Hayden. CIT is notoriously conservative about such things. With so much government funding in play, they don't want to be associated with the sensational or anything that might tarnish their upstanding reputation. If Ben's disappearance causes too much of a media sensation—if I get too much attention for the wrong reasons—I know they will choose someone "less complicated" to lead the next space telescope mission.

I leave his office in a whirl of emotions—confusion mixed with anger and uncertainty. In less than twenty-four hours, my stable and reliable life suddenly feels volatile, careening out of control.

I'm a fizz of nerves as I drive back home, but I try to distract myself from that buzzy feeling by calling Ben's sister, Julia, from the car.

I explain everything. It's easier this time, maybe because I've had a chance to say it aloud a few times already. But the words still sound surreal as they race out of my mouth.

"Oh my god," she shouts into the phone. Julia is known for being effusive, but this is loud, even for her. "Did anyone check the hospitals?"

"I'm sure police are checking. Why?"

"Maybe he had another kidney stone."

"What do you mean *another* kidney stone?"

She sounds annoyed. "He had one four days ago, didn't he tell you? How come you don't know?"

"I was in DC presenting at NASA Headquarters. I didn't talk to him while I was gone."

"He went into the ER on Saturday. Called me on the way saying he thought he was maybe having a heart attack. Didn't he tell you this, either? Didn't Zack know?"

"Zack was away on a class environmental trip until Sunday night."

"I told Ben that if he were having a heart attack he wouldn't be able to call me. I had a kidney stone a few months ago, so I told him that's what I thought it was. I checked on him later and he said I was right. Kidney stone, wouldn't you know it."

I'm having a hard time wrapping my head around her story. "Then what happened?"

"Told me he passed the stone and the doctors sent him home. But those kidney stones are wicked. Maybe he's back in the hospital with complications or something? Could be that's where he is."

Her theory, as wacky as it sounds, actually takes my anxiety down a notch. "Why wouldn't the hospital call me?"

"Our whole medical system is messed up, that's why," she says. "Don't get me started about the time I went to the ER with pneumonia."

CHAPTER FIVE

"No, we've checked all the hospitals. He's not there," Detective Dawson says. He arrived at my house ten minutes before I got back from CIT and is waiting on the front porch. "Not in the county jails, either."

"Jails?"

"We got to cover all the bases. Some missing persons end up there."

He has a thing about the Christmas tree. Sits right across from it this time, staring at it as though it's a rare artifact in a museum.

"You guys get a real Christmas tree every year?" he says absently, but it feels planned to me.

"It's been a few years . . . but we had one every year when Zack was little."

"Not for me. Too much hassle with all the needles and the watering . . . you think a guy who's getting ready for a big trial wouldn't have time to do all that . . . and decorate it like this, too."

I'm not sure what he's getting at, and I'm tired. "It's a family tradition. Ever since—"

"How come you didn't know about the kidney stones until now?"

"Like I told you before, I was making a presentation at NASA. Those meetings are always intense, and given our major discovery, this one was particularly eventful."

"It's kind of a big deal. Kidney stones. Is it like him to keep something like that from you?"

I shift in my chair. "What could I have done about it except worry from twenty-five hundred miles away?"

"And your kid—Zack, is it?—he didn't tell you his father was in the hospital for kidney stones?"

"I'm thinking he didn't know. He was on a school trip until Sunday night."

"Did your husband tell you about the 911 call he made Monday night?"

My stomach tightens. "911?"

He looks at his notes. "The call came in at 11:53. Your husband indicated that he had seen an intruder on the property."

"In the house?"

"In your backyard. By the time officers arrived eleven minutes later, the intruder was gone."

A chill runs up my spine.

"I talked with Ben's assistant—Will Wright—and he says Ben took out a seven-million-dollar life insurance policy, naming you as the sole beneficiary, several months ago. What can you tell me about that?"

"I don't know anything about the amount," I say. "I don't know how Will knows something like that, either."

"That's a lot of money for someone like you to come into. I'll bet seven million is more than you'll make for the rest of your career."

I stare—actually glare—at him and notice the way he's looking at me. And realize he's baiting me.

"You don't *actually* think I might be behind his disappearance because he took out life insurance and named me, his wife, a beneficiary?"

"*The* beneficiary."

"Statistically, have there ever been women who made their husbands go missing? To get their life insurance money?" He looks at me but doesn't answer. "Except in the movies," I add. "Or tabloid TV shows."

He doesn't blink. "We haven't ruled you out."

"Seriously?"

"You two have a prenup?"

"What does that have to do with anything?"

"From what I understand from Will, you have a prenup that says that you are entitled to inherit everything only after you've been married fifteen years."

"You're allowed to ask personal questions like that? And people have to answer?"

"They can if they want. And they usually do. Is it true your fifteenth wedding anniversary was a few months ago? And that your husband is heir to the Mayfield Department Store empire in Chicago?"

"Are you asking me or telling me?"

He softens his tone. "I'm asking you to confirm you're now free to inherit one hundred percent of his tremendous wealth if he dies."

If he dies. What is he talking about? Ben is just missing. He's coming back. There's no way he's dead.

———

I know where Detective Dawson's going with his line of questioning. Forget my reputation as an astronomer working on a three-hundred-fifty-million-dollar space telescope for NASA. Forget my groundbreaking discovery of the Trojan asteroid. He's trying to paint me as a gold digger who stands to get not only my husband's family fortune but also a seven-million-dollar payout if Ben dies.

Why he's doing that when there are other suspects puzzles me. Perhaps he thinks I'm in collusion with his embezzling partners? Or maybe he just has to prove—like I do in all my research—that he's asked every question, examined every piece of evidence, and followed every lead. Even the dead-end ones. Even the stupid ones.

I'm worried he's going to find out that we had discussed divorce. Maybe Ben told someone. And if he did, the detective seems clever enough to get people to tell him that kind of stuff.

I know what he'll assume. I know what everyone will assume.

They'll assume that if a woman is suggesting divorce or spending time with some man who isn't her husband, that she is also bat-shit crazy. That she's somehow responsible for whatever tragedy is unfolding. Maybe she also struggles with drugs or alcohol. She's unreliable. She'll do dangerous things.

If our kid is in trouble at school, if our husband cheats, if we like someone who isn't our husband, or if we can't have children or don't want children, we are so weak that we have no boundaries for our behavior, no willpower, and we are nearly guaranteed to make atrocious decisions. We become sociopaths-in-training.

His theory plays into the belief that behind the facade of any successful woman, mother, or wife, we are all hiding our shallow, fickle, dumb, gullible, and controlling selves. Not because any of this is accurate or true, but in a crisis like this, assumptions become truth.

It's even worse for me. I'm the significant other to an immensely popular, handsome restaurant owner with a famous movie-star partner. Why would any sane woman be unhappy with someone like him? Of course I have something to gain from his disappearance. Of course I'm somehow responsible.

———

My email inbox has 157 unread messages from the last twenty-four hours. Many are work related, but there are dozens from our friends expressing shock at the news and offering support. They don't want to bother me by calling, but I wonder if hearing a friendly voice on the other end of the line might actually help settle the gnawing, buzzy feeling that's rocketing through my body.

My friend Lauren texts me, offering to coordinate anyone who wants to help. She's setting up a Facebook page and will post updates that friends can share. She wants to prevent people from "barging in with casseroles and dessert trays and wasting your time prattling on about stupid stuff or asking prying questions." I smile—Lauren is never coy about her feelings—then take her up on her offer by forwarding all the what-can-I-do emails to her.

When I first met Lauren at a mutual friend's son's bar mitzvah, we had struck up a real conversation at dinner—surprising because those events usually only encourage polite, often awkward, small talk. But Lauren ran a high-end 3-D printing firm, and I was fascinated to learn about the flexible artificial bone she was working on that could be used in place of bone grafts. So when the party DJ started blasting techno funk music and insisting that everyone get up and dance, Lauren snatched a bottle of wine from the table, grabbed me by the arm, and we ditched the boom-and-yell party room for the quieter and cooler outdoor patio where our conversation turned into a friendship.

I'm about to set my phone down when an email in my inbox catches my attention. "A secure message from Old National Bank." At first I think it's junk mail:

> We've sent an important communication to your Secure Message Center, available on Old National Bank Online or on the Old National Bank Mobile app.
>
> The subject is: Your $1,000,000.00 payment from BENJAMIN A MAYFIELD is in your available balance.
>
> You can sign in to review this communication in your Secure Message Center.
>
> Thank you for being a valued Old National Bank customer.

One million dollars.

After Zack was born, I'd opened the account at a bank near where my mom lived in Indiana. I'd stashed away a few thousand dollars over the years, imagining Zack using it to buy a car someday or putting it toward college.

Why had Ben deposited so much money in an account neither of us had used for more than a dozen years? Is this the money his partner claims Ben stole?

I stare at the date of the transaction on the screen. Today's date.

I call the bank and fumble through the security questions with the customer service rep. I don't know the account number, which triggers several other security questions including my mother's maiden name and in what city I worked my first job. Luckily, I pass the tests and ask her if she can tell the origin of the large deposit.

"What I can see is that it was a wire transfer initiated by Benjamin Mayfield."

"When? Today?"

I hold my breath, hoping she'll say yes. Proof that he's alive.

"No, not today," she says, her words slicing through my hopes. "The request was made yesterday but came through after the wire transfer cutoff time, which is why the funds hit your account today."

"Wire transfer cutoff?"

"If a bank receives the transfer request after the cutoff—usually six p.m. Eastern—funds are credited to the receiving account the next day."

"So he made the request *yesterday . . . Tuesday?*"

"Yes, the request was received Tuesday afternoon at five."

There's a moment on a roller coaster ride where you've crested the top, you've hung there for the briefest of moments, and then the car plunges to the bottom.

That's exactly where I am. My body is in free fall, and I'm terrified this ride is never going to end.

Why did Ben leave one million dollars in the bank yesterday less than an hour before he disappeared? Why did he leave behind a gun? If he knew he was in danger, why wouldn't he call me? Or at least leave me a note.

Then my mind takes a sharp detour. Am *I* being framed? Is it possible that Ben had left all this evidence—the gun, the erased DVR, this money—to make it look like I am responsible for his disappearance? Maybe he had been so angry at me for suggesting divorce that he planned this whole scenario to get back at me.

That's not the Ben I know. Whatever angry feelings he might have about our discussion, I can't imagine he'd put me and Zack through all this.

But could he?

———

My sister texts me for an update and offers again to fly in from San Francisco. It would be good to have more help, but I'm hiding so many things from police—the gun and the DVR—that I don't want her here, prying around, asking nosy questions. My sister and I are the product of school-teacher parents—my dad taught high school math and my mom was an English teacher—so we grew up following the rules. Of the two of us, Rachel is more rigid in her approach to problem solving, and I'm sure she won't approve of the decisions I've made. And being three years older, she'll act like it's her place to set me straight.

Not yet. Will reach out when it's the right time, I text her as the doorbell rings again. I open the door, and this time it's Stuart Baxter returning with Christie Miller, an attorney who is to advise me on how to handle the media. Christie is tall, nearly six feet, wearing what appear to be three-inch heels, with wavy blonde hair that falls to just above her shoulders.

"Reporters are looking for any action they can hang their theories on, so be careful with every word you say," she says as they settle into the couch in the living room. "Every expression. I'm working on an outline of a statement for you to make tomorrow. And after that, we're going to get you on all the news channels so that you can ask for help on the airwaves."

"Can I say that we think Ben's disappearance is related to next week's trial against his Aurora partners?"

"Absolutely not." She straightens the collar on her white blouse. "The subject is off-limits for reasons we'll get to in a moment. Your job is to let the public know that you are fully cooperating with police. And that you're enlisting their help to find your husband."

I don't know much about what happens in cases like this. A few years ago, a young pregnant wife went missing in Southern California, and even after weeks of searching, her body was never found. I'd been so busy with the work we were doing on the space telescope that I missed most of the insistent media coverage, but I do remember that every time I turned on the news, her family members were pleading with viewers to help find her. Should I organize Ben's family to talk to the media?

Christie seems to be reading my mind. "We want to avoid this turning into a media circus, so let's keep it simple. I don't want a lot of voices talking about Ben."

Stuart leans forward, rests his elbows on his knees. "Now, here's why you can't talk about the upcoming trial. First, we don't want to prejudice potential jury members and force a change of venue because the partners can't get a fair trial here in LA. Separate from that, we don't want the media to get distracted by the partners' involvement right now. We've got to leverage the media to help us find Ben. And last, we've heard from the partners' lawyers that if we come out and speculate that they're somehow responsible for Ben's disappearance, they're going to retaliate and tell the media that it's *Ben* who has been stealing millions from Aurora."

"Richard Jenkins called me to say that very thing."

Stuart frowns. "Richard called you? Not okay. From now on, I don't want you taking any calls from Richard or the other partners. They all have the same agenda. They want to take the heat off themselves by claiming that Ben was stealing."

I'm silent for a long while, choosing my words. The only sound is the ticking of the old-fashioned clock on the mantel. A gift from Ben's father on one of our anniversaries. "Is it possible Ben *was* stealing?"

Christie and Stuart look up from their papers.

I pause for a long moment, gauging how much I was really prepared to tell them. "Yesterday, Ben transferred one million dollars into an account I have at a small bank in Indiana."

Stuart's face falls. "What the hell is going on here?"

CHAPTER SIX

The invitation from Aaron comes to my private email account. It's a link to a secure and encrypted server, and I have to jump through a few hoops to set up a username and password and then verify my email address and password a second time before it will let me view the email he's sent to me:

Follow the link below to read or reply to your secure message from Jules Verne.

I smile. Aaron loves Jules Verne stories, especially *Journey to the Center of the Earth*, so it makes sense that he would set up a user ID with that name.

I click on the link and see that Aaron/Jules has recovered another seventeen-second clip. This one is from the camera in the family room, taken at 9:13 a.m. on Monday, the day *before* Ben disappeared. I immediately recognize our friend Matt Shepherd in the shot. He's dressed as though he's headed for the golf course, wearing neatly pressed chino shorts and a crisp white polo shirt.

"It's used to treat Parkinson's and some gastro disorders," he's saying. "Can cause all the symptoms you mentioned. Tachycardia, palpitation, dizziness. Especially given how much we found in your blood. Four times the safe dosage."

Matt is a doctor of internal medicine at Cedars-Sinai Medical Center. His son, Henry, became friends with Zack in kindergarten, sharing a mutual obsession with robots. When our boys became inseparable, Ben and I ended up hanging out with Matt and his wife, Kim, over barbecue and craft beer while our boys rode bikes, swam, and played all things robot.

From this camera angle, I can only see the back of Ben's head, but I hear him say, "So I had food poisoning?"

"Belladonna isn't a form of food poisoning. Someone deliberately—"

The clip stops.

Is Matt saying that Ben had been poisoned? I watch the clip several times more and blast the volume so that I don't miss any words.

Was this why Ben was in the ER? Not for kidney stones, like his sister, Julia, had said. But for belladonna poisoning?

I look up belladonna online and see that it comes from the leaf and the root of a plant in the deadly nightshade family, and it's a drug that blocks functions of the nervous system.

I consider sending this clip to Detective Dawson, but I'm certain it'll make him demand to see the entire drive. And, for now, I have to assume that Ben had a good reason to erase the drive so that *no one* would see what's on it.

I call Matt's cell phone, but it goes straight to voice mail. I leave him a message.

As I watch the clip again, I wonder why Ben didn't call to tell me he'd been poisoned. I could see why he might not want to disturb me about the intruder on the property, but the poisoning is exactly the kind of news I would've expected him to tell me. Yet he didn't call or even text once.

Maybe he didn't want me to worry, especially since there was nothing I could do from twenty-five hundred miles away.

Or maybe because I'd suggested divorce, he thought I wouldn't care.

———

Matt rings back thirty minutes later.

"Sarah," he says. "Sorry, I was with a patient when you called. I heard Ben's missing. Any news? Tell me he's home and that his car broke down or something simple like that."

"He's still missing."

"Crap. I'm so sorry."

"Do you think the belladonna poisoning might have something to do with his disappearance?"

"Possibly. I can't tell police because Ben didn't give me permission to discuss it with anyone. But I was on the phone with my attorney early this morning seeing how I could share information, now that he's missing. Technically, I'm not supposed to be talking to you about it, either, Sarah. But given the circumstances and since you already know . . ."

"Why didn't Ben report it to the police himself?"

"He said he had a plan to figure out how it got into his food. Didn't say what the plan was, though. But he definitely didn't want anyone to know about it. I think he was even going to tell his sister he had kidney stones."

"He did. But he didn't tell me how he came in contact with the drug. Do you know?"

"Yeah, no. It's very strange. Because it's not the kind of thing you accidentally ingest or that accidentally gets, you know, mixed up in your food. He said he ate lunch at a restaurant near your house, then started feeling terrible about a half hour later. Thought he was having a heart attack . . . you know, just like his dad did around his age. So once we confirmed the poisoning, the only thing I could figure was that the drug was put into what he ate at lunch."

"So you think it was . . . deliberate?"

He pauses. I know then that what he's going to say isn't going to be good. "Yeah. This wasn't accidental. I think someone was trying to poison him."

After I hang up with Matt, I call Detective Dawson and tell him about the poisoning. As he details the places he's going to check again—the hospitals, the emergency rooms, the morgue—I imagine Ben alone, struggling to stay alive somewhere. A wave of nausea hits me, forcing me to brace myself against the kitchen sink.

———

"Dad didn't tell me anything about being poisoned," Zack says, eyes wide with shock. "He seemed fine when I got home Sunday night after the environmental trip. He even made me his World Famous Grilled Cheese."

"Maybe he had recovered by then . . ."

"Why wouldn't he tell me, though?"

"He probably didn't want to worry you."

That answer seems to bring his anxiety down a notch because he heads into the kitchen to fix himself a snack.

I glance at my watch and my stomach knots. In a few minutes, I'll make my statement to the press. I've revised the draft five times already, trying to find words that will sound natural so I don't appear to be reading a prepared statement, even though I am.

Until then, we're trapped in the house. Reporters are camped on the parkway, and from my living room window I can see the raised antennas of two TV news vans. I suddenly wish I'd chosen black-out curtains in the living room instead of off-white sheers because every time I pass one of the windows, I know the reporters can see movement through the drapes.

Los Angeles is a nonstop news town, so a story like this can be sensational today but utterly forgotten tomorrow. I know I need to capture viewers' and readers' hearts, make them feel for Ben's situation, so they won't just graze on the sizzle factor of this story and move on to the next sensational one. I have to convince them to help Ben. To be on the lookout for him in case he's disoriented or sick from the poisoning. I have to believe that someone out there can help.

It's a tall order. I'd spoken to the news media many times before, most recently about a bus-sized meteor that streaked across the sky in Moscow and blew up. That kind of interview was easy because I had facts to rely on—how fast the meteor was traveling, how big it was, how rare it was.

But here I have no facts. Ben was here. And then he wasn't. I couldn't tell reporters about the gun or the large deposit in my bank account. Or anything to do with the Aurora lawsuit.

I pace the hardwood floor in the living room then gaze at the Christmas tree, thinking over Detective Dawson's question. How did someone who was about to testify in a high-profile trial find time to decorate a Christmas tree? And not just a few strings of lights and ornaments slung onto it. This was a careful production—vintage lights woven throughout, our family's ornaments carefully placed, and tinsel artfully clinging to the branches. I touch my fingers to the San Francisco Trolley ornament Ben and I picked out in a tourist shop on Pier 39 when we spent our first anniversary there. Down below it hangs a surfing Santa ornament from Maui, where we went for our "babymoon" three months before Zack was born.

Ben had started the Christmas tree tradition the year we were married, spending hours scouring stores for lights, ribbon, tinsel, and ornaments. Not because they were part of his own tradition—he grew up in a Jewish household—but because they were mine. Every year he strived to replicate the classic Christmas tree of my memories: the silver tinsel, popcorn garland, candy canes, and big-bulb colorful lights.

And he succeeded. Each time we switched on those Christmas tree lights, I felt like I had stepped back in time, flooded with memories. I could smell my mother's gingerbread cookies coming out of the oven and hear my father's voice telling Rachel not to pull the ornaments off the tree that stood by the bay window in the living room. "Ho ho ho," he'd say, then scoop her up in his arms and fly her away from the tree.

I always felt the fully decorated tree was his best gift to me, and here it was again. A gateway to the past. To happier times.

Why had he decorated the tree in the midst of the chaos of his trial? After being poisoned.

And while so on edge that he had bought a gun.

———

I'm about to make a statement to reporters when a new email from Aaron flashes across my cell phone: *Follow the link below to read or reply to your secure message from Jules Verne.*

I shove the phone in my jacket pocket, hoping my look of surprise hasn't been captured by the cameras that are trained on me.

I stand on my front lawn alongside Detective Dawson in front of a bank of microphones and a sea of reporters.

Stuart and Christie stand off to the side, largely inconspicuous in the growing crowd. I haven't engaged them to represent me not only because they're litigators, not defense attorneys, but also because I worry what reporters will assume. In the court of public opinion, it seems to me that you are automatically guilty if you hire a defense attorney in situations like this.

When I'd left NASA Headquarters just days ago, I'd expected to be making announcements to the press about our Trojan asteroid discovery, not that my husband is missing. As I speak the words aloud—Ben Mayfield is missing—the realness of what's happening sinks in and my voice shakes. I realize that I haven't cried or shed a tear since this all began. I'd skipped over the shock and the fear and gone straight into problem-solving mode. Now I'm worried that I'm going to lose it—dissolve into tears or maybe have my voice tremble uncontrollably—in front of all these reporters.

It's a tough crowd. Only a few reporters, like Kate Bradley and another reporter from the *LA Times*, show anything that resembles sympathy. The rest are ready to pounce with questions.

"The outpouring of support from our friends and family means so much more than anyone can know," I finish, my voice hoarse with emotion. "Thank you for that and for understanding how difficult this is for our family."

A reporter with a blonde bob points at me. "Earlier today, chef Ann Lyman, who worked with Ben Mayfield in the past, said, and I quote, 'The timing is very suspicious. Ben was about to win that lawsuit against his partners, but before he got his day in court, he vanished. I believe if Ben hadn't filed the suit, he would be here today.' Do you agree with her theory?"

Christie shoots me a look of caution. I wait a moment before answering. "I know Ann and appreciate her passion for wanting to figure out why Ben is missing," I say. "We all do. But I can't comment on any connection with the trial. There aren't enough facts to posit any theories yet."

I suddenly worry that I appear too calm. Composed even. I want to break my CIT-trained habit of speaking in full sentences because I think it makes me sound too calculated. Too strong.

A reporter wearing a light-blue polo interrupts. "Are *you* a suspect in Ben Mayfield's disappearance?"

I'm surprised by the question, although I shouldn't be. "No. I was out of town in Washington, DC at NASA Headquarters at the time when we think Ben went missing."

I look at Detective Dawson and immediately realize I've said too much. I should've stopped at "no" because by giving them facts—by laying out an alibi—I automatically sound like I'm on the defensive.

"*The lady doth protest too much, methinks,*" I imagine one of the headlines reading. Well, one of the smarter publications anyway.

———

It's early evening and my house is full of people. There are Ben's attorneys, of course, and Lauren, plus a handful of friends who are in the process of making flyers to post around our neighborhood and at Aurora. Lauren has assembled a small team to post on social media and tells me she's recruiting more volunteers to "tack flyers on every wall, window, and flat surface in LA." She's also plowing through a checklist of things police have requested that will aid in the search: recent photos, personal items with Ben's scent that will help search dogs find him, and a contact list of family members and close friends.

The kitchen is full, too. Even though Lauren asked people not to send gifts, there are cards, flowers, and baskets of cookies and muffins from friends, Ben's colleagues and mine, our neighbors, and even Zack's school. All expressing words of encouragement and hope.

I've completed interviews on several radio stations, answered questions from three LA news publications, done interviews for the local morning news shows, and because of Ben's connection to movie star Michael Hayden, I've talked to several entertainment-industry trade publications. I've juggled requests from another half-dozen bloggers and social media sites until my voice is raw, and I'm tired of hearing myself talk, certain that I've begun to sound like a wound-up robot, repeating the same lines over and over.

Behind every interviewer's eyes, I feel the silent question: *Are you in on it?*

The *LA Weekly* reporter isn't as coy. "Everyone is wondering if you're involved in Ben's disappearance, but the suspicions are often dismissed because you are a CIT astronomer," he says. "Yet there are rumors circulating that you had a prenup that would entitle you to a significant chunk of the Mayfield Department Store fortune after your recent fifteenth anniversary. So if your husband isn't found, you have quite a lot to gain."

He leaves his statement hanging there. It's not even a question.

My voice is steady, even if on the inside I'm not. "The rumors you mention take the focus away from the crucial message we need people to know. And that is, we need everyone's help finding my missing husband. He may be sick or injured. Someone out there may have seen him or talked to him—and we need them to come forward."

When we wrap up the interview, he thanks me for my time, but the way he looks at me leaves no doubt that he thinks I know more than I'm saying.

Back in my kitchen, Lauren, her blonde hair tossed up in a messy bun, is the ringleader of the team of friends and volunteers developing the flyers. She insists on including an image of Ben's missing car, but despite looking through thousands of photos in our digital archives, she can't find one.

"It's not like we took photos of the car," I tell her. "It's a dark-blue Audi, but I don't remember the model number."

Lauren jumps online. "Was it an A6? Maybe the A8? Or could it have been the TT Coupe?"

She shows me the photos on the screen, but I don't know the answers to her questions. I didn't go car shopping with Ben, and in the haze of the moment, all the models appear too similar to make out which one is his.

I hand her a binder that contains all the important information about our cars. Still, I know what she's thinking. What they're all thinking. I'm a crummy wife. I can't tell you what kind of car he drives. I don't have a favorite photo of him as my phone screensaver. I hadn't talked or texted with my husband for three days before he went missing.

I have absolutely no idea what was going on in my husband's life.

Tears cloud my eyes. I'm becoming someone I never thought I'd be. Scattered. Weepy. Unfocused. I feel like there are a hundred things I should be doing, but I'm doing none of them.

Lauren spots my leaky eyes. "Why don't you get something to eat? Debra brought your fave—scones and lemon curd."

I don't have an appetite, so I head to the guest bathroom to collect my thoughts. Even with the door closed, I can hear the muffled inflection of voices—rising and falling—drifting from the kitchen. And clattering dishes. One of my friends is cleaning up my kitchen, I think, which is wonderful, but just plain odd.

I glance in the mirror and, in the unflattering glare of the overhead lights, notice a web of mascara smudged beneath my bloodshot eyes.

I splash cold water on my face, dry it with a towel, then call Ben's voice mail and listen to his low, measured voice. I hang up and listen again. It sounds like he recorded it in the early morning when his voice is always a bit hoarse. I imagine him sitting in the living room, wearing his favorite navy-blue sweatpants and drinking espresso.

Where is he?

Then my eye settles on the tub and I can see three smudged footprints, as though someone—Zack?—had stepped into it with their shoes on. I move the wooden blinds aside on the window above the tub. It is definitely closed enough to let us activate the alarm. But the latch is not in the locked position.

We hadn't installed a camera in this guest bathroom for obvious privacy reasons. Were these footprints evidence that Zack was bringing friends through the window to avoid being recorded by the cameras?

Or was this proof of something more sinister? Something to do with Ben's disappearance?

I close the latch and resolve to ask Zack later. Then I click on the email from Aaron. This clip is taken in the living room on Tuesday, the day Ben went missing. The camera takes in the whole room, including the Christmas tree, which, in this shot, is fully decorated.

Ben and Zack are standing in front of the tree, their backs to the camera, putting something in the branches. Ben pats Zack on the shoulder. The Burl Ives song "Holly Jolly Christmas" is playing on the living-room speakers and drowns out anything they might be saying. But there's no mistaking that they're laughing as they position Santa Claus in the tree.

CHAPTER SEVEN

"Why didn't you tell me you and Dad worked on the Christmas tree together?" I ask Zack, avoiding the word "lie" because I know it'll upset him.

He's sitting on his bed doing his algebra homework, wearing a set of green headphones. The cat lounges at his feet.

"What do you mean?" he says, looking up from his homework and removing one of his headphones.

"I know that you and Dad worked on the tree together. You did, didn't you?"

I don't like the tone I'm using. It's accusatory, the same tone I used when we found him passed out drunk. Only this time we're talking about whether or not he decorated a Christmas tree.

He looks down and slumps a little. I've caught him in a lie. "Yes."

I lower my voice. There are a dozen people downstairs and I don't want this conversation to get out of hand. "Why did you tell me that you *didn't* work on the tree with Dad?"

"I don't know . . . I figured Dad would tell you."

"Why didn't you just tell me the truth? You're never going to get in trouble for decorating the Christmas tree with your dad," I say, settling beside him on the bed.

He looks away. "I was asleep when you asked, okay? And I didn't want you to make a big deal about it."

"You didn't want me to make a big deal about what?"

He sighs. "I knew you'd think that if I worked on the tree that it meant I'd forgiven you and Dad."

"Forgiven *us*? Zack, you're the one who's been grounded for drinking and smoking pot here with your friends. What do you need to forgive *us* for?"

He folds his arms across his chest. "You don't trust me about anything anymore. I'm grounded forever." He waves a hand in the air. "And it's like I'm in prison with all these cameras everywhere. And you and Dad checking them all the time to see what I'm doing."

My face crumples. I place my hand on his. "Zack, we did all this because we're worried about you."

"I just want things the way they . . . were."

I take in a deep breath, slowly exhale. "We're—I'm trying," I say. "Let's keep trying . . . together. And just so you know, it makes me really happy that you helped Dad with the Christmas tree."

"Dad drafted me." His eyes well with tears. "He promised the tree would bring us all back together again."

I can't speak. Instead, I reach out to hug him, and when he hugs me back, a shudder comes over me, then tears slip out of my eyes and slide down my face. "He said that?"

"Yeah. Then he told me a story about how I pulled the whole Christmas tree over when I was three . . ."

I smile and wipe my eyes. "Your dad wasn't always the best at applying physics principles to figure out how wide the Christmas tree base should be. So when he made the base really small, you pulled on the tree and it toppled right over on you." I kiss his forehead. "Now, where did you and Dad find the Wedding Santa?"

He brightens. "We tore apart the attic and found him way in the back under some of my old toys."

The Wedding Santa was given to us as, yes, a wedding gift. Even though our wedding was in June. It showed up on the gifts table without a note or explanation. Ben and I could never figure out who it came from, but we thought it was such an odd wedding gift that each year one of us hid it in the Christmas tree and challenged the other to find it.

Ben was the most creative at hiding it, wrapping it in a tangle of lights one year or secreting it high in the boughs another. Once the Wedding Santa was found, Ben would grab me by the waist and kiss me until we were both breathless.

Twelve years into our marriage, the Wedding Santa went missing. We searched every corner of the house looking for it, but unlike when we'd lost the infinity ring years before, we couldn't forgive each other for the Wedding Santa's loss, and we each blamed the other.

"Why won't you admit you accidentally threw it out," I had said angrily.

"You're the one who put it away last year."

It was a meaningless fight, and we both knew it wasn't just about the missing Wedding Santa. We were exhausted and stressed. Drifting apart. Our connection consisted almost entirely of taking care of Zack and the deadening routine of making and managing a home. Add to that our busy travel schedules—Ben was working to set up restaurants in Chicago and New York, and I was on the road twice a month for NASA meetings and other research sessions. And when we were home, there was the inevitable dinnertime conundrum when one of us planned to be home to cook something, but neither of us made it there early enough to prepare anything. With two demanding work schedules, our discussions were invariably stressed, flaring with anger as the juggling grew even more complicated.

I'm about to leave Zack's room when I remember to ask him about what I saw in the tub.

"Do you know anything about the footprints in the downstairs bathtub?"

His eyes cloud over. I know it must sound like I still don't trust him. "No, why?"

"Could your—"

"No, Mom. I never use that bathroom. And neither did my friends."

"Okay," I say gently, wanting to believe him, but still not entirely sure I can.

I leave his room after that and slip unnoticed into the living room. Though the steady hum of voices floats from the kitchen, this room is hushed, silent. I scan past the silvery tinsel and lights, through the branches, to where I'd seen Ben and Zack place the Wedding Santa. When I don't find him, I search more methodically, pushing aside fat-bulb lights and shiny ornaments, scouring each sector of the tree from the top down. The Wedding Santa is gone.

Disappointed, I step back from the tree. I cannot imagine where the Wedding Santa had disappeared to in the twenty-four hours since Ben and Zack put it in the tree.

And then I see it. Hiding in plain sight. Obscured by the brilliant halos from a clump of multicolored lights and a trio of wooden snowman ornaments we'd picked up on a trip to Germany ten years ago.

I lift him out of the tree, and a memory surfaces of Ben's face, his laugh, when we first pulled the cheery Santa out of the wedding-gift box that warm summer evening. He'd kissed me then and said, "Merry Christmas, my amazing wife!"

Santa's black boots and red jacket have faded over time, and his belt buckle is tarnished. But his cheeks are still rosy, and he smiles at me, just like he once did.

———

My telescope is trained on the moon, watching for an event at dusk that's barely visible, even with a telescope. It's the penumbral lunar eclipse, where only a part of Earth's shadow—the lighter penumbra—falls on the moon's face. It's difficult to observe because there's not a dark bite taken out of the moon like we'd see in a regular lunar eclipse. In a penumbral lunar eclipse most people will notice nothing at all. At best, some might notice a dark shading on the moon's face.

Tonight the eclipse eludes me. Even though I know where to track the Earth shadow's movement on the moon's surface and the subtle gray shading to look for, I can't see it. I feel as though I wouldn't see it even if I had the strongest telescope.

Still the moon beckons me, its cool light playing on the water in the pool. It seems to be calling me to distant memories.

I took Ben to a lunar eclipse on our first date. At twilight, we walked atop Mount Tamalpais amid the groves of smooth red-barked manzanita and oak while hawks swooped across the dusky sky. Then, underneath the inky canopy of stars, with the smell of wild fennel and eucalyptus riding on the wind, we watched the Earth's shadow devour the moon. We stargazed atop that chilly mountain, our eyes and telescope trained on the cobalt-blue zenith above until we noticed the first glow of the approaching sunrise and the stars melted ahead of it, as though darkness itself were dissolving.

The first time I saw Ben he was sitting across a crowded lecture hall in an English class at UC Berkeley. He had striking good looks—blue eyes and wavy brown hair that fell to his shoulders—and wore a black denim shirt and destroyed jeans, before jeans like that were a thing. I imagined he was a musician. In a rock band.

When he spoke to me after class one day, I actually thought he was talking to someone else. Guys with looks like his didn't often talk with girls like me. They hung out with girls who wore makeup and their cutest pair of flats to class. Girls who bought Starbucks drinks with fifteen-syllable names and carried around PalmPilots to keep track of their busy social calendars.

I was more of a nerd, my brown hair tied up in a messy ponytail, peering out from trendy-but-still-nerdy two-tone glasses. I rarely wore makeup and was always reading, usually sci-fi novels by authors no one's ever heard of.

"That's one of my favorites," he said, nodding toward the book in my hands.

I was sure he was kidding. This was a story about quantum mechanics, about science and faith and space and time—with some brain-explosion-causing philosophy thrown in. I laughed, just in case he was being sarcastic.

"Have you got to the part where she finds the tincture?" he asked.

He wasn't kidding. "Yes, and she's in deep trouble. The building has disappeared."

We ended up talking for nearly an hour. I liked the way he looked at me when I spoke, as if it mattered to him what I said. Still, it crossed my mind several times that this was some kind of elaborate gag, that I was being punked. Instead, he invited me to go to dinner at an Asian fusion pop-up restaurant he wanted to try. I told him I was planning to watch the lunar eclipse, and without missing a beat, he invited himself along.

That night, under the red eclipsed moon, I learned he was a sociology major, a talented cook secretly hoping to own his own restaurants someday, and that hidden behind those impossibly handsome good looks, Ben was a true nerd. We had both read the encyclopedia for fun, played Dungeons and Dragons in middle school, liked Brown Sugar Pop-Tarts for breakfast, and could name all of the actors who played Doctor Who.

But Ben really earned his nerd cred when he texted me before our next class together . . . in Klingon: *thlhIngan Hol Dajatlh'a'?* he wrote, which means "Do you speak Klingon?"

Hlja', I typed back. Meaning yes. I'd actually bought and studied a book on how to speak Klingon, the language of one of the most prominent alien species on *Star Trek*.

quSDaq ba'lu"a'? he texted.

I was stumped. And impressed that he knew more Klingon than I did.

The next thing I knew, he was standing next to me, phone in hand, grinning. "It means 'Is this seat taken?'"

I don't remember a single moment of that English class. I was brilliantly aware of him sitting beside me, his arm oh-so-lightly brushing up against mine now and then. I was seduced by his smell. Likely just Old Spice, but he wore it like an intoxicating potion. I tried to appear unruffled, but every time I glanced at him, I felt off-balance.

Then, in the middle of class, he began scribbling something on a piece of paper. I peered over to see what he was writing, but he covered up the paper with his hand and flashed me a mischievous smile. My heart raced as he slid the paper in front of me.

The page was filled with an incomprehensible jumble of letters. Definitely not Klingon.

I felt the heat rise in my cheeks as I shot him a puzzled look. He smiled, then sat back in his chair, as if to say, "Figure it out."

While the professor droned on about Mark Twain, I scanned the string of letters, trying to make sense of them. Then I realized that he had written me a message in a code—a simple substitution cipher that relied on transposing all the letters in the alphabet so that the resulting alphabet is backward. The letter *A* was decoded as the letter *Z*, *B* actually meant *Y*, and so on.

Ben watched as I decoded each letter of the phrase. It read:

Can I make you dinner?

———

DAY TWO

Detective Dawson looks ill. His skin is ashen gray, and the hollows around his eyes look dark and puffy as though he hasn't slept in days. You wouldn't know it by his handshake, though. It's a strong grip that jams my fingers together so hard I actually pull my hand back and shake off the pain.

He doesn't notice.

It's late—nearly eight at night—and his presence on my doorstep tells me he must have something important to tell me. And the minute he sees my friend Lauren sitting at the kitchen table with her laptop, he asks her to come back later. Polite. But there's no doubt it's not a request.

"Could I stay?" Lauren asks. "She's going through a lot—"

"She'll be okay with me," he says with confidence, although I'm not sure I will be. I don't know what the detective needs to tell me that can't be said in front of my best friend.

Lauren scoops up her things, wraps me in a quick hug, then heads to the back door. "I'll be back whenever you need me."

The detective leaves the kitchen and makes a beeline for the Christmas tree again. He looks over the ornaments, and his eye settles on something.

"Diamond Icicles," he says, breaking into a smile. "My grandparents had these."

He lifts up a twisted metal "icicle" that's about five inches in length.

"Ben got them at a garage sale years ago. He has them in every color."

I can see his hand shake a little as he puts the icicle back. He's nervous. There's something he wants to tell me. Or ask.

I'm not wrong. "You might want to sit down."

Oh god. Does he have bad news about Ben? I drop in slow motion on the couch and feel my body sink into its soft cushions, which suddenly feel like craggy rocks.

"Have you . . . have you found him?"

He shakes his head. "Your husband hired a bodyguard on Tuesday. A man named Antonio Spear. Did you know about this?"

Nausea burns at the back of my throat and I feel light-headed. "I had no idea."

He speaks slowly as though that might lessen the blow. "Spear worked for World Intelligence Network, a private security firm. You heard of them?"

I nod. "A few of the celebrities that come to Aurora use that service. I've met the owner a few times."

"Tuesday afternoon at five thirty, Spear picked up your husband at your home. Later that night, he was found shot to death in a security-company-owned Toyota SUV."

It feels like he has just driven an icicle into my heart. "Was Ben with him?"

He draws a deep breath, closes his eyes for a second. "Three shots were fired, one of them killing Mr. Spear. We've analyzed the blood found in the car, and some of it belongs to your husband. Since Ben was no longer at the scene, we believe he was abducted by whoever shot Mr. Spear. We think they hopped back on the freeway to make their getaway."

I'm not one for hysterics, but I suddenly feel like I'm going to cry, or wail, or fall on the floor. Or all three. My body feels disconnected from my mind. Out of my control.

"But it's possible . . . Ben could've escaped on foot," I say, even though I know the theory isn't plausible.

"We found no sign of that. But we did find his broken cell phone by the SUV."

The walls begin to close in on me then, and the room begins to spin. How will I tell Zack? "This can't be true . . ."

"Ben did manage to make a call that night. But not from his own phone. From Antonio Spear's phone." He flips through his notebook until he finds the page he's looking for. "He made that call at 9:08 that night."

"Who did he call?"

"I think you already know," he says. "You."

———

I know exactly where I was at 9:08 Tuesday night, and I have a feeling Detective Dawson does, too.

"I didn't get a call from Ben . . ."

He doesn't believe me. I can see it his eyes. He thinks he's caught me in a lie. "Would you bring me your phone?"

I go to the kitchen and get my phone out of my purse and hand it to him.

"There's a voice mail, isn't there?"

"Not from Ben," I say. "There's no caller ID, and when I played it, there was a lot of white noise and I couldn't make out any words."

"That's the call Ben made from Spear's phone," James says. "Which explains the lack of caller ID. Ben made three calls in quick succession from his bodyguard's phone that night. The first call at 9:06 was to 911, and dispatch records indicate that call was too garbled to understand. The second call was made to you, but it went unanswered. The third and last call was made to you again, and that's when Ben left this voice mail."

His words drive a cold stake into my heart. Ben *had* called me. But what was he trying to tell me? If I'd picked up, could I have helped him?

The detective's voice brings me back to the moment. "The phone was issued to World Intelligence Network, who gave us access to his cell phone records and voice mail. Now our sound technicians are working to make out what Ben is saying, and I should have those results in the next day or so."

He flips through the pages of his notebook, then looks up at me, a stony expression on his face. "There's more, Sarah."

The air leaves my body. What could possibly be worse than finding out your husband has been shot and abducted?

"The belladonna poisoning we talked about doesn't appear to be an accident. We're investigating the restaurant where he had lunch that afternoon. The Parkway Bistro."

"We've been going there for years. I can't imagine they'd be responsible."

"My point is, someone has tried to kill your husband—twice." He looks down and taps his pencil on his notepad. "And the first place we need to investigate is whoever has the most to gain from killing Ben Mayfield. You're the sole beneficiary of his life insurance policy and heir to his family fortune."

The breath stops in my throat. "What are you getting at? I can't be a suspect. I wasn't even in LA when my husband was poisoned."

"You've got a rock-solid alibi, but that doesn't mean you didn't hire someone to do it."

My anger flares. "That's ridiculous. I didn't—"

"What I'm constructing now is a timeline of where *you've* been, Sarah. Let's start with what time your flight from DC came into LA that night."

My entire body tenses. I know where his questioning is heading. "I'm not sure the exact time. But I can check."

"Were you back in LA when Ben called you at 9:07 and then again at 9:08?"

"Yes, but I never heard—"

"We checked the airline schedules, and the last flight from DC arrived at 8:15 that night. So why wouldn't you have heard his call? Where were you?"

I've already told him I didn't get home until one in the morning. Traffic in LA can be bad, but there's no way it took five hours to get from LAX to Brentwood.

"I was having a drink at the airport with one of my CIT colleagues," I say.

"For four hours?"

"We had a lot of catching up to do on the Trojan asteroid discovery and the NASA presentation."

"And you couldn't 'catch up' during work hours?"

"We were celebrating . . . it's a major discovery—"

"And your colleague's name is?"

I hesitate, wondering if I'm required to tell him and worried that I'll be dragging Aaron into this investigation with me. But if I don't tell him, I know it'll look like I have something to hide.

"Aaron. Aaron McCarthy."

"You two have more than a friendship going on?" He asks it casually, looking down at his notepad. "I mean . . . four hours."

"No."

"Is that your vice?" he says quietly.

"My what?"

"For some it's booze, pills. For others, it's gambling, overspending. Everyone's got one. Some people cheat on their spouses. Is that your vice?"

"That's an inappropriate question, Detective Dawson. You realize I've been married fifteen years. Ben and I have a son. I'm an astronomer at the Carnegie Institute of Technology—"

"Doesn't make you any less human than the rest of us."

I swallow hard. "So what's yours?"

He looks up and fixes a stern gaze on me. "My what?"

"Your vice."

"This isn't about me."

"But it is. You come in here and make a declaration that everyone has a vice—without, I might add, any research or evidence to back that up—and then accuse me of cheating on my husband. If everyone's got one, what's yours?"

He opens his mouth to say something. Then shuts it.

"Just because my husband is missing and you're wearing a badge doesn't mean you can speculate about me and my vices. Not unless you're prepared to talk about your own."

He stands, pretends he didn't hear me. "So for the record, you were on a plane to NASA Headquarters the day your husband was poisoned with belladonna."

"That's correct."

"And, for the record, after your husband was involved in a shooting that killed his bodyguard, he tries to call you at 9:08 Tuesday night. And you don't answer. Because you are sitting in an airport lounge until well after midnight with a . . . guy from work. Is that correct?"

I feel a pang of guilt but keep my voice steady. "I didn't hear the call."

"If there's something going on between you and this guy, you'd be smart to tell me now rather than wait for us to dredge it up later."

"There's nothing going on between me and Aaron."

CHAPTER EIGHT

After the detective leaves, I head up to Zack's room and share the news with him. At first he looks at me as though he can't understand the words I'm saying. Then his pale skin turns pink and tears well up.

"Do they think that Dad got away?" he asks, full of hope.

I stroke his hair, smoothing the cowlick at his left temple. "They're not sure. They're looking into whether the person who shot his bodyguard abducted him."

"Why would someone . . . abduct Dad?"

I ache to have answers for him, Still, I resist the urge to give him ones that sound plausible yet may not be true. "They're not sure. We're going to find out, though." My voice is full of hope, and even though my heart is racing, I'm able to summon a calm tone.

My lack of answers troubles him as much as it does me. Zack likes things concrete and certain, which, like me, is why he gravitates to math and science, and the indefinite nature of everything that's happened clearly unsettles him.

He wipes his eyes, and suddenly he reminds me of Ben. The downward slope of his eyes, the strong cheekbones. I hug him, but unlike when he was little, I know that no measure of hugs is going to make this hurt go away.

After he goes to take a shower, I head out to the patio. Beneath the starlight, my breathing usually slows and my thoughts flow more easily. But tonight as I gaze up at the night sky, the stars can't work their usual magic on me. They look like dull, hazy dots in the sky.

Unreachable, like Ben. Where is he? Is it too much to hope that he somehow escaped the shooting? Or was it more likely that he had been abducted? Or was even dead?

Tears burn my eyes.

I can't escape the heavy feeling that I let Ben down. While I was drinking tequila with Aaron, Ben had been shot and witnessed his bodyguard's murder. He had called me in crisis and I wasn't there for him. If I had answered the call, maybe I could have done something. Maybe Ben would be here now.

Am I responsible for Ben's disappearance?

I gaze again at the stars and try to draw a deep breath, but it feels like my chest is wrapped in a vise.

I remember an Isaac Asimov story, *Nightfall*, about a planet where daylight is so pervasive that the stars were visible only once every two thousand years. So awesome was the sight of darkness and the stars that many people descended into ecstasy and madness when they viewed them for the first time. On Earth, where we can see the stars every night, we often glance casually at the cosmos and then quickly down again. Ignoring its rhapsody.

But not me. When I gaze at the night sky, I often *feel* infinity, even though it's a concept I don't use. Despite its seductive allure, we have no direct observational evidence for infinity. And yet I've felt it.

The night before Zack was born, Ben and I waited for my contractions to become regular before we headed to the hospital. It was after midnight and the air was particularly clear, swept clean by the Santa Ana winds that had blown fiercely earlier in the day. As we stepped outside on a moonless night, we both noticed the Andromeda constellation blazing in the sky above us.

Some might call it a boring constellation, just two lines of stars. But tonight it seemed brighter than usual, and we could actually glimpse the fuzzy patch in the sky just to its side: the Andromeda Galaxy, home to one trillion stars.

"Will you look at that," he whispered.

As we held hands under the canopy of stars and galaxies, waiting to become parents, the world seemed to swell, and it felt as though we were woven together in infinite time.

———

"Mom," Zack is whispering.

"Mom." More insistent now.

I jolt awake, realizing I've fallen asleep atop my covers. Zack is standing over me, and even in the dim light of my bedside lamp I can see the terrified look on his face.

"There's a man sitting in a car in front of our house."

"What time is it?"

"Midnight. I was about to go to bed when I heard a car door slam. I thought . . . I thought it might be Dad, so I looked out the window. There's a guy . . . sitting there."

I follow him to his room, my heart beating like I've just drunk five cups of caffeinated cola. His bedroom light is off, which gives us the advantage of seeing clearly into our front yard and the street. There's a black car, parked facing the wrong way, in front of our house. And a man sitting in the driver's seat.

For a moment I allow myself to think it's Ben—that he's home—but then I see the red glow of a cigarette in the man's hand and realize it can't be. Ben doesn't smoke. And why would he just be sitting there?

"Maybe it's plainclothes police . . . ," I say, but my voice is wobbly.

"There was a guy sitting in a car in front of our house the night Dad went missing, too."

"What? Why didn't you tell—"

"I didn't think anything of it at the time. But it's the same guy. I know it. We have to call 911," Zack says.

"He's just sitting in a car . . . they won't come for something like that."

"Are the doors locked?" he asks.

I try to recall. I'd fallen into a dead sleep on my bed. Around eleven? I remember letting the cat out through the front door, but I had not locked it, thinking I'd have to let her back in in five minutes anyway.

We hear a dull metallic thud, coming from downstairs. We both freeze, listening. The silence in the house is deafening, booming in my ears. I don't breathe.

Then a sound pierces the silence—the steady and unmistakable click of someone trying to slowly turn the doorknob on the front door.

"Call 911. Now," Zack insists.

We race into the office and lock the door. I yank my cell phone out of my back pocket, but my hands are so shaky that I enter the wrong passcode to unlock the phone. I try again, and then with trembling fingers I punch in 9-1-1, but instead of a live dispatcher, we get an automated response and we're placed on hold.

I slam my palm on the computer space bar and pull up the camera feeds. Except for the floor lamp in the living room, all the lights on the first floor are off. Even though the cameras allow us to see up to sixty feet in complete darkness, all I can really make out are vague shapes that could just as easily be a piece of furniture or a person down on the floor.

Camera one shows us a clear shot of the inside of the front door, and light spilling from the living room is enough for us to see that the deadbolt is horizontal—the door is unlocked.

My stomach lurches.

Zack points at camera two. His voice is a sliver. "Look."

Peering into the kitchen window is a man wearing a gray baseball hat. The hat shadows his face, but he's built like a linebacker, muscular with broad shoulders.

My mind flashes to the gun that's in my nightstand, but I don't know how to use it. And my whole body is trembling so hard that I doubt that I could aim it properly even if I did have training.

"What's he doing?" Zack whispers.

The man moves from looking into the kitchen window and out of camera range. Now we see him on camera three, and he's peering into the living room window.

"We have to get to the panic button," I say.

Zack looks at me wide-eyed. The alarm panel is next to the front door.

He makes the word "no" with his lips, but no sound comes out.

I'm afraid to go downstairs. And I know he is, too. Yet I stride into the hallway, phone in hand, and head to the stairs. I see the alarm panel at the bottom to the left of the front door, but it feels like it's a mile away. My heart is pounding so hard I can hear it pulsing in my ears.

I glance at my bare feet, draw a deep breath, and race down the carpeted stairs, lunging at the panel and jamming my finger on the panic button until the loud sirens blare inside and out.

I hear footsteps running down the brick driveway. Then the screech of tires on the street. I lock the front door and bolt the living room window.

The car is gone.

CHAPTER NINE

DAY THREE

The gun is more fearsome in the morning light. I've cleared a place on my desk and set it more than an arm's length away from me while I watch YouTube videos on how to use it. I'm relieved there are near-dummy-proof safety features that prevent anyone from accidentally shooting it unless they have a full grip on the trigger. Still, there's something about the hard, heavy metal that sends a shudder through my body.

It's a machine whose primary purpose is to kill.

I spend a lot of time around machines. Computers and telescopes, of course, but also sensors, cameras, and satellites. Yet none of them—even the Giant Magellan Telescope being built high atop a mountain in Chile and weighing over one thousand tons and housing nearly four thousand square feet of mirrors—could unleash the destruction equivalent to a single shot from this thirty-ounce hunk of metal.

Could I use it for its intended purpose? Could I actually point it and pull back the trigger?

I rest my chin on my clasped hands and take in a few deep breaths. Activating the alarm panic button had brought police to the house, and after they checked the property with guns drawn and found no one,

Zack and I had reset the alarm and eventually fell back into restless sleep. I woke every hour, burdened throughout the night with disturbing dreams about intruders in the house. But in the dreams, whenever I pulled the trigger, I'd hear a tiny click and nothing would happen. The hard gun in my hand would suddenly become a plastic toy pistol like the ones Zack played with when he was little.

The brightest star in the known universe is the Pistol Star. It's ten *million* times brighter than our sun and unleashes as much energy in six seconds as our sun does in an entire year. But the brightest star in our universe can't be seen—not even with our most powerful telescopes—because it's hidden behind a great dust cloud.

It's like this gun, whose reason for being here is hidden from me, brought here because of events I don't yet understand.

I know Ben left me this gun for a reason, but I also know it can't stay in the nightstand by my bed, invading my dreams with its very presence. Instead, I open the metal case for one of my telescopes and pull back the gray foam inside the lid. I slide the gun behind it. I snap the metal latches closed and thrust the telescope and its errant passenger back in the corner.

But knowing the gun is there should I need it again isn't enough to quell the gnawing anxiety that grips my entire body. I pick up the phone and dial World Intelligence Network, the security service that Ben had hired, and ask for their owner, Travis Rollman. I tell the woman who answers the phone that I'm Ben Mayfield's wife, that I'd met Travis a few times at Aurora, and need to speak to him on urgent business. I sit on hold for several minutes until she comes back on.

"He's not available right now. But he'd like to speak with you. Can I have him call you back?"

"No," I say, my voice sounding bigger than I feel. "Tell him that I'll meet him in his office in half an hour. I'm on my way."

As I step into the World Intelligence Network's suite, with its polished concrete floors and high exposed ceilings on the twenty-second floor of a sleek office building on Sunset Boulevard, I feel like I've just walked off a cliff.

I've never been like this before—careening from thought to emotion, acting seemingly on impulse. Even when we were little, it was my sister Rachel who was the dramatic one while I was steady and predictable. Now, after last night's intruder, I'm a whisper away from coming unglued.

I gaze out the windows at the Hollywood Hills skyline, seduced for a moment by its glamour. This is what Ben grew to love about LA—the adrenaline-soaked hum of the city and towering structures of concrete and glass.

I spy the verdigris-domed Griffith Observatory perched high atop the Hills, remembering a trip there with Ben a few months after we had started dating. We fixed our eyes on the gentle swaying of the bronze ball in the observatory's Foucault Pendulum. As the minutes passed, the pendulum knocked over a succession of pegs—proof of the Earth's rotation. Watching this elegant scientific instrument, we tried to wrap our heads around the idea that even while we stood still holding hands, the Earth was spinning below us at over a thousand miles per hour.

Movement and change are happening all around us, even if we can't see it. Ben and I were happy together once . . . and then we weren't. But it wasn't a seismic shift that had changed us—it was the slow, inevitable rotation of things. The Earth shifts below our feet, bringing forth not-so-subtle changes—lightness and dark—but after a while, we cease to notice them.

"Sarah," Travis says, rushing out of his office. He's dressed in a trendy blue sueded jacket with a red printed T-shirt underneath, and sporting blue-tinted glasses. He greets me with an awkward hug, which tells me he isn't the hugging type but, given the circumstances, thinks he should pretend to be. "You didn't need to come all the way here. I've been planning to call you."

He ushers me into a glass-walled conference room with a commanding view of the famed Hollywood sign, then hands me a chilled bottle of water from a small refrigerator.

"You look pale, Sarah. Can I get you something else besides water? Coffee maybe?"

"No, but thanks," I say, realizing that I'd forgotten to apply any makeup this morning. I'm pretty sure that my hair has a slept-in look, too, even though I made a half-hearted attempt to run a brush through it.

"I've been planning to reach out to you, but with Antonio's death, it's been nonstop looking into what happened."

"I'm just . . . trying to understand why Ben hired you. Why he hired Antonio."

He motions for me to sit in the chair next to him. "Ben thought he'd been poisoned at the Parkway Bistro and wanted to question the kitchen staff about it. We didn't think it was safe for him to go there alone, so I assigned Antonio to go with him. They questioned everyone there—and came up with nothing."

"Nothing?"

"It's a small staff that's been together for about two years with little turnover. They work in extremely tight quarters—practically elbow to elbow—so it'd be nearly impossible for one of them to slip in a poison without being seen. And the way the kitchen's set up, it's not like an outsider could sneak in there unnoticed, either."

"Is it possible that someone paid the Parkway Bistro team to poison Ben?"

"I don't see how anyone could get in that restaurant to do it, honestly."

"But someone could've been smart enough to figure it out . . ."

His neck muscles tighten. "I've been over it again and again with them. That theory doesn't pan out. Your husband knows everyone there. He's friendly with all the staff, and everyone likes him."

I know this is true about Ben. People like him. Within minutes of meeting someone new, he always found a way to connect with them about a quiet passion of theirs. He could bond with complete strangers over classic Hollywood movies, a deep-dive discussion about civil rights, or even a shared passion for off-road BMX racing.

"Maybe Ben was poisoned somewhere else?"

He takes a swig from his water bottle. "After our investigation at the Parkway Bistro, that's what we're thinking. The problem is Ben isn't here to tell us what else he consumed that afternoon. Do you have any idea?"

I shake my head. "I was out of town at NASA Headquarters, and my son was on a school trip." My head begins to throb. "I need your help, Travis. We've had several intruders on the property since Ben disappeared. Last night Zack and I saw a man looking in our windows, and then he tried to open the front door. Something similar happened Tuesday night, the night Ben went missing. And on Monday night, apparently, Ben made a 911 call about an intruder on the property."

A muscle twitches in his jaw, and now it's his turn to turn pale. "You're not safe," he says. "And if something happens, police may not be able to help you in time." He leans forward, clasps his hands. "In a perfect world, I'd like to hide you and Zack away somewhere safe while we figure out what's going on—"

"I can't disappear. I need to be here to work with the police and the family and friends helping search for him."

He nods. "Then let me put a couple of my top guys at your house twenty-four-seven to keep an eye on things. I'll give you my best. No charge."

"Really, Travis, I can afford—"

"It's the least I can do for Ben."

"Then thank you."

He stands. "My guy—Brad—will make his presence known. We want to send a loud message for whoever is behind this—Ben's disappearance, the shooting, the poisoning—to stay away from your family."

———

The front door is locked. I've armed the alarm, even though it's noon, and Brad is patrolling the perimeter of my property. I'm still rattled about the prowler and consider asking Brad to show me how to use the Glock.

I lean on the kitchen counter, watching the images of Ben's story play out on the television news. Channel Eleven reporter Kate Bradley is talking about the life insurance policy that Ben took out naming me the sole beneficiary. "If Ben Mayfield isn't found," she says, "his wife stands to not only gain the proceeds from his seven-million-dollar life insurance policy but become heir to his vast Mayfield Department Store fortunes."

I can't figure out how she knows any of this. But I'm also shocked at the photo of me that they choose to feature in the story. Not my official photo, where I'm wearing a suit and had a stylist do my hair and makeup, but a candid shot—perhaps one from the bowels of social media—where I am makeupless and blurry. I look on the edge of crazy.

I text the detective to tell him I've hired a security service. Seconds later, a text flashes across the screen. But it's not from the detective. It's from Aaron.

I looked.

Then: *Wonder if I should be doing this?*

Damn. What has he seen?

Can you send the clip? I text.

No.

Calling you now. I type.

Wait.

I see the blue bubbles on screen as he starts typing something else then deletes whatever it is. No response.

My first thought is that he's seen more of the news reports about Ben's disappearance and he wants—needs—to distance himself from all of it. But then I reread his texts and wonder what he's seen on the DVR that has made him question whether he should be helping me.

Has he found a clip that will explain what Ben was hiding? Why he erased the DVR?

His response comes a full fifteen minutes later: *Can you stop by the office soon?*

Heading into work feels like a herculean task. Even the simple act of turning on the electric tea pot and opening my email feels exhausting. What made me think I could actually drive into work today?

I'm annoyed at Aaron. Why didn't he just send me the clips he didn't think he should be seeing?

Want to just send the data? I text.

I see the blue bubbles again as he's typing something, and it feels like forever until it comes through: *Not a good idea . . .*

I feel light-headed as I race to CIT under gray skies. Rain is rare in LA, but the clouds that had been looming behind the San Gabriel Mountains are emerging as black storm clouds, spawning a wall of darkness ahead of me that mirrors my mood.

The threatening rain keeps many CIT employees and students indoors, making it easier for me to get to Aaron's office largely unnoticed. He's waiting for me when I arrive, dressed more casually than usual, in a black polo and jeans.

I close the door behind me.

He turns to me and I see the veil of nervousness in his eyes. "Sorry. Paul was in my office when you were texting me."

Paul is one of the top brass at CIT, heading the Space Systems Laboratory. Besides being an engineering genius, one of his many strengths is what he calls MBWA, Management by Walking Around.

Without notice, he'd pop into your meetings or into your office, just to catch up briefly with what you're working on and what challenges you were facing.

"I didn't want you to call or come in while he was here," Aaron says. "He would definitely ask why you're calling or meeting with me, especially when everyone here has seen your husband's disappearance all over the news."

"I'm sorry to be putting you through this. Maybe we—"

"No, I want to do this for you, Sarah. But I think I've seen something I shouldn't have." He hands me his iPad and presses the play icon on the screen.

This twenty-eight-second clip is from the camera in the office next door to our bedroom. Ben is standing with a woman whom I instantly recognize as Simone. The time stamp reads Tuesday at 11:45 a.m., just a few minutes after the first clip I saw of the two of them together.

I press pause. "I'm not sure I want to see this."

He looks at me, holds my gaze. "It's not what you think. But it is troubling." He holds his hand over the play button and waits for me to nod my approval.

"Okay," I say finally.

"No suspects yet," Simone says. They're right under the camera so her audio is clear. I can even see the starlike pattern on the necklace she's wearing. "But they found fingerprints on Rebecca Stanton's purse and on her countertop. And the neighbor gave police a description of the man they saw leaving her apartment around six thirty that morning."

The clip stops.

"I don't . . . understand." I play the clip again, paying close attention to her words and the motion of her hand as she gives Ben a piece of paper.

"Take a closer look at the paper," Aaron says.

He enlarges the image enough that I can read "New York Police Department" at the top of the page. But the rest of the words are too blurry to make out.

"My guess? This woman is some kind of private investigator," he says, tapping on the screen.

My mind is racing. *Why is Ben talking to a private investigator about a police report for a woman in New York?*

Aaron's voice is unsteady. "I googled Rebecca Stanton in New York."

He taps on the screen and pulls up a four-day-old article in the *New York Post*. A photogenic blonde apparently on vacation in Hawaii or some other beach paradise smiles from the photo. She's wearing a white tank top and colorful skirt, holding a small dog up in the air. I read the article:

"New York police are investigating the death of a popular restaurant owner who was found shot to death on the rooftop patio of her Manhattan apartment on Saturday morning. The woman has been identified by police as 36-year-old Rebecca Stanton. About 6:45 a.m., paramedics responded to a medical emergency call and when they arrived, they found Stanton with a fatal gunshot wound to her upper torso. The co-owner of Paragon on 55th in Manhattan and graduate of Duke University, Stanton lived a seemingly picture-perfect life of high-end parties with celebrities like Justin Timberlake and Emma Stone."

The air leaves my lungs. A woman is dead. Murdered. Why was Ben looking into her murder hours before he went missing?

"Do you know who she is?" Aaron asks.

"No," I say, barely above a whisper. My heart jumps. Was Ben involved in Rebecca Stanton's murder? If so, maybe that's why he contacted a defense attorney. Perhaps he erased this drive because what's on it would incriminate him.

"What's on this drive?" he says. "If we continue to keep it a secret, we could both be in serious hot water. Not just with police. But here, too."

I feel off-balance. I know what he means by "here." CIT has a code of conduct, and its twelve principles include "obeying the law." Hiding this potential evidence could jeopardize both of our careers. "I'm sorry. I should never have brought you into this."

He touches my arm. Heat moves up my throat. I glance at his hand and make the mistake of meeting his gaze. I'm not imagining the concern in his eyes. And something else.

"What do you think we should do?" he asks.

"You've already done more than enough. Let me get the drive out of here."

I reach for the drive on the corner of his desk. And then he does something I don't expect. He places his hand on top of mine. "Wait. Let me . . . let me do one more pass. There's another utility I haven't tried yet. I'll send you whatever I come up with. That way you'll have everything."

"You really shouldn't," I say quietly. "It could get you in a lot of trouble."

I notice how close we are standing. The air between us vibrates with possibility.

His words are soft, almost caressing. "I know what's at risk. And I want to do this for you."

I know better than to look at him.

CHAPTER TEN

"Some things hide in plain sight," I'm telling the reporter on the phone. "We often can't see or observe them because we're blinded by the light of other objects. Light is sometimes the enemy. And there can be other invisible but strong forces at play."

"It wasn't easy to find, then?" the reporter asks. Jonah is a journalist from AstronomyScience.com. He's not asked me a single question about Ben being missing. He's asking about 2010 TK7, the Trojan asteroid.

"Extremely difficult to find. That's because its location—at Lagrangian 4, the place in space where the gravitational forces of the sun and Earth are equal—is bathed in tons of sunlight. It took a highly advanced heat sensor to pick up its existence through all that blinding light."

Jonah jumps into another question, but my attention drifts. *Blinding light.* I wonder if in my search to find Ben I am being blinded by sunlight—by his popularity, his good-guy personality, and what I think I know about him—unable to see what's right in front of me.

He stops talking and I suddenly realize he's done asking a question, but I have no idea what it was.

"Would you repeat that?"

"When you spotted it with the space telescope, did you know immediately it was Earth's first—and maybe only—Trojan asteroid?" he asks.

I shake my head. "I was completely blind to it at first. All of us were. We didn't recognize the telltale signatures on the graphs. All the evidence was there, but it took days of analysis to realize what we had found."

My research assistant, Grace, waves at me from my office door. I ask Jonah to hold.

"Shane Russo is in the lobby. He's not on the list . . ."

I smile for the first time that day. Shane was Ben's roommate when we were all at UC Berkeley, and the three of us often got together and solved the world's greatest problems over greasy late-night pizza. Like many college friends, we'd lost track of each other, but we reconnected nine months ago when we found out we were living just a few blocks apart in Brentwood.

Shane and his wife, Diane, were high-level executives in finance—mergers and acquisitions—and their office was less than a mile away from CIT, in Westwood. His wife did a lot of business in Europe, so we rarely saw her, but Shane was around the house a lot lately, helping Ben map out a business plan for the new restaurants he wanted to build or acquire.

"Tell him I'll meet him there in five."

No one can visit the research labs at CIT without presenting a government-issued ID and being on a roster that's authorized by an approval team days before the person is allowed on the grounds. Somehow Shane had talked himself past the security guard at the main entrance and into the lobby. But that's as far as he'd be allowed to go without prior security clearance.

I finish up the call with Jonah, then rush downstairs to meet Shane. With thick brown hair streaked with gray and dressed in a tailored black suit and burgundy tie, he could easily pass for a NASA boss. Maybe that's how he talked himself onto the grounds?

"You've got some security," he says. "You think they'd let me go to your office if I submitted to a retina scan and donated a pint of blood?"

"You're a sight for sore eyes." I motion to the chairs in the corner of the lobby. "But how did you ever get past security?"

"The guard was busy helping a bus maneuver out of the lot. I told him I was already late for an important meeting with you. I guess I looked like I belonged here because he waved me through."

Hardly anyone sidesteps security that easily, so even though I smile, I make a mental note to bring it up at our next staff meeting.

"I stopped by your house, and Zack said I'd find you here." He lays an expensive leather briefcase on the chair next to him. "How are you holding up?"

"Okay, considering. I'm not sleeping much. And I have a perpetual ache in my stomach."

He looks around the lobby. "But . . . you're back at work?"

"Not really. I'm only here for an hour to do a quick interview and grab some stuff. We have a proposal due in a week. Megaproposal. Given what's happening with Ben, my team here is stepping up to handle most of it. But there are still a few parts that I'm not ready to hand over because of where I am in my analysis."

"And still no sign of Ben?"

I shake my head. "Nothing."

I tell him how Ben was traveling in a car with a bodyguard when someone attacked them and the bodyguard was killed, but Shane has already heard this on the news.

"Do they have any idea what happened to him after that? Any clues that he might still be alive?"

"They think he was probably abducted by whoever shot him."

"Then he might still be alive somewhere. Have you seen any activity on his charge cards? Cell phone?"

I shake my head. "Everything stopped."

"I guess I was hoping that maybe he had just skipped town for a bit. To get away from the heat of the trial and all. What can I do? How can I help?"

"There are already big search parties . . . people scouring parks and hospitals. Friends posting on social media and flyers on practically every tree and lamppost in LA. Police are looking everywhere. There's not much else you can do right now."

"The media is saying that Ben's partners may have something to do with his disappearance. Is that what police are pursuing?"

I nod. "But that doesn't stop them from questioning me because they think I have something to gain from his disappearance. Things like life insurance and his inheritance. As if it's not the twenty-first century and I have my own career and my own savings."

"You need to tell them that you've got a relative who's a high-powered defense attorney. Like maybe the one who represented Ryan Seacrest a while back. I'll bet that would make them leave you alone."

I laugh. In college, Shane often embellished his background, leaving out the parts about his dad being a construction worker or that his parents didn't go to college, and focusing instead on a supposed uncle he said was a hedge-fund manager at Goldman Sachs. When some of the wealthy kids bragged about their Porsches or their no-holds-barred spring-break vacations on the other side of the world, Shane would concoct his own big stories, then laugh about it with Ben and me. Because Ben came from a wealthy family, he thought Shane's stories were a hilarious fake-out on the other rich kids, but I always felt his stories were kind of sad. My roots as the child of schoolteachers are humble, too, and I seriously doubted people would like me any better if I made up an extravagant fairy tale about my life. But Shane disagreed. "If they think you don't have the right connections or money, they'll walk all over you."

"When did you see Ben last?" I ask.

He shifts in his seat. "Friday night. In Manhattan. He was in a good mood until Rebecca started asking about the Aurora lawsuit."

"Rebecca?"

"Rebecca Stanton. She's the co-owner of Paragon, the restaurant he's trying to buy."

———

My words are caught in my throat. I want to tell him everything. About the clip where Simone is telling Ben about a man who was seen leaving Rebecca's apartment on Saturday morning. I want to tell him that Rebecca Stanton is dead.

I don't.

As far as I know, her murder hasn't become a big national news story, so I can see why he doesn't know. Still, it strikes me as odd that Ben didn't tell him. Or that someone from Paragon didn't notify him.

My mind is zooming. I have a sense—an instinct—that I shouldn't talk about anything I've seen on that security-system DVR. If the police knew it exists, if they found out I had knowingly kept it from them, I'd be in serious trouble. The kind that would not only get me kicked off the space telescope project but also might land me in jail.

I cough and pretend to need water. I buy time opening the water bottle I'm carrying and take a long gulp. I'm a bad actress. Shane probably knows I'm uncomfortable, but I'm hoping he'll just chalk it up to traumatic stress.

"It's not what you're thinking," Shane says. He mistakes my discomfort for fear that Ben is cheating. Isn't that what all wives do?

"I'm not—"

"It's not like that between them. They argue. Last week they were fighting about why she couldn't get her father to part with his share of the restaurant. When I was in Manhattan a month ago, they were fighting about—" I guess my face must look chalk white because he stops talking. "Look, I didn't come here to . . . well, this isn't anything we need to talk about now."

93

"What is his relationship with Rebecca?" I know what he's going to say. Even if he thinks Ben was straying, he's going to protect his long-time friend. His roommate from college. And he's going to be careful not to rattle me, especially now.

"She's just a business relationship. A contentious one. And you've got nothing to worry about."

But the way he says it makes it clear that I do.

———

My eyes are bloodshot and bleary. I've sifted through every drawer in Ben's desk, scoured his work emails, flipped through the binders in his cabinets, and searched through the contacts on his laptop. I'm not entirely sure what I'm looking for, but I'm in a hurry because I've snuck into Ben's office at Aurora over the busy lunch hour, using his key card and a spare key to the back door that he kept on a metal ring with a Lego wizard on it.

Ben is a very organized businessman. What few papers he has are neatly stacked on his desk, and although he has one drawer of old-fashioned file folders, it appears that most everything else that runs Aurora is stored digitally, using a password that I don't know. I try guessing a few times—Zack's middle name, our first street address—but nothing works. I can access his email without a password, and while there are thousands of emails, there seems to be an intricate system of filing them, even though I can't figure out what it is.

I look for indications of Ben's relationship with Rebecca Stanton, and in all their recent emails, there's definitely tension between them. "This has got to stop," Ben said in one email. "Every time I don't agree to your terms, you always threaten to back out of the deal entirely." In another, Rebecca accuses him of moving too fast. "Slow down. We don't have to close this deal today. We'll get there, but I need time to convince my father. GIVE ME TIME."

There were a couple of flirty messages, too: "Morning, Gorgeous!" Rebecca wrote. "Saw they snapped your pic at the Vanity Fair party. Wow." Or another where Rebecca seems to be blurring business with something else. "I can't think of anyone else I'd rather be doing this with. You amaze me every day." But the one thing I can't find is evidence that Ben ever returned the compliments. Most of the time he didn't respond to her flowery emails at all or, if he did, he kept it friendly but professional. "Amaze? I think you mean amuse. Anyway, any idea when your attorneys will have assembled the bank docs?"

I'm also eager to learn more about the private investigator named Simone I'd seen on the security clips. I type "Simone" into the search bar on his contacts list, and two names pop up. One is based in London and represents Guaranty Alliance Bank. Probably not her. And the other is an attorney named Simone. Could this be her? I search his emails for any correspondence from her and find several, but they're dated four years earlier and related to some trademark applications. It feels like a dead end.

I sit back in his chair, defeated. My eyes drift to a photo on Ben's desk, and my breath stops in my throat when I realize what it is.

———

Most people put photos of themselves with their family on their work desks. But not Ben. Sure, he has a cluster of photographs of Zack on his credenza—Zack at six, face sprinkled with freckles, eating a yellow Popsicle. And another of me and Zack when he was around nine and we had ridden the monster roller coaster at Knott's Berry Farm.

But what sits on his desk—what he looks at every day—is a photo of the Perseid meteor shower he took in Indian Cove at Joshua Tree National Park. With two primordial, crooked Joshua trees in the foreground and a sprinkle of silvery stars in the background, he captured a meteor shooting across the sky in one-thirtieth of a second.

Ben is not a photography buff. But I know why the photo is here.

The warm night in August when that photo was taken, we had bundled baby Zack in the car and arrived at Indian Cove just past three in the morning—the best time to view the meteor showers, but also when only the diehard meteor fans remained. I went to work setting up my telescope, like I had done with him dozens of times before. After I punched the longitude and latitude into the computer to track the sky, I needed to type in the date and asked, "What's today's date again?"

When he didn't answer, I glanced up and saw him looking at me. Even beneath the starlight, I could see a faraway look in his eyes.

"What?" I said with a laugh. "Did I already ask that or something?"

He stepped closer and touched his hand to my hair. "No . . . it's just the way you hold your head when you're setting up your telescope."

I pushed my hair away from my face. "I'm a total geek, aren't I?"

He smiled. "And it's the way you look at me when you ask me if you're a total geek."

And just as he was about to kiss me, one of the Perseid meteors dazzled the skies above us.

"Never change," he whispered. Then as the meteors rained across the sky, he pointed his camera at the heavens and captured this stunning shot, the silhouettes of the spike-leaved Joshua trees giving the photo a feeling of having been taken at the dawn of time.

"I want to remember this night forever," he said. "Years from now, when we're both really, really old, I will make sure you remember it, too."

"How are you going to do that?" I said, wrapping my arms around his waist.

"I have my ways," he said slyly, then kissed me.

My eyes well with tears. He did have his ways. The photo was proof of that.

Detective Dawson is bringing me coffee. From some hipster joint called Tail of the Tiger. He's standing on my front porch, and his hair is neatly combed today. He's wearing what looks like a new light-brown sport jacket. That can only mean he wants something.

I glance at my reflection in the mirror next to the front door, frustrated with the puffy dark circles beneath my eyes.

He fumbles a little when he hands me the paper cup. Still hot. "You seem like the type that would like a cappuccino."

"There's a cappuccino type?"

He shrugs. "They're usually perfectionists, and they like being in control. Sound like anyone you know?"

"There's no place for a perfectionist in astronomy." I take the cup but don't have the heart to tell him that I can't stand coffee.

"You have a minute to talk?"

He follows me into the house and then heads straight to the Christmas tree even though the living room is completely dark. I flip the tree-light switch, and the room—and his face—are suddenly bathed in red-and-green glow. He stays standing, looking at the tree, his back to me.

"The sound technicians have analyzed the voice mail from your husband. The cell coverage was really spotty, but we've been able to make out two words in the entire clip: 'summer' and 'angle.' Is that someone's name? Does it mean anything to you?"

"Summer and angle? No. Were the words close together or separated?"

He pulls out his phone and plays the clip. The sound technicians had taken out the white noise and isolated the voice. It's a stressed voice—is it Ben's?—saying "summer" then a white noise beat and "angle."

"Our team is wondering why someone who had just been shot and had his bodyguard killed in front of him would call his wife and talk about 'summer' and 'angle.' Think about it. He has seventeen seconds to tell you something. Seventeen seconds. And in that extremely limited time, he works in the words 'summer' and 'angle.' Why?"

I search the databanks in my brain for any connection to "summer." There's the season, of course. And summer solstice.

"I've got nothing."

"Is that some kind of astronomy talk? We looked it up, and you being an astronomer and all, we were wondering if he was talking about the angle of the sun in summer."

"Why would he be talking about solar altitude after he's been shot and his bodyguard is dead? Ben's not even a scientist."

"But you are."

"Even astronomers don't go around talking about the sun's angle in summer."

"What is a 'summer angle,' then?"

"There really isn't such a thing. The only thing that comes to mind is that the solar altitude—the sun's angle—is forty-seven degrees higher at the summer solstice than it is at the winter solstice. But that's not something anyone would talk about in an emergency."

"Think about it, Sarah. It could help us get the break we've been looking for in this case."

He settles on the couch and motions for me to sit next to him. Then he clears his throat and riffles through his notebook.

"Just a couple of more questions here, then I'll let you go. I need you to fill in some blanks about the night Ben went missing. What's the name of the airport bar where you and your colleague—Aaron, is it?—were Tuesday night?"

I take a seat on the couch, trying to look calm. "I don't remember."

"There's only one in the American Airlines terminal. Was it Angel City Brewery?"

"Could be. I'm not sure—"

"The bartender remembers seeing you there Tuesday night."

"He does?" I say, but of course the bartender remembers me. I sat with Aaron at the very end of the bar for hours, engrossed in conversation, laughing, tossing back shots of tequila, and chasing them with sangrita. No doubt he remembers that we drank all of their Calle 23 Blanco, so he had to crack open a brand-new bottle.

I'm sure he saw the kiss.

We were laughing about something we'd seen on the TV above the bar, then his lips were on mine, soft and warm, erasing everything that had come before it. I closed my eyes and soaked in the perfection of the kiss—the smoky taste of tequila, the way his hands held my face, and what his lips were doing with mine. It was the kiss of a lover, expressing a meaning I couldn't yet grasp.

"Any idea what else he saw?" James's voice brings me back to the moment.

"I have an idea, yes," I say quietly.

"How long has that been going on?"

I feel the heat rush to my face. "I don't have to answer that."

He rubs the back of his neck. "We're going to need to monitor your phones, your cell phone, your personal email."

"Why? Because you think that what the bartender saw somehow has something to do with Ben's disappearance?"

"Actually, I do."

My mouth goes dry. "We were celebrating. We had too much to drink and things got out of hand."

"You're oversimplifying the situation, Sarah. I got a call from one of your husband's partners, Richard Jenkins. He says Ben's lawsuit is a smoke screen to cover up the fact that Ben was stealing millions from *them*. They say he disappeared with the money."

"Richard told me the same story. But where's the logic in his theory? If Ben was stealing money from them, why would he disappear, leaving his wife and son behind?"

He cocks his head to the side. "Maybe things are not so great between him and his wife."

The weight of my own guilt presses down on me. I'm silent for a long moment. "Even if you believe that theory, what about our son? You think he'd leave Zack behind?"

"Marriages, families, relationships are complicated. People don't always act the way you think they will." He drains his coffee. "The way I see it, if Ben did steal the money from the partners, and if there was trouble between the two of you . . ."

"Shouldn't you be looking instead into what happened to Ben after he was shot and his bodyguard was killed? Was he abducted? If so, by whom? Where did they take him?"

He laces his fingers behind his head. "Several of my partners are chasing down those leads. But my focus? My focus is you, Sarah. I need to understand everything that was going on in Ben's life before he disappeared. And you are the key to that."

"I've told you everything I know."

"You know what I find most of the time? The truth is often obscured by the facts that are directly in front of us. The truth lies around the edges. And that's where I'm going to keep looking." He tucks his notebook into his jacket pocket then abruptly changes the subject. "What do you know about his new partner in New York?"

I feel like I'm outside my body, watching from a distance. I make sure every word I say is true. "Ben has been trying to buy restaurants in New York and Chicago, but he never said anything about any particular partner. Why?"

"Richard claims Ben's working with this new partner to hide the money. Any idea who he's talking about?"

"He's trying to blind you with sunlight."

"What do you mean, 'sunlight'?"

"He's distracting you with some shiny and unexpected premise, forcing you to chase down useless theories in order to keep the focus off of himself."

He shrugs. "Sounds like you're doing the same thing. You're telling me your husband never told you the name of his new partner in New York?"

"Do you have a wife, Detective?"

"Not yet. No."

"Well, if you did, I don't think you'd bore her with the details of every person you spoke with during your workday. Especially if you've been married for fifteen years. Especially if she had her own demanding career. And if you did share those details, you can bet you wouldn't be married very long."

His lips curve slightly but he doesn't smile. "If you ask me, that sounds like an excuse for not knowing much about your husband. You don't talk to him for three days, you ignore two phone calls from him because you're . . . drinking with a colleague, you don't know who he partners with, what kind of car he drives. You don't even know he hired a bodyguard. Tell me, Sarah, what *do* you know about your husband?"

His words slice through the air, leaving me breathless. "The things I know about my husband . . . are the things that aren't . . . relevant right now."

He rises from the couch and faces the Christmas tree. "They're probably more relevant than you think."

The words slip from my mouth before I can stop them. "I know that he loves Formula One racing, he's religious about eating granola with blueberries for breakfast, he's completed six marathons in the past three years. He loves our son, sucks at math, makes a mean tri-tip on the Fourth of July, and . . . he decorates one helluva Christmas tree."

My eyes well up with tears, but I blink them away. I'm describing a life I once lived. A life that suddenly feels far away, as though I had dreamt it. How long has it been since I sat with him while he ate granola and meandered through the Sunday paper? When was the last time we'd spent the Fourth of July at home, instead of on opposite sides of the continent on business?

He stands. "I'm sending some technicians over later this morning to set up the monitoring of your emails. And your phone."

I place my coffee cup on the table next to his. I haven't taken a single sip. "I want to consult with an attorney first."

"If you don't have anything to hide, this shouldn't be a problem. Or, think of it another way. You can either agree to it, or I can get a warrant to make it happen."

CHAPTER ELEVEN

Anyone who studies the cosmos must accept that darkness is an inescapable fact—an astronomical certainty. We need darkness in order to experience the light of the stars. Still, I cannot understand the blackness and confusion that has descended on me. After my presentation about our discovery of Earth's Trojan asteroid, I'd been elated that we'd unlocked a secret of our solar system. Now I feel a heaviness in every step. It's as though a massive gravity pull has drained all the light from my world.

I fix my gaze on Jupiter, shining like a promise in the evening sky. I train my telescope on it and look past its tawny bands to locate its moons—tonight I can see three of them, hovering like bright fireflies.

Where is Ben? Can he see Jupiter and its moons tonight? I don't—won't—allow myself to think that he's dead. But I have no narrative for where he is if he is alive.

I try to focus my attention on Jupiter and its moons, but the questions swirl around me like giant clouds of dust. What is Ben's connection to the dead Rebecca Stanton? Was it just a coincidence that he met with her Friday night and she was dead Saturday morning?

I step off the patio and into the garden, where the scent from the pathway lined with sprawling lavender envelops me. Ben had spent a fortune to hire one of LA's foremost landscape architects to design the backyard gardens. She'd planned them to stimulate all the senses—plants in an array of colors bloomed in every season; citrus and fruit trees hung heavy with guava, avocados, tangerines, and lemons; and countless plants and herbs threw their scents into the nighttime air—rosemary, lavender, jasmine, and the sweet, haunting fragrance of lilac. Ben had grown up in Chicago, where lilac flourishes everywhere, but in the warm temperatures of LA, only low-chill varieties grow, and they are fussy, requiring extra care from the gardener.

In the moonlight, I notice one of the small lilac bushes has fallen over, perhaps dug up by a neighbor's dog or one of the many raccoons that sometimes roam our yard after feasting on the koi in a neighbor's pond.

As I push the lilac back into place, I notice a glint in the dirt. At first I think maybe it's an illusion caused by the moonlight reflecting off some sandy soil, but when I look more closely, I can see something metallic just under the surface. I kneel down and sweep my hand across the dirt.

Beneath my fingers is a gun.

This isn't like the one I found in the bedroom. It's smaller, not new. Not loaded.

I suddenly know what shock feels like. My mouth goes dry, and I'm not sure if I want to run or hide. My mind cannot grasp why the gun is here, hiding in plain sight. It'd be so easy to spot in the daylight. It's as if someone deliberately left it here. For me to find?

My heart feels like it's stopped beating. I lift the gun out of the dirt and drop it on the smooth brick path. It makes a metallic thud, then lies there, taunting me with its mystery. In the mocking moonlight, I stare at it and feel sick, as though I've just exhumed a body.

All capacity for rational thinking vanishes, leaving only the reptilian part of my brain to respond—adrenaline jolts blood through my veins, and my entire body breaks out in a cold, nervous sweat.

I don't have to examine the gun to suspect that it's the weapon that killed Rebecca Stanton. But I cannot think through whether Ben hid it or whether someone deposited it here to frame Ben. Or to frame me.

For a brief moment, I consider showing it to Detective Dawson. But if this is the murder weapon, handing it over to police will surely seal Ben's fate as the prime—and perhaps only—murder suspect.

Is this why Ben erased the DVR? Because he had killed Rebecca Stanton and he didn't want any evidence that he'd buried the murder weapon here?

As I peer at the gun in the moonlight, I decide there can be only one conclusion. *The gun must not be found.*

I race to the garage and grab a shovel. I dig out the lilac and, with what feels like superhuman strength, hollow out a deeper hole, a foot deep, perhaps.

With the sweet scent of lilac rising up on a warm breeze, I lift the gun and carry it in my outstretched palms. I feel as though I am making an offering, a silent prayer that this gun is not what it appears to be. Using a lilac leaf, I remove any possible fingerprints, and with a trembling hand, lower the gun into the hole.

My breathing is shallow as I cover the gun with dirt then replant the lilac. I run back to the garage for a broom, sweep away any telltale dirt on the pathway, then race to return the tools to the garage.

"Mom." Zack's voice startles me from behind.

I whirl around and clutch a hand to my chest. "You scared me."

"Some guy from the FBI is at the front door."

CHAPTER TWELVE

Zack is wrong. There are two FBI agents on my doorstep. The tall African American man is carrying a large plastic bottle of water, nearly empty. The petite woman next to him wears a black suit, her long dark hair parted on the side. Her blue eyes are so pale they remind me of the eyes of white ibis I'd seen wading in the Gulf in Florida.

"Samuel Nelson, FBI," he says, shaking my hand.

"Elizabeth Elliott," she says.

They both produce their gold "Federal Bureau of Investigation" badges, which, in the soft light from the porch sconces, look real enough. I peer at the photos in the identification cards next to the badges. They also seem real, even though the moment doesn't.

"It's late," I say, nodding toward Zack beside me. I'm pretty sure FBI agents aren't supposed to show up on your doorstep unannounced late into the night.

"Yes, and we're sorry," Elizabeth says, as though she means it. "We had intended to get here earlier but got stuck in some serious traffic on the 405."

I can't figure why FBI braved the 405 freeway during rush hour to come to my house unannounced.

"Do you have a moment to talk?" Samuel asks.

"About what?"

"About your husband." He has an accurate way of speaking, as though he wants there to be no ambiguity about what he's saying.

"I'm already talking with LAPD."

"Yes, we're working with the LAPD, and we have those records," he says.

"We have a few questions we'd like to ask you. They might help us locate your husband," Elizabeth continues.

She says it casually, as if the questions they're going to ask are about Ben's favorite color or where he likes to vacation.

"Do you know what's happened to him? Is that why you're here?" Zack asks.

Elizabeth smiles without showing her teeth. "If it's okay, we'd like to continue this discussion with just you, Mrs. Mayfield."

"We've brought coffee," Samuel says with a forced smile.

———

"Let me turn on some lights around here, then I'll meet you in the kitchen," I tell the FBI agents, disguising my trembling stomach with a cheery tone.

I follow Zack upstairs to his bedroom and reassure him that I'll tell him everything in the morning. Then I stumble through the house turning on lights while making a quick call to Stuart, filling him in on the FBI's visit. He suggests an attorney who could accompany me during the interview. If there was any time to hire a defense attorney, it feels like it would be now. Still, I resist. I know that the top brass at CIT and others would see that hire as proof that I had something to hide.

I hang up and gaze into the living room, where moonlight drifts through sheer curtains, casting black and silver shadows on the walls.

Have I made a mistake hiding the gun? If it is evidence against Ben, I think I'm doing the right thing by burying it. Or am I merely helping a dead man?

That thought sends a chill through my core. I have a sense Ben is not dead. We scientists call that "motivated reasoning"—believing something because we want it to be true, even if the evidence mounts up otherwise. I'm aware that my belief is a defense mechanism, a way to protect me from the unthinkable. My motivated reasoning silences my scientific mind, the part of me that would examine the data and seek to reach an accurate conclusion.

I wonder if I've been building a family—a life—with someone who is capable of murder. Was everything I knew about Ben an illusion?

I part the living-room curtains and gaze at the moon one last time. I know that its light is an illusion, too. Moonlight is actually the reflected light from the sun, bouncing off the moon. Still, I sense hope in its rays.

———

"An asteroid?" FBI agent Samuel Nelson asks. "Following Earth around?"

"Well, actually, it's the other way around. The Trojan asteroid dances *in front of* Earth, getting closer then farther as it orbits," I say.

"Closer then farther." I've lost him in the abstractness of my description. "So it might crash into us someday?"

"Nope. Like a good dancer, this asteroid always avoids blundering into its partner."

"Dancing, huh?"

I know he's stalling, trying to appear engaged before he asks his questions.

"Right. *Earth* is playing follow the leader," I explain. "We're chasing this dancing asteroid around the sun."

We're sitting around the kitchen, seemingly old chums catching up over tea and coffee. Samuel is wearing a tan suit that's two sizes too big for his narrow shoulders.

He and Elizabeth wanted me to be somewhere comfortable, some place we could talk. The kitchen is that, although at this hour only the pale moonlight trickles through the mullioned windows. Even the bright pendant lights over the table can't throw off enough light to cast away the gloom.

"We want to ask you a few questions about Ben." Elizabeth says his name with soft emphasis. "He was in New York last week. Can you tell us why?"

"He's been looking to open up another restaurant in Manhattan."

"Do you know who he was meeting with while he was there?" Samuel asks.

"I've already told Detective Dawson that I don't know about his business dealings. Ben really doesn't share that with me."

Elizabeth mimics the placement of my hands on the table, palms down. "What did he talk about when he returned from New York?"

"I only saw him briefly before I had to leave for the airport. We talked about, you know, married couple stuff. Our son, house repairs. Mundane things." I leave out the part about discussing our broken marriage.

"There is . . . evidence that Ben was present at a crime scene. Did he mention anything to you?" Elizabeth asks.

Present at a crime scene.

My palms are sweaty, and my mind flashes to the DVR where I first saw Ben talking with Simone about Rebecca's murder. What if that DVR has actual evidence that Ben *murdered* Rebecca?

"No. What kind of crime scene?"

Samuel takes a long slug of his coffee. "A woman named Rebecca Stanton was murdered—shot to death—on the rooftop patio of her apartment building in Manhattan."

"Murdered? What does this have to do with Ben?"

Elizabeth leans forward and lowers her voice. "What we're getting at here is that your husband had met with her earlier the night before.

We understand he was in the midst of buying the restaurant she owns, Paragon, but she severed the deal just hours before she was found dead."

I know my cheeks are scarlet now. "Are you sure you're talking about my husband? Ben Mayfield?"

"Witnesses saw them arguing Friday night," Samuel says, evading my question.

"And we identified his fingerprints at the crime scene," Elizabeth adds.

The room goes dead silent. I look from Elizabeth's face to Samuel's, trying to understand what they're getting at. My voice is a raspy whisper. "Are you saying Ben is somehow involved in this woman's murder?"

"We're not in a position to say what his involvement is yet," Samuel says curtly. "But we can say that we have an eyewitness who saw someone matching your husband's description leaving Rebecca Stanton's apartment early that morning."

Their evidence explains almost everything. Ben's disappearance has nothing to do with the lawsuit against his partners or their accusations that Ben was stealing from them.

Rebecca severed the deal with Ben to buy Paragon.

Ben killed Rebecca Stanton.

The gun in the garden is the murder weapon.

Or is the gun I found in the nightstand the murder weapon?

My mind is racing so fast to process it all that I excuse myself and stumble into the bathroom in a fog. I find a washcloth and run it in cold water, then press it hard against my upper lip to stop the waves of nausea.

I cannot accept their conclusion that Ben killed Rebecca Stanton. He couldn't have actually pointed a gun at anyone and pulled the trigger.

Once when Ben and I were returning to our car after dinner in Koreatown, two teens approached us and demanded money, their fists balled up in their sweatshirt pockets as if they might have guns in them. When the bigger one shoved me, Ben's face reddened and the veins bulged in his neck. He grabbed that kid by the arm and twisted it sharply. "Don't you touch her," he growled in a voice I didn't recognize. If he'd had a gun then, I could imagine he would've brandished it. But I still can't see him pulling the trigger.

I can't breathe. My lungs feel like they've turned to concrete, and I can't draw a breath.

I try to remember what Ben did—what he said to me—when he returned home Saturday morning. We were together for only thirty minutes before I left for the airport. When I told him I'd been unhappy in our marriage for months, his face had turned parchment white, but I had been so consumed with what I had to say that I don't remember if he had been acting different before that.

How does someone act if they just murdered someone?

I glance at a set of photos tucked in the corners of the bathroom mirror. A friend had thrown a Halloween party and took photos with a vintage Polaroid camera. We'd been too busy to find costumes, so Ben and I went as California cowboys. Ben wore a dusty cowboy hat, a faded blue handkerchief looped around his neck, and a suede jacket that made him look like he was straight out of *The Magnificent Seven*. Only in this picture, his hat is tipped forward, casting a shadow on his face. His lips are pressed together in a straight line. At the moment the camera captured his image, he looks decidedly grim.

I lift the photo off the mirror and shudder. It's like looking at a stranger.

CHAPTER THIRTEEN

An hour later, four agents wearing black FBI vests descend on my house and produce a search warrant. After giving me a minute to make sure it's referring to our property, they instruct me and Zack to wait in the living room with Elizabeth while they search the premises. When I explain to Zack why the FBI is here, his eyes widen and he looks like he might cry.

I hug him tightly and force a calm in my voice that I don't feel. "We'll figure this out." Then I call Stuart, who tells me I must comply and instructs me not to give them any information that isn't contained in the warrant.

I hang up and scan the paper—now smudged from my sweaty hands—but my mind cannot focus long enough on the words to make any more sense of it. I can see that it gives them the right to search everything on the property plus Ben's texts, emails, and phone calls, but since his phone is not here and his laptop is at work, they focus their attention on going through every room in the house as well as the front and back yard.

"Beautiful tree," Elizabeth says, running her fingers through the silver tinsel. "You and Ben do this every year?"

This is not a casual question, even though she asks it as though we're old friends. I know she's starting the conversation to gather more information about Ben and our family.

"If you think Ben had something to do with Rebecca Stanton's murder," I say, "how does that explain everything that happened to him—to us—since then?"

She looks at me, her lips pursed.

"You know he was poisoned?" I continue. "That he and his body-guard were shot Tuesday night. And there have been a number of intruders on the property—once when Ben was here and once when Zack and I were alone at night. In light of your theory about Ben, how do you explain any of that?"

She answers slowly, carefully choosing her words. "We're investigating those incidents, too. It's possible they are in retaliation for Rebecca's murder. By someone who knows what your husband did."

Zack looks up from his phone, a startled expression on his face. I don't like him hearing any of this about his dad, but I'm powerless to shield him from it.

"What they *think* he did," I say. "Where does the FBI presume my husband is now?"

Her voice is flat, devoid of emotion. "That's why we're here. We're looking for information that may help us find him."

Or convict him, I want to say, but I clamp my mouth shut.

I can't take the stress any longer. I lean my head against the back of the couch and close my eyes, signaling that the conversation is over.

I hear occasional thumps overhead as two men search the second floor. But I'm focused on the sounds the agents are making in the back-yard. My hearing seems heightened, and I think I can actually hear their footsteps shuffling on the garden brick, even though the geography of the grounds makes that scientifically impossible.

I hear the garage door squeak open. Are they lifting the shovel off the wall, or is that scuffle and scrape the sound of them pushing a metal cabinet around? Fortunately there isn't much to see in the garage. A few years back, Ben and Zack had organized it like something off of GeekDad.com so they could build crazy gadgets. Most of the time their projects didn't work, but after many failed attempts to get it right, they did manage to make a small drone quadcopter one summer and a wooden catapult the next.

The sound of heavy footfalls on wet grass in the garden brings me back to the moment. I imagine the agents unearthing the gun and feel like a knife is twisting in my gut. Do FBI agents dig up an entire backyard looking for evidence? I wonder if they have metal detectors and whether I've buried the gun deep enough to avoid detection. Or if my fingerprints will still be on the gun even though it's been buried in the loamy dirt. The logical part of my brain knows that's impossible, but that doesn't stop my heart from banging against my ribs.

The clock on the mantel announces the eleven o'clock hour—sixteen notes of the Westminster chime melody, whose sweetness seems to be mocking the grim circumstances. The song is followed by eleven delicate tones marking the hour, each of which grows progressively louder, beating out my destiny.

If they find either of the guns, should I pretend to be shocked? That would be the best course of action, but I'm a lousy actor.

"Almost finished here. You got a recorder hooked up to the camera security system?" Samuel asks, stepping into the living room.

"We just got the system. But the DVR malfunctioned and wasn't recording anything."

That answer seems to satisfy him, but it takes nearly a half hour for my pulse to return to normal.

I feel prickly impatience as the minutes then hours tick by slowly. I don't see Samuel or the other agents again until they rush down the stairs toward the front door. I catch a glimpse of the black bags in their hands. Whatever is in there must be what they think is evidence—but I have no idea what it is.

———

DAY FOUR

My sister is crying. Her eyes are red and swollen, and her voice is thick and raw from tears.

"I had to come."

It's early Saturday morning and Rachel has arrived on my doorstep, dragging a shiny blue metal suitcase behind her.

"I know you said you'd tell me when you needed me to come, but I thought that even if you weren't going to ask for help, you probably needed it." She pulls me into a hug, and the tears fall some more. "I took the first flight out this morning. Is there any news?"

"There's a lot to tell you."

She steps inside and rolls her suitcase into the corner. "Can I stay in your guest room? You won't have to entertain me or anything. I'm here to help out."

I hesitate. "It's been chaotic. You might be better off getting a room at that hotel a few blocks away."

I'm not entirely sure I want her at the house. My sister is nosy. When we were teens, she'd steal into my room and read my diary. She once ratted me out to our parents after I wrote about sneaking out at midnight to watch a meteor shower with some friends.

Her prying will appear innocent, of course. She'll say she's looking for a brush or moisturizer and look through all my cabinets and drawers. And she'll definitely sneak a peek at the texts on my phone and eavesdrop on my conversations.

She's also a perfectionist. She would notice that the lilac bush was tilted or the soil was disturbed. Her garden won some award and was featured in the *San Francisco Chronicle*—so I wouldn't put it past her to dig around the lilac to give it some extra fertilizer or make it stand straight.

And find what's buried beneath it. If it's still there.

She senses my reticence. "I'll only stay as long as you want me to."

Now I feel bad for hurting her feelings. Both our parents had died in the last three years, and since then Rachel has been more needy, more quick to tears. "We're orphans," she'd often cry in panic when we talked on the phone. "Things will never be the same again." It's not that she missed them more than I did, but she definitely spent more time focusing on our loss.

"It's good to have you here," I say with surprising calm. My mind is still racing to figure out what evidence the FBI took away last night. I knew it wasn't the Glock that I'd hidden in the telescope case. After they'd left, I'd checked and the weapon was still there, hidden beneath the gray foam. Now I'm anxious to head into the garden—alone—to see if the FBI has dug up the gun. I'd wanted to look ever since they'd left, but I'd resisted the impulse, determined to wait until daylight when I could more easily see what they'd done.

"Have you even been eating?" She asks, bringing me back to the moment. She places her hands on her hips. Even after enduring a flight from San Francisco and without a stitch of makeup, she looks like she could be a model—glossy red hair that falls in waves to her shoulders and pale white Irish skin. "You look like you've lost weight. Let me fix you something."

"I don't have much of an appetite right now."

"What can I do, then?"

"I'd love a quiet soak in a bubble bath," I say, remembering lounging in bubbles for hours when we were kids, soaking until our hands turned pruney. "Then I'll tell you everything."

She rubs her hands together, excited to have something to do. The minute she heads for the bathroom to fill the tub, I rush outdoors and into the garden. In case she's watching from one of the windows, I stretch my arms over my head and yawn, as if I'm just out there getting some relief from the stress. I pluck a tangerine off one of the trees, cast off its thick skin, and sink my teeth into its juicy flesh.

Fruit in hand, I inspect the lilac bush and feel a surge of relief when I see it's exactly where I left it, undisturbed. The entire flower bed and the soil around the bush look completely untouched.

The agents had not found the gun. But they'd found something else inside and taken it away.

What was it?

———

As I shove the telescope case back into the corner the doorbell rings, and I hear my sister scurry down the stairs to answer it.

"Yes, she is, but I don't . . ." I hear her say quietly. Then she calls out to me, her tone demanding. "Sarah, you need to come down here."

When I arrive at the door, Rachel looks more than a bit overwhelmed as Brad stands in the doorway, his hand firmly gripping Shane's right arm.

"Sarah, tell him I'm a friend of yours," Shane says.

"He's okay, Brad."

"He looked like one of those reporters that try to sneak up here all day long," Brad says, releasing Shane's arm.

I thank Brad again and close the front door.

"Wow, that's some security you have there," Shane says, rubbing his arm.

Rachel clears her throat. "I'm Sarah's sister, Rachel. Visiting from San Francisco."

"Shane," he says, shaking her hand. "I've heard a lot about you from Ben. I've been friends with your sister and Ben since college."

He gives me a brief hug. Even though it's Saturday, he's dressed like he's headed to the boardroom, wearing a navy-blue power suit that highlights his broad shoulders. I can see why Brad might have mistaken him for one of the better-dressed reporters. "Pecan sticky buns. Straight out of the oven," he says, presenting me with takeout from a nearby bakery.

"Smells delicious."

My sister takes the bag and heads to the kitchen to find a place for it on the counters overflowing with food and flowers.

"I just want to check to see how you're holding up. Do you need anything?"

"I've called his voice mail about thirty times just to listen to him speak. Does that make me crazy?"

Shane shoots me a half smile. "I think that's pretty normal, actually."

"The longer he's missing, the harder it's getting . . . but I'm hanging in there."

We head into the living room. He nods at the camera in the corner. "With all the security you guys have, you'd think they might have seen something."

"Yeah, we probably went overboard when we put in the system. And somehow its hard drive was completely erased."

I fill him in on the latest from the FBI, and he looks at me in utter disbelief when he hears Ben is a suspect in Rebecca Stanton's murder.

"There's no way Ben murdered anyone," I say. "He couldn't have pulled the trigger. I'm sure of it."

Shane's face turns ashen. When he finally speaks, his voice is low and shaken. "Sarah, you might want to sit down."

"Why?" I ask, but I don't sit.

He rubs the back of his neck. "Ben owned a gun. *Guns.* I never saw them or anything, but he told me he bought a few. Said he stored them at one of the gun clubs in Manhattan."

My voice is not much louder than a breath. "He stored guns in Manhattan? What for?"

"He never told me. And I would never have believed he could pull the trigger, either. Except when I saw him Friday night he'd been drinking . . . and when Rebecca backed out of the deal at the last minute, he was slamming his fists on the table. Knocking over glasses. Yelling at Rebecca. Saying stuff like 'You can't do this to me,' and 'You're going to regret this.' Good thing she ran out or . . . I don't know what would've happened."

My words sound wooden. "Are you . . . are you saying you think it's possible Ben killed her?"

His face softens. "I can't imagine Ben hurting anyone. I mean, c'mon, this is Ben we're talking about, right? Even back in college when we'd hit the bars and the parties, remember Ben was the golden boy. He never got into any kind of trouble, even when the rest of us did. But that Friday night? That's a Ben I've never seen before. That's someone who was really angry. Amped up on drugs and had too much to drink. He was capable of anything."

CHAPTER FOURTEEN

It's ten o'clock in the morning, and both the sun and a pale half-moon ride high in the sky. The moon is visible in daylight nearly every day with a few exceptions, but most of us don't take time to notice it. I gaze at the two spheres, feel the warm sun on my skin, and then I'm grounded in the familiar. The constant.

A casual observer of today's sky might assume that the sun and the moon are the same size. They certainly appear that way. But in reality, the moon is so tiny compared to the sun that it would take sixty-four *million* moons to fill up the sun. They only *appear* to be the same size because in a unique coincidence, the moon is 1/400th the size of the sun, but it's also about 1/400th as far from us as the sun.

Most things are not as they appear.

Ben appeared to be a successful restaurant owner, married for fifteen years with a teenage son and well-liked by everyone who knew him. But behind that facade lurked evidence he murdered Rebecca Stanton.

And then there was Shane's description of Ben being drunk and angry the night she was murdered. That didn't seem like the man I knew, either. Sure, he liked to relax with a few beers or shots of his favorite Japanese bourbon, but I'd never seen him go much beyond that. *Was Shane exaggerating, or was this who Ben really was?*

I had no idea how to explain the FBI's accusations to Zack. This was his dad, the man who used to frighten away monsters that hid under his bed, who was an all-star at the hiding part of hide-n-seek, and who made breakfast waffles smothered in whipped cream and drizzled with chocolate, straight out of a young boy's dreams.

So when I told him, gently explaining why the FBI had come to our doorstep, his face crumpled and he cried thick tears, like glassy jewels that slipped out of his brown eyes.

"You don't believe any of it, right, Mom?" he'd asked.

"I don't," I'd whispered, hugging him tight.

My thoughts are interrupted by a swift knock at the garden gate. "Sarah?" a woman's voice calls out to me. The gate is tall—six feet—so I can't see who's on the other side. "It's Elizabeth Elliott. From the FBI. I tried ringing your doorbell . . ."

The scents of lilac and lavender rise up in the midmorning heat as I head through the garden and unlatch the gate. I'm not sure why Elizabeth thinks it's okay to stop by again unannounced, but I also know that I haven't been answering my phone, either.

Even on a Saturday, Elizabeth is dressed in a conservative gray suit with a white blouse, her dark hair falling in gentle waves. It's a carefully cultivated look that makes her seem far more imposing than her five foot three inches.

I point out the half-moon and the sun in the sky. "Is that . . . normal?" she asks. I get the impression she spends little time looking at the sky, because she seems almost spooked by the sight.

"Pretty much every day, except for when it's close to a new moon or is a full moon."

She nods like she understands, but I'm pretty sure she's not listening. "Have a minute?" She lifts her tone at the end of her sentence to make it sound casual, but the firm set of her jaw makes it clear it's not.

"Actually, I was about to get going . . ." Unless she has a search warrant, I want nothing to do with Elizabeth and her questions.

"I have some new information to share with you."

I'm not sure I can handle any more information from the FBI. I close the gate behind her and feel the energy drain out of me. "Come on in."

She follows me to the seating area on the patio, then waits for me to sit before choosing the chair directly across. She leans forward and pushes aside the arrangement of succulents on the coffee table, as though they might somehow get in the way of our discussion. "When did you ask your husband for a divorce?"

Her question catches me by surprise. "What do you mean?" I ask calmly, but I can't stop my cheeks from flushing red.

"A few days before his disappearance, your husband told his mother, Catherine Mayfield, that you had asked him for a divorce."

"What do you—"

"Is it true? Did you ask your husband for a divorce?"

"We discussed our marriage. Divorce was mentioned. But no plans were made." My voice sounds thin, weak.

Her perfectly tweezed eyebrows arch over blue eyes. "And you didn't disclose this to anyone before? Not to police. Not to us."

"This was a private discussion between my husband and me. I don't imagine Ben thought his mother would tell the FBI about it. It's not material to what's going on."

"Actually, it is. You're in line to inherit the Mayfield Department Store fortune. Not to mention that you're the sole beneficiary of Ben's seven-million-dollar life insurance policy."

I roll my eyes. "I've already been through this with Detective Dawson. Just because I stand to benefit financially from Ben's death doesn't mean I'm somehow involved in it."

"I didn't say you were involved. Or that Ben is dead."

It feels like she just slapped me in the face. "Then what are you asking?"

"Is it possible that your boyfriend—Aaron McCarthy—has a role in this?"

"Let's be clear. He's not . . . my boyfriend."

"This is the man you were with in the airport bar the night your husband disappeared?" She glances at some other notes. "The man the bartender said you were kissing long after midnight."

I shut my eyes. "Aaron is not involved in any of this. That kiss was a one-time thing . . . a mistake."

"A mistake," she says quietly, then flips through her notepad. "And yet, the CIT records indicate you met with him just hours after your husband's disappearance. Just after eleven the next morning."

My heart thumps loudly in my chest. "You have the CIT access records?"

"I'm not at liberty to say what records we have. But we know you met with him within hours of reporting Ben missing. Why?"

I shift in my seat. "We needed to discuss several things. We've just announced a major discovery of a Trojan asteroid in Earth's orbit—"

"Are you saying that not long after you discovered your husband was missing, you left your home and traveled all the way to CIT in Pasadena in order to discuss . . . an asteroid?"

"Yes. That's what I'm saying."

"In person. You couldn't do that by phone?"

"Right."

She leans back into the cushions of the couch, studying me. "Why are you protecting him?"

"I'm not protecting anyone. Aaron had nothing to do with Ben's disappearance."

"How well do you know Aaron McCarthy?"

"I've worked with him for a few years. Two maybe. Why?"

"So you know about his bankruptcy a few years ago?"

I shake my head. "I don't. And what does it matter? Being bankrupt doesn't mean you go and murder your colleague's husband."

"It matters if your 'colleague' would become an extremely wealthy woman when her husband is dead. I understand your stake in the Mayfield Department Store fortune would be valued well into eight figures."

I'm frustrated and dumbfounded at her line of questioning, but letting her know I'm feeling any of that is a losing battle. "You're wasting your time looking into a discussion between a husband and wife about their marriage. Or my brief . . . incident with Aaron McCarthy."

"Odd you should use the word 'brief' because it doesn't appear that way. Apparently the two of you were seen together a couple of times since Ben went missing. Twice at CIT. You can see how that appears."

I want to tell her that Aaron and I had been meeting to recover the security footage on the DVR but I know that admitting to hiding potential evidence would not go over well. Might even land me in jail. How else to explain why I met with Aaron?

I sit up straight, as though I'm ready for her to leave. I want to take the conversation in a different direction. "I thought you said you had new information to share with me."

Her face darkens. "I do. We have the results from Rebecca Stanton's autopsy." She's silent for a long moment. "She was pregnant."

The news hits me hard. Sucks the breath out of me. Elizabeth doesn't have to say anything more in order for me to fill in the blanks: Maybe Rebecca's murder wasn't just about a business deal gone sour. Or an affair. Maybe Ben killed Rebecca because she was pregnant and threatened to tell. To tell me. And if I found out, Ben was worried I would divorce him and walk away with half of his Mayfield Department Store fortune.

I glance up at the pale half-moon, still floating with the sun across the sky and try to calm my nerves.

Things are not always as they appear.

———

"Mom?" Zack says.

I jolt awake and realize I'd fallen asleep on the couch in front of the Christmas tree after dinner. I'm disoriented and unsure of the time.

Then reality comes in like a roar, stealing my breath. For a few moments of sleep, my body—my brain—had been lulled into forgetting. But now the truth comes rushing back.

Ben is missing.

A wave of deep longing and sadness engulfs me, and I'm powerless to stop it.

Ben is a murder suspect.

I sit straight up.

"Are you okay, Mom?"

I nod, trying to steady my emotions. I feel like I might burst into tears.

"Yes, what's up?" I say, trying to conceal the sadness in my voice. I'm guessing he's here to complain about Aunt Rachel. Since he was little, she had a habit of going into his room and organizing the clothes in his drawers and the books on his shelves. It's a compulsion of hers, and while he welcomed it when he was five, I'm betting that now he doesn't want his aunt to mess with his stuff.

"I'll talk to you in the morning."

I rub my eyes, trying to will my heavy eyelids to remain open. "No, I'm awake. What did you want to tell me?"

He's halfway out of the living room and stops to look at the Christmas tree. He seems to be weighing some kind of decision. "If I tell you something, you promise you won't get mad?"

I swallow hard. "It depends on what it is."

He starts to say something then closes his mouth.

"If I'm mad about what it is, I promise to stay calm about it." I hold up my hand. "Promise."

He ambles over to the chair beside the couch and sits down. "I lied about where I was the night Dad . . . went missing."

A tight knot forms in my stomach. "What do you mean?"

"I know I told you and the police that I went to karate then got home at nine. But the truth is, I skipped karate, my friends came over, and I stayed out with them until about nine thirty."

"Zack—"

"I *know* I was grounded. And I was pretty sure you'd bust me. But you weren't home until really late, either."

Busted. I try not to look guilty. "What were you doing with your friends?"

He shakes his head. "*It's not what you think.* We got something to eat. That's all."

I'm relieved even if I'm not sure I believe his story. "I'm far less 'mad' about you breaking your grounding than if you were making poor decisions with your friends."

He's focused on a spot on the carpet. "That's not everything. There's something I didn't tell you about that night."

I stare at him, waiting for him to continue. I'm not sure if I should be scared or angry or both.

"I know Dad told me to set the security alarm, and I know I'm *supposed* to set it when I leave . . . and I did it that night. But when I came back, the alarm was *off*."

His eyes are wide, and for a moment he looks like a seven-year-old in a teenage body. "Maybe you didn't actually set it, but you think you did. That happened to me once," I say, trying to lighten his mood.

It doesn't work. "I remember hearing the alarm beep when I left the house. I *know* I set it." He draws a panicky breath. "And when I came in that night, I had the feeling . . . well, it felt like someone was in the house."

My face is rigid with shock. "What do you mean? Did you call the police?"

"I kind of thought I was imagining it at first. Spooking myself out. I mean, I didn't see anything or hear anything. It was just a feeling. So I went upstairs to my room." He pushes the hair back from his eyes. "And while I was up there, I heard a . . . shuffling sound downstairs."

"Where?"

"Back by the kitchen."

"Maybe from the guest bathroom?"

"Yeah, around there . . ."

"Like someone was shutting the window in there?"

He locks eyes with me. "Maybe like that."

"Remember when I noticed dirty footprints in the tub? The window latch was open. As if someone had snuck out the bathroom window."

He puts his hand to his mouth. "Who?"

My mouth is dry. "I'm not sure. Did you call the police when you heard the sound?"

"No, I waited and listened for a long time, and when I didn't hear anything again, I thought that maybe it was just the cat or something. But now that Dad is missing, I thought . . ." His big eyes are pools of shining hope in the dim light. "Do you think maybe Dad came back and was in the house that night? Maybe that's why the alarm was off when I came home? Maybe that's who I heard."

I don't want to dash his hopes but I have to. "Not your dad. The shooting happened sometime after nine. Even without traffic, there's no way he could have made it back here before nine thirty. No way."

"Maybe he did, Mom. Maybe it's proof he was here. That he's alive."

"If it were your dad, he wouldn't have been hiding from you."

I hear the tremor in his voice. "Unless . . . what the FBI thinks he did is true?"

I rest a hand on his shoulder. "It wasn't your dad, Zack."

His whisper is full of fear. "Then who *was* here?"

———

I don't have an answer to Zack's question, but I want to reassure him we're safe, even though I don't believe we are. It's nearly midnight but I make him some popcorn, his favorite snack, and while it's popping in Ben's ten-year-old oil popper, I make sure Zack sees me say a hearty goodnight to David, the bodyguard who's sitting outside our front door, then set the alarm. All of that seems to have a calming effect on him, but the opposite effect on me.

I want to believe Zack's theory. Even though it's physically impossible. Believing is far better than thinking about who was hiding in the house the night Zack came home.

Once I get him back to bed, I try to play out Zack's theory. I trace the steps I imagine Ben would have taken from the front door if he came home. What would he do next?

I head upstairs to our bedroom, then shake my head. If he did come home after the shooting, he would surely have taken the gun out of the drawer. For protection.

Or was that when he deposited the gun? For Zack's and my safety.

I stop in my office and scan all the surfaces. There's no sign that he'd been in here.

I pad back downstairs and into the living room. The green and red colors of the Christmas tree lights dance on the walls in the darkened room. I lean on the edge of the couch and gaze at the tree, trying to slow my racing pulse and throttle my thoughts that are spinning out of control.

As much as I want to believe Zack's theory, I cannot see any evidence that Ben survived the shooting and returned home that night. If he were injured, as police say, surely there'd be signs of blood somewhere, too. That means, someone—not Ben—was in the house when Zack came home that night. As the realization sinks in, I feel my pulse quicken again, and suddenly our quiet, calm home feels eerily unsafe.

Then my eye falls on the present beneath the tree. I hadn't given it much thought the first time I'd seen it, but now that Ben is missing, could the gift offer any clue to what happened to him? I pick it up and study it. Ben has written my name neatly in black Sharpie, like he always does. But his gifts always appeared on Christmas Eve—not a moment before—wrapped in gorgeous luxe paper and expensive silk ribbons by the store where he'd purchased them. This paper looked like he'd bought it himself at the drug store, and judging from the imperfect tape, he had wrapped it by hand. In the midst of the chaos of the trial and after being poisoned, how—and why—had he made time to buy and wrap a gift for me?

I lift the tape off one end and begin to unwrap it. For a moment, I feel guilty, like when I was six years old and secretly unwrapped part of my Easy-Bake Oven two days before Christmas.

I can't believe what I see. It's a polished gray-and-white stone in a silver setting on a chain. A card inside the box indicates that the stone was taken from a four-billion-year-old meteorite discovered in Namibia in 1836, where it likely had fallen in prehistoric times.

A meteorite.

In second grade I'd started collecting pieces of distant asteroids and comets that have fallen to Earth in the form of meteorites. Much of my collection, like a piece of the meteorite that created the Meteor Crater in Arizona, was ordinary. A few were rare, like a fragment of the Allende meteorite, whose mineral-rich inclusions are older than the sun and Earth. But this meteorite was flawless and big, about two inches long and a half inch wide.

In the flat plane of the box, the faceted meteorite is dull, nonreflective. But when I lift it out, it shines with a mysterious, subtly distorted beauty.

I turn the meteorite over and notice that the silver back is engraved: Q'U AWZZG. TWDM, JMVRQ

Is it in code?

I feel the air leave my body.

If Ben is using a Julius Caesar cipher like he used when we were dating and newly married, then all I had to figure out was what the letter shift was. If the shift was three, that meant *A* would be encoded as *C* and so on.

I work with lightning speed, remembering the heady feeling of decoding the first message he wrote back in English class. I shift each letter by two then three then four . . . then eight.

And realize what he's written:

I'M SORRY. LOVE, BENJI

CHAPTER FIFTEEN

The words vibrate with double meaning. Is Ben saying he's sorry for killing Rebecca Stanton?

Or is it a deeper message, unrelated to her. About us?

After Ben and I had been married for a few months, we'd made plans to go out to dinner with friends, only Ben arrived at the restaurant nearly two hours late. The next morning he spelled out the words "I'm sorry" on our dining room table . . . with two dozen red roses. In our first years of marriage, whenever either of us needed to apologize, we'd surprise the other and write the words using whatever we could find: pretzels, rocks, paper clips, sometimes chocolates. Ben was far more creative than I was with apologies. Once he even wrote "I'm sorry" in Klingon.

A wave of sadness washes over me. At least five years had passed since either of us apologized this way. The tradition was long forgotten, replaced with angry texts or more often silence.

And how long had it been since he signed his name "Benji," a nickname I gave him when we were first dating because it sounded like the name of a cute, freckly five-year-old playing in the mud, when Ben was the polar opposite, a young man who looked like he was completely out of my league with his thick wavy hair, eyes the color of the sky, and a wide, nice-guy smile. As we left our twenties and drifted into our thirties, the cute nickname vanished, but here it is again. In code. Engraved on the back of a meteorite that was nearly as old as our planet.

"Everything okay?" My sister's voice startles me. "You're up late."

She's standing in the doorway, dressed in red flannel pajama bottoms and a T-shirt and holding a glass of red wine.

"I'm fine," I say, but my voice is pitched high.

She steps into the room, her eyes on the gift. "What's that?"

I slide the necklace back into the box. I'm not ready to explain to her what the coded message means. Mostly because I don't understand it myself. "I'm just . . . trying to take my mind off things."

"I honestly don't know how you're holding it all together," she says.

I'd already told her what the FBI suspected. I'd left out the parts about the guns and the million dollars in the bank but told her everything the FBI said about Rebecca Stanton, her murder. The color had faded from her already pale cheeks, and she was so rattled, she didn't move the entire time I spoke. Then she made me repeat every word I'd said.

"I'm not." I place the gift back under the tree. "Holding it together, that is."

She sits on the couch, pulls her legs up to her chest, and rests her chin on her knees.

"Can I ask you something?"

Can I ask you something is how Rachel tells you that a whopper of a question is coming. When we were teens, she'd always asked prying questions about things I did with the boys I was dating, whether I'd smoked pot, or if I got drunk at a friend's party. They were always prefaced with a simple *Can I ask you something?*

"It's late . . ."

She places her glass on the side table. "Was Ben cheating on you with Rebecca Stanton?"

I draw a deep breath. Rachel never liked Ben. After I married him, she warned me that someone with looks like Ben's was never going to be faithful. She predicted that his family's money would either make him lazy and unfaithful or a workaholic and unfaithful. "I honestly don't know. I should have a theory of some kind, but I don't."

"Did you ever have any suspicions? Were there clues that he might be cheating?"

I shake my head. "Marriage is complicated. Especially when you get to the fifteen-year mark. You stop noticing things. You stop noticing *the other person*. You know it's an ebb and flow, but a year goes by and you're unhappy, and then another . . . and the next thing you know, you've been unhappy with your marriage a long time. And maybe all along they have been unhappy, too. You just didn't know it."

She frowns. "That sounds like you're letting him off the hook for cheating."

"I'm just trying to analyze something complicated here . . . and the truth is, I don't have enough data. I don't know what Ben was thinking. Or doing."

She takes a long sip of her wine. "What I don't know is how you guys stayed married this long in the first place."

"Rachel, don't—"

She tosses back the rest of her wine. "I promise this isn't a rant against Ben. Even if he is a damn cheater. And even if I thought you should never have married him. But the two of you work crazy hours, seven days a week. And then you have Zack . . . and the problems you've been having with him. And then you've got this ginormous house to take care of." She waves her arms around. "What's that chaos theory thing you always talk about?"

"You mean the theory that small changes can have large, unpredictable consequences?"

"That may be how you scientists describe it. But I think of it this way. The more things you've got going on, the more likely one of them is going to fail."

Fail. Heat rushes to my cheeks. That's not how I'd like to describe my marriage. But suggesting a divorce *is* saying that your marriage failed, even if it's a term—and a feeling—I don't like.

"I heard you tell the FBI agent that you had talked to Ben about a divorce."

My face flushes. "Were you eavesdropping?"

She lets out a deep sigh. "I didn't mean to. Honest. I was reading on the balcony when she came over. Is it true?"

"We discussed it, yes."

"Because you knew he was cheating?"

"No. It's more complicated than that."

"But he was. Cheating. It's the only way any of this makes sense. Why would he go over to Rebecca's apartment and kill her simply because she backed out of a business deal? Then there'd be no way she could move forward."

"I've thought of that." I can't bring myself to tell her that Rebecca Stanton was pregnant. That would just add fuel to her theory—a theory that was making me break out in a cold sweat.

"Which means it had to be a crime of passion. Something was going on between them. Maybe she threatened to tell you about the affair . . ."

Tears sting the corners of my eyes. "This isn't really the time to—"

"Sorry, I didn't mean to make everything worse. But I'm worried, Sarah. I read up about Rebecca Stanton. And her father . . . has a reputation for doing some really violent things."

"Like what?" I'd been meaning to go online and research Rebecca Stanton and her family, but I hadn't found time. Clearly Rachel had.

She hesitates. "I read a *New York Post* article about some of the brutal crimes the Stanton family has been associated with. I'm too spooked to say them out loud. Have you seen what Gary Stanton looks like?"

"What do his looks have to do with anything?"

Her voice shakes. "He has the face of someone who might kill you. Or have you killed."

"You're being melodramatic."

"Don't dismiss me like that. I'm serious. He served time for drug trafficking and money laundering, and one of his sons is in jail for murdering two guys in Chicago. I can't stop thinking—what if he wants to get back at Ben for killing his daughter and comes after you and Zack?"

"You watch too many crime TV shows. That stuff doesn't happen in real life."

"But it does, Sarah. You don't know what went down between Ben and Rebecca. You don't know *why* he killed her—"

"Ben didn't kill Rebecca Stanton." My voice is too loud. Brittle.

She draws a deep breath, softens her voice. "You're fooling yourself, Sarah. And you know what? If I were you, I'd be in denial, too. But someone saw him leaving her apartment after the murder, and his fingerprints are at the scene. All that's missing is the murder weapon."

I draw a deep breath and think about the gun buried beneath the lilac bush. Is it the murder weapon?

"You don't understand. Ben isn't capable of killing anyone. That's not who he is."

She's silent for a long moment, picking at the cuticle on her left thumb. "We didn't think Dad was capable of leaving us and starting a whole new family somewhere else, either. But he did."

"This isn't the same . . ."

She looks down at the floor. "Sometimes we really can't know the people we love."

Her words are the killing blow. I feel the tears well up and spill over the rims of my eyelids and onto my cheek. The words I want to say are caught in my throat. I want her to go back to being my nosy sister asking prying questions, not treating me like I'm a fragile, broken woman whose husband has cheated on her. Whose husband is a murderer.

Rachel sees my tears. "I didn't mean to make you cry."

I wipe my cheeks. "Ben is not Dad. This is *different*."

She crosses the room and envelops me in a hug. "I want to believe that. But you, of all people, know that you can't ignore facts and proof."

———

The day my father left, I slammed out the back door and into the woods behind my house. I ran the narrow path through red maple and sycamore then past the pond bursting with tall reeds and cattails. I raced among the grove of sprawling oaks, the wind whipping at my face, my breath coming in shallow waves, trying to make sense of why my father would us leave behind and start a new life with another family in another state.

When I reached the path's end—the deep woods—I kept running as fast as my bony twelve-year-old legs would carry me. I knew every rise and fall of its hills, even where to find the clean and cold stream that bubbled up amid the spires of white-barked birch trees and fed the pond below. I knew that beyond the knoll topped by towering eastern pine lay pristine Lake 14, reachable only when the pond froze over in winter.

As the woods grew denser and the trees more crowded, I slowed a little. Shafts of sunlight flitted through the trees then burst forth in a clearing, blinding me for a moment. I stopped and caught my breath. Except for the crunch of dry leaves beneath my feet, the woods were silent. I lifted my eyes to the warm sunlight, watched the particles of dust rise up into the light, and felt my future with all its promise of joy and growth, untouched by the loss of my father.

Unsettled by the events of the day, I climbed thick honeysuckle vines up into a tree and nestled my body in the crook of a limb, resting my back against the rough bark. I looked past the wild fern that gathered along the pond's edge and watched the algae on the surface of the water shift and change—at once mottled with mounds of green then suddenly glassy and clear like a mirror, reflecting the blue skies above. As I sat in the tree, my breath slowing, I felt the vastness of the woods and the universe. I grasped, in a rudimentary way, my very small place in it.

The woods were undergoing constant renewal and change but in a rhythm, in patterns, I could understand—unlike people, who changed their minds on a whim or wanted to start over because they were disappointed with where they had ended up in life.

I was hungry to understand everything about the one place that was in balance—perpetual—and spent many hours there that summer, collecting plant specimens and examining pond water samples under a microscope. After my uncle sent me a telescope for my birthday, I would run to a clearing in the woods at twilight to watch the stars, charting the constellations in a spiral notebook. In time, the stars no longer felt distant or obscure. I knew exactly where I was when I looked up at the night sky. In their unveiling and fading, in their movement and life cycles across the heavens, the stars were alive to me. They were my home.

In the daytime, too, I scanned the skies with my telescope.

"The stars don't shine during the day, silly," Rachel would say, laughing.

But stars do shine during the day. They're right there where they've always been. We just can't see them because we are blinded by sunlight.

CHAPTER SIXTEEN

DAY FIVE

My sister is flirting with an FBI agent in the front garden. She's playing with the ends of her hair and smiling, the trill of her laughter piercing the early morning quiet.

I've just returned home after walking to the coffee shop to get a croissant and a hot tea latte. And a jelly doughnut for Zack, who's still sleeping. The croissant is still warm in the bag, and I'm eager to sit in the kitchen and enjoy it. It's the first time in days that I've had any kind of appetite.

My sister has good taste. The man is handsome. Sandy brown hair. Fit. He looks like he could play an FBI agent in a movie.

She's pointing to a glossy red heart-shaped flower with a yellow spike in the center. "It's called *Anthurium*. I know it looks like the fake stuff you see in the malls and office buildings, but this is the real deal."

They make a beautiful picture, standing in bright sunshine in the middle of my front yard, surrounded by a garden in full bloom. A lone butterfly flutters past them.

Rachel doesn't see me walk up the sidewalk, but her botany student does. He interrupts my sister's monologue and walks toward me.

"Scott Lautner," he says. "FBI." He takes out his badge, but I don't look at it because agents Samuel Nelson and Elizabeth Elliott step off the porch to greet me.

"Sarah," Elizabeth says. "Your sister said we could wait on your front porch."

"That's as far as I allowed them," my sister says. I can't fault her for not thinking to call me immediately when the FBI showed up. She's been divorced for four years, and the agent's blue eyes probably made her forget what she was supposed to do.

"Where is Brad, my security guard?" I ask.

"He's aware that we're here, and we asked him to wait in his vehicle so as not to interfere with the investigation." Scott nods to Brad's white sedan in front of the house.

"Look, before we begin, we want to tell you that we are officially investigating Rebecca Stanton's father, Gary Stanton, in Ben's disappearance," Elizabeth says. "As you may already know, he's the head of one of New York's notorious crime families. And if he suspected Ben was responsible for his daughter's murder . . . that could explain why Ben is missing."

The implications of what she's saying are chilling, and I feel myself go cold. But I'm puzzled. The FBI came all the way out here to tell me they're investigating Rebecca's father in Ben's disappearance? They must be softening the blow for something else they want to tell me.

"And the other reason we're here," Samuel says, "is that we have a second search warrant." He hands me the papers, and I glance at them, my vision blurring.

How is this happening again?

I look at my sister, and her smile has disappeared. I can see she feels bad for letting them on the property.

"What's this about? Didn't you get everything you needed last time?"

"I understand how disruptive this is," he says, as though he's reading from a script.

"My son is sleeping. Can you come back after he wakes up? You can imagine how disturbing this will be for him. *Again*."

He fiddles with the watch on his wrist. "This is a search outdoors. In the backyard."

I feel the blood rush to my face. "In the backyard?"

"I'm going to ask you to stay with Agent Elliott while we investigate," Samuel says, then he and Agent Lautner quickly head up the driveway.

I don't know how much time goes by while I process what's happened. I'm shaking inside, and once I realize I don't have any words to say, I storm onto the porch and sink onto the wooden bench. A moment later, Elizabeth and Rachel catch up. Rachel sits next to me, taking my hand in hers, just like when we were kids.

It doesn't take the agents long to find the evidence they're looking for. Within a few minutes, Agent Lautner rushes down the driveway with a black evidence bag.

"We're finished here," Samuel says, stepping onto the porch and removing his disposable gloves. He can't hide his triumphant tone.

The clock inside the house chimes eight notes, indicating the bottom of the hour.

———

"What do you think they found?" my sister asks.

"I have no idea," I say with surprising conviction.

I'm distracted by emotion. Everything in the flowerbed has been dug up. The lilac tree is dumped on its side next to a large hole. "You'd think they could've at least put the poor shrub back. It's probably already in shock," she frets, then heads to the garage. I'm guessing she'll get a shovel and replant it.

I don't have to look into the hole to know that they have found the gun. Of that I have no doubt. But I cannot figure who would've known the gun was in the yard. Who could've told the FBI with enough detail and veracity that they not only secured a search warrant but found the weapon within a few minutes?

Zack comes out in the yard, rubbing his eyes. It's Sunday and he's slept late. The cowlick at his hairline is sticking straight up. "What's going on?"

His eyes are scanning the yard, the lilac bush on its side, and I can see panic rising.

"FBI came here with a search warrant."

"What for?"

"They didn't say. Were any of your friends out here in the last few days?"

He looks at me, crosses his arms on his chest. "When?"

"Like anytime since Dad came home from New York."

"I told you, I had a couple of friends here Tuesday night. The night Dad went missing."

"Who?"

"Does it matter who?"

"I need to know who was here."

He stands there a moment, not blinking. "Cole and Bryan."

My voice is low and steady. "Cole and Bryan." *The friends who'd gotten high and jumped in our pool.* "Were you guys—"

"No, Mom. Why don't you trust me? We just hung around the pool for a few minutes before we went to get something to eat."

"Did either of them walk around through the garden?"

He looks at me like I might be wearing a tinfoil hat. "*No.* Do you think one of them had something to do with the FBI coming here?"

"I don't know what to think."

Rachel returns with a shovel and a bag of organic compost. Before she puts the lilac back, I glance into the hole and see that it's empty. The gun *is* gone.

"We can't always be sure what people are capable of," I say.

———

Years ago when Swiss scientists found the first widely recognized Earth-like planet—what's called an exoplanet—orbiting a sunlike star, it marked a breakthrough that ended decades of searching. Its discovery was one of the most profound in human history. Before our discovery of this planet we named 51 Pegasi b, scientists had no evidence that planets existed outside of our solar system. Finding it made astronomers question everything we thought we knew about our universe.

All big discoveries lead us to rethink what we know. That's true here, too. The gun in the backyard. Ben's fingerprints at the crime scene. The eyewitness. All these discoveries make me question everything I know about Ben.

In fifteen years of marriage, I never once thought him capable of any criminal act. Certainly not murder. But what are the signs of being a killer?

When Zack was a toddler, I remember waking many times at night to find Ben missing from his side of the bed only to discover him in Zack's room, awash with moonlight. The two of them would be fast asleep in the rocking chair, Zack snuggled in Ben's arms, his mess of blond curls sprawled across his dad's chest. Could such a father be capable of murder?

Ben has changed since then. Since he opened Aurora. He'd become obsessed with the restaurant's success, working until the late into the night most days. He traveled often, hunting for new restaurants to acquire in New York and Chicago.

At home, he was increasingly distracted by texts, early morning emails, and late-night meetings. At Zack's birthday dinner, Ben didn't laugh once when Zack told a goofy story about his Spanish teacher interrogating the entire class about a box of Toblerone chocolates missing from her desk. Instead he kept a sober gaze fixed on his phone, where he was following a crisis unfolding at Aurora.

Still, becoming consumed with success doesn't mutate you into a murderer, and even with Ben's slow transformation into someone I barely knew—even with our growing distance from each other—I never saw signs that he might be capable of murder.

But there's another reason I cannot accept Ben's involvement in Rebecca Stanton's murder. It would mean I must also accept the real possibility that Ben himself is dead, the victim of some kind of retaliation.

That's a discovery I'm just not ready to make.

———

Channel Eleven's Kate Bradley is reporting from our parkway again. Live. I have to admit she's the best in the group of reporters who gather daily on the streets and sidewalks in front of our home. She's measured when she speaks, not like the breathy reporters from Fox and TMZ, who shout as though every new development is sordid and sensational. I've seen her so often reporting on this story that I'm beginning to feel like I know her.

"FBI and police have expanded the search for missing restaurant owner Ben Mayfield to include the Inland Empire and the San Fernando Valley," I hear her say on the TV in the kitchen. "Mayfield was last seen five days ago getting into a Toyota SUV driven by his bodyguard, Antonio Spear, who was later found shot to death off the 405 freeway, about a mile from Mayfield's well-known restaurant, Aurora."

And then the report includes a photo of Ben. Tanned, handsome, bathed in seemingly golden light and surrounded by a bevy of celebrities that frequented Aurora. An empty heaviness comes over me.

"It's unknown if Mayfield was able to escape on foot or if he was abducted by whoever shot his bodyguard," she continues. "But what has police stumped is this. What happened to Mayfield's car? Police have stepped up the search for his blue Audi A8, as they hope it will offer clues to what happened to Mayfield."

I swallow the lump in my throat, wondering when these reporters are going to find out that Ben is suspected of murdering Rebecca Stanton.

Agent Elliott assured me that they were not releasing any further information about Rebecca's murder because it would compromise the investigation, but the story is too sensational to remain hidden for very much longer. How soon until that news is leaked?

At least I'm no longer an official suspect in Ben's disappearance. The FBI is monitoring my phones and texts because they're looking for Ben, not looking at me. I am relieved that they've set aside their assumptions about me, but I can't help but wonder: If they're right that Ben did kill Rebecca Stanton, what happened to him? Was he dead, his body lying somewhere police haven't looked yet? Or was it possible that he was still alive, abducted for reasons we don't know yet? A ransom, perhaps. The heir to the Mayfield Department Store fortune could be worth a hefty sum.

As I watch Kate Bradley's seemingly endless coverage continue, my cell phone rings. It's my CIT boss, Steven Webster. I mute the sound and answer the call. After a few minutes of casual banter about the space symposium panel he just moderated, he launches into business.

"We've decided to delay further publicity about the Trojan asteroid discovery," he says. "Right now we think the announcement will get lost in the sensational nature of what's happened to your husband."

"I'm disappointed but understand," I say, watching as Channel Eleven clicks through photos of Aurora on its opening night a few years ago—limos, klieg lights, a parade of celebrities and accompanying paparazzi.

"I hope this doesn't sound insensitive, but how are you coming on the projection for the proposal?"

I don't want to admit I haven't spent any time finishing one of the calculations we need for it. The space telescope will scan two hundred thousand of the brightest stars, but we need to estimate how many planet "candidates" we expect to find and how many of those we expect will be Earth-sized. "I'll have everything along with the methodology to you later in the week."

"Would you like to assign that task to someone—"

"No. I've got it under control." I glance at the continuing coverage, and my blood pressure rises when I see Kate Bradley is now interviewing Ben's sister, Julia, in Chicago via satellite. I suck in a breath. There's no telling what Julia will say, especially with cameras trained on her.

I steady my voice. "How's the top brass feeling about all the news coverage?"

He pauses a long moment. Then gives it to me straight. "It's making some of them very nervous. And rightfully so. Your name is about to be listed as the principal investigator on this one, and some of the news we're seeing . . . well, we all know the decision makers don't like even a whiff of controversy when they're thinking about handing out a quarter billion dollars."

"Would it help the project if I—"

"No. We're not going to hand this over to someone else just because your husband is missing."

I close my eyes and draw a deep breath. I want to tell him that Ben isn't just missing. He's a murder suspect. That will surely change his mind about everything. I open my mouth to begin an explanation, but his next words make me lose my nerve.

"I hope they find your husband soon," he says quietly. "Alive and well."

After I hang up, I turn up the sound on Kate Bradley's interview with Julia.

Julia's wearing a tank top and striped leggings, which isn't what you'd expect to see the family member of a missing person wearing on TV, or in December in Chicago. But Julia has never been predictable.

"What can you tell us about the investigation into your brother's disappearance?"

"Why the LAPD can't find him or his car is beyond me," Julia says calmly, but her eyes have a wild, high-strung look to them. "Makes me wonder if they're really doing enough to find him. Or, you know, if they're just incompetent."

Kate raises an eyebrow. "Police seem to be quite competently overseeing dozens of officers and volunteers who are searching the area," she says. "How are you and his family holding up now that Ben has been missing for five days?"

"My mother isn't doing well. She had a stroke a month ago, and this tragedy is slowing her recovery. I'd be out there searching for Ben myself, but I need to take care of my mom."

"What's the situation with Ben's suit against his Aurora partners?"

"Yeah, I'm not up to speed on that, but I warned Ben not to get into business with them. Never trusted any of them. Because I can tell you this. No matter what they're saying, they know exactly what happened to Ben."

I sigh, hoping Richard Jenkins and my CIT bosses aren't watching.

———

I cannot remember the combination for the safe. I've tried the ones that Ben and I had always used—our birth dates and our anniversary—but the door remains locked. I know what mundane things to expect behind the steel door: our will and living trust agreements, life insurance policies, the deed to our house. But I suspect—based on nothing but a gut instinct—that the safe holds clues to what happened to Ben.

I'm not surprised the FBI didn't find the safe when they searched the house, because it's concealed in concrete behind a rusty metal cabinet next to the water heater in the basement. You'd need x-ray vision to even speculate it might be there.

Ben had grown up seeing his family lock their jewels, expensive watches, and important documents in a safe, so it seemed completely natural to him that we'd lock up our essential papers this way. But this safe went overboard with its safety specs: half-inch steel doors that could supposedly withstand .50-caliber bullets, seventeen-hundred-degree heat for ninety minutes, and even impalement by a one-ton steel I-beam. Ben's mother was close friends with the owner of a luxury safe company, so this "starter" safe arrived as a gift a few weeks after we moved into our Brentwood home.

The safe is only large enough to house a foot-tall stack of papers and a few showy jewels Ben had inherited from his grandmother. I try another three-number combination, Zack's birthday, but the lock still doesn't move. The brushed-steel dial seems to be mocking me for continuing to try.

Had Ben changed the combination?

If so, then that could only mean he had something to hide. From me. That thought makes me even more determined to figure out the code. Simple math says that if I devoted every waking minute to cracking the code, it would take me working around the clock for up to sixty days to try all the possible combinations. I attempt a few dozen more until my fingers begin to feel numb and my attention drifts.

Then a text from Aaron flashes on my phone, but this one isn't a link to a clip from the security-system DVR. Instead it's a photo of a Piggly Wiggly store sign, a smiling yellow pig wearing a little white paper hat. At first I think he sent me the photo by mistake—I've never been to a Piggly Wiggly—but then I notice that right above the lighted sign, hanging high in the night sky, is Venus, and directly above that glittering planet is a brilliant and slender crescent moon.

I smile for the first time in days. There's something quirky and funny about the rare sky show—the alignment of Venus and the moon—playing out above the happy-faced pig sign.

I think about Aaron sending this to lift my spirits, then my mind inevitably drifts to our kiss, this time outside the airport Tuesday night.

"What . . . are we doing?" he had whispered.

I met his gaze for a long moment, but instead of doing the right thing, I leaned in to kiss him again, certain—positive—that it wouldn't be the same this time. That the surprise of it all was what made it . . . powerful.

It didn't work. Because this kiss was exploring, questioning. Both of us trying to understand the force that was drawing us—pushing us—together. I leaned into him, felt his arms enveloping me, and the blood rushed hard to my ears, shutting out all the airport sounds around us. He drew me closer, and it felt as though the two of us had done this dance together before, even though we hadn't.

I couldn't catch my breath. It was stuck high in my chest, somewhere inaccessible to my vocal cords. The words came out breathy, a voice I barely recognized. "We can't . . ." I touched my lips to his in the softest kiss. A kiss goodbye.

"The problem is . . . I like you too much." The way he was looking at me made me think it was true.

I took a step back. "I shouldn't have . . ." I said, trying to sound normal.

As if I could ever get back to normal.

CHAPTER SEVENTEEN

"Sarah, Aaron's here for you," Rachel calls out to me a half hour later.

I draw a deep breath. After the Piggly Wiggly photo, Aaron had texted to let me know he was on his way. He didn't say whether he was coming over to talk about new data he's recovered from the DVR or work business, but with police and FBI monitoring all my communications, I don't risk asking him why.

I head downstairs, and I notice Aaron is watching me. I can see he's not used to seeing me dressed like this, barefoot and wearing jeans and a slim-fitting T-shirt.

I feel his admiration and my chest swells. I'm determined to feel nothing, to squash and flatten all my emotions, if that's possible, so that I can talk with him like nothing happened between us. As if I can control that.

"You've met my sister, Rachel," I say, and I'm relieved that my voice sounds . . . normal.

"I did," he says. "I brought the . . . data we talked about."

"Great, come on up to my office."

"You two can work down here. I won't be in your way," Rachel says. Even though it's not true. She'd definitely eavesdrop.

"My office will be easier," I say, but realize it won't be. Not for me. The thought of being behind a closed door with Aaron is making me jittery.

I can feel Rachel watching me as Aaron follows me up the stairs. I sense her sister-radar is on high alert and she's wondering why a good-looking colleague is here on a Sunday when Ben is still missing.

I open the office door and let Aaron in. "Nice," he says.

My office has two enormous skylights that drench the room in sunlight by day but allow me to peek at the stars at night. Several telescopes cluster in one corner, but the room is dominated by a set of bookshelves labeled with subjects like Asteroids, Optics, and Exoplanets, and an entire shelf devoted to my collections of meteorites.

He sets his leather bag on the couch and looks over the meteorites, notices a small crystal among them, and picks it up.

"My latest obsession," I tell him. "That one's not a meteorite . . . it's zoisite. Looks blue, right?"

He nods without taking his eye off the stone.

"Now move it into the natural light."

"It's . . . red," he says in a half whisper.

"It's a pleochroic gem, which means it's one of the few stones in the world that have two or more colors, depending on the direction of the light."

"It's kind of . . . mesmerizing. I can see why you love it," he says, then gently places the crystal in my hand. I meet his gaze and get the feeling he's thinking about Tuesday night. "How are you holding up?"

"This isn't how I was expecting to spend the week after our big announcement." That sounds glib, so I add, "You know what's the worst part?"

"What?"

"I don't know what data to rely on. The FBI has evidence that my husband was involved in Rebecca Stanton's murder. But that's in direct conflict with the person I've known all these years. And then there are

Ben's attorneys, who think his partners are behind his disappearance. That seems more probable, but there isn't any evidence to support it."

"I might have found something that will shed more light." He pulls a flash drive from his bag. "But I had to look, Sarah. I know you asked me not to, but it was the only way to figure out what I recovered."

"I don't want you to get in trouble because you're helping me."

"I feel kind of . . . involved. I mean, we were together and then your husband . . ."

I realize what he's asking, even if he's not saying it. "What happened Tuesday night was entirely my fault. My doing."

"That's not how I remember it." His eyes drop briefly to my lips. "It was me who wanted it to happen—who *made* it happen . . ."

I let his words hang in the air. I can't admit my feelings, but I can't pretend I didn't have them, either.

"I should never have kissed you."

My words land hard on him. It's not the answer he's hoping for. "I . . . can't stop thinking—"

"We can't . . . ," I say softly.

We both know the reasons we can't repeat what we did that night. But knowing something is impossible or wrong doesn't make you want it any less. It doesn't put an end to the feelings.

He shifts his tone. Professional now. "I saw on the news where the FBI is involved, so I figured they're monitoring your email and texts. That's why I didn't send you any more data by email link, even though it's encrypted."

"Good thinking. What were you able to recover?" I ask, anxious to see.

"Your cameras are voice or motion activated, so sometimes the system recorded nonevents, like when you or your family came in the front door or went outside." He sits on the couch, pulls a laptop out of his bag, and turns it on. "I put those kinds of clips in a folder of their own. You should look at them later. But there are three that you need to see."

I sit beside him, and he inserts the flash drive into his laptop's USB port. "Let's start with this one since it's time-stamped the afternoon your husband went missing."

He clicks on a link and we see Ben sitting in front of my computer in this very office at 5:05 p.m. on Tuesday, just a few minutes before he left with his bodyguard. From a vantage point behind my desk, this camera was positioned to capture the entire office but especially the small liquor cabinet that Zack and friends had once raided.

And then there's Ben.

He's dressed for work in a white shirt open at the collar and a midnight-blue blazer. A three-day beard graces his jaw. I can't take my eyes off him. When he looks up from the computer and glances in the direction of the camera, he seems wholly different than I remember. There's a tenderness in his eyes that I haven't seen in a long time.

Something remarkable happens when you observe someone and they have no idea they're being watched. It's as though they're uncloaked for a moment and you can see them as they really are. Ben doesn't look like someone who just committed a murder. He looks as though he's carrying a joyful secret.

A few seconds later, Zack steps into the frame and points to something on the computer monitor. "Once you click 'Continue' you'll erase all the data on the security system's DVR. Are you sure you want to do that?"

There's a brief silence, then I hear Ben say, "Positive."

———

Ben had deliberately erased the DVR. It wasn't accidentally corrupted or mistakenly erased. He had planned it. And gotten Zack to help.

"What's on this drive that Ben didn't want anyone to see?" I ask, but stop there. My theory, the one I don't dare speak, is that somewhere on this hard drive is proof that Ben killed Rebecca Stanton.

"You need to watch it again," Aaron says. "Look closely this time at their computer screen and you'll see they're only using the program's internal delete function."

He plays the clip again, and I notice the familiar blue-and-gold security-system banner.

"If this is all the deleting they did, it would've been far easier for us to recover than it has been. The way the data has been corrupted, they must've run a more powerful scrub utility *later* to wipe the drive clean."

"Why?" I look at Aaron and suspect he has his own theory about Ben, even if he won't say it. The two have never met, and I wonder if it's awkward for him to speculate about the man who is my husband.

"Luckily for us, whatever utility they used wasn't entirely recovery-proof." He clicks on another clip. "This next one is very odd. But maybe you can make sense of it."

This segment is time-stamped Monday night at 11:54, the day before Ben disappeared. The camera is pointed at the pool in the back-yard, but it's late at night and the pool lights are off, so all we can really see is the outline of the pool reflected in the ambient light. For a brief second, there's shadowy movement on the right side of the frame, then the camera is awash with bright white light. The light shifts for a moment, then settles down, obscuring everything.

"At first I thought this was a by-product of the data deletion, but look at it again."

He plays the clip and points at the corner of the screen. "You can vaguely make out the shape of someone standing here. It looks like they've deliberately positioned a very bright light—maybe upwards of ten thousand lumens—on some sort of tripod to blind the security camera. If you throw enough light at the camera . . ."

"It can't process the weaker reflected ambient light. The light creates a blind spot."

"Any idea why someone would want to blind the camera aimed at your pool?"

A wave of prickly heat rushes through me. The camera is aimed at the pool, but its field of vision also includes the garden. The part of the garden where the gun was hidden. Whoever placed the gun in the garden that night knew exactly where the security camera was and blinded it with an ultrabright spotlight.

Was it Ben who had buried the gun there? Could this be what Ben didn't want anyone to discover?

———

I'm done looking at clips. They make my mind run through so many possible questions that my head starts to swim. If it was Ben who buried the gun in the garden, it made no sense for him to blind the security camera when he could more easily stop it from recording with a click of his mouse. But here was proof that Ben had gone even further and deleted all of the security-camera footage. That could only mean there was something else on that DVR that Ben didn't want anyone to see.

Aaron's voice brings me back to the moment. "I know this is a lot to take in. There's just one more clip I think you should see. You okay?"

I nod yes. But I'm not okay. I lean my head against the back of the leather couch and close my eyes for a moment, my frustration rising swift and thick. When I open them, he's looking at me, a puzzled expression on his face. My eyes meet his, and for an instant, the scientist-colleague version of him is gone, and in its place is the man I kissed in the airport. I gaze at him a moment then force myself to look away. I know what it would be like to let this moment take on a life of its own.

I don't.

"What's next?" I say, but my voice hitches.

He looks at me for a long moment as if he's going to say something, then instead clicks on another entry: Tuesday 12:41 p.m. Hours before Ben went missing.

This shot is taken from the camera over the front doorstep, where Ben's partner, Richard Jenkins, stands dressed in a dark sport coat.

Ben's back is to the camera, but we can hear him say, "We've been over this a thousand times already."

Richard's voice is silky. "Let it go, Ben. The only people who are going to profit from your lawsuit are the lawyers."

"You want me to look away while *you* siphon off millions? Remember when we started this together and everyone else predicted we'd be shuttering the place within eighteen months? Instead, we made it—*I* made it—a huge success by every measure, bigger than any of us ever imagined, and yet all the profits are gone."

Richard pushes a finger in Ben's chest. His voice is a low growl. "If you don't stop now, it's not going to end well for you. You're going to regret it."

Then he looks straight at the camera above Ben's head.

———

Richard Jenkins made good on his threat. Or so it appears.

Ben's car was found in the desert, in the remote Pinto Basin of Joshua Tree National Park, just 175 miles east of Los Angeles. The keys were still in the ignition, and the tank was completely empty.

At least that's what Detective Dawson seems to be saying as he stands in my living room later that afternoon. I'm foggy and unfocused. It feels like the words slip out of his mouth in a hazy jumble and my brain has to assemble them like a puzzle into a coherent sentence.

"No sign of him yet," he continues. "A search of the area by helicopter with special heat-sensing equipment turned up nothing. We have over fifty officers, volunteers, and eleven teams with search dogs combing the park. The area's been having unseasonal high temperatures these past weeks—over a hundred degrees—so we're working fast. If he's fallen or been injured, we need to get to him quick."

Joshua Tree is over a half-million acres of unforgiving wilderness shaped by strong winds, unpredictable torrents of rain, and extreme climates. Even with hundreds of searchers, it would take weeks to scour every acre.

"It's possible that he could be nearby." I hear my lack of logic, but it doesn't stop me from continuing. "That he just left the car and is coming back."

The detective draws a deep breath, rubs his cheek. "We found the car around Porcupine Wash, a really remote area of the park. Out in the open. It appears as though it has been abandoned for a few days. And there was a lot of blood on the front seat. Consistent with an injury."

My sister hugs my shoulders tightly. I glance over and see tears in her eyes. "I'll call Lauren now, and we'll get friends and family to help with the new search," she says calmly, though I know she's anything but. She's imagining the worst, like I am.

"Please don't," Dawson says. "The sheriff's office has been getting lots of offers for help. But with the temperature hitting 105 again today, they're only working with trained volunteers."

My legs are so wobbly I sit down on the couch. The detective settles beside me.

"On the front seat, we found a slip of paper with your name and cell number."

He hands me his phone and shows me a photo of the paper. Even though the writing is scrawled, I recognize the handwriting.

"Is it Ben's?" he asks.

I nod, shaking all over, fighting back tears.

Everything turned to chaos after that. More news media turned up on our front lawn. Lauren had banded some of our friends together and raised ten thousand dollars to offer to anyone with information that brings Ben home safe. Then social media lit up with people—complete strangers—offering to search for Ben at Joshua Tree and being turned away by the sheriff's office.

I dig through my closet searching for shorts for daytime and layers to throw on for the cool desert temperatures in the evening, then toss water and snacks into a backpack. I'm lacing my boots when my sister comes into the room.

"You're not going," she says.

"Why not? I've got to do something."

"You need to be here. In case he comes home . . ."

My voice catches in my throat. "How would he get home if his car is in the desert?"

She looks flummoxed for a moment. "Maybe he could hitchhike. I don't know," she says then breaks into tears. "He still can find his way home." She doesn't believe what she's saying. She's afraid they'll find him—his body—when I'm out there searching. She's worried how I'll react if I see him dead, hundreds of miles from home. She's not wrong about that. My nerves are hanging by a thread, and I'm not sure how much more I can handle.

"Besides, you heard the detective. It's not safe. They're turning everyone away."

"I can't just sit here, waiting for news. I need to—"

"You can't go, Sarah. Zack already has one parent missing. If nothing else, you need to be here for him."

Zack. How am I ever going to explain to him that his dad's car—with blood on the front seat—has been found abandoned in the remote desert? He'd stayed home again, looking pale and exhausted, and mostly remained in his room all day.

I head to Zack's room. It's only four thirty in the afternoon, and he is sprawled on his bedcovers, the cat sleeping in a nest of blankets he's made for her at the foot of the bed. He looks so peaceful, I decide not to wake him.

I place a light blanket over him, and when I go to switch off his lamp I notice a plastic snowman by his cell phone.

I haven't seen it in over ten years. It's the casualty—or should I say the survivor—of a snow globe accident. When Zack was three, maybe four, years old, Ben had given me a snow globe for Christmas. Inside was a dapper snowman holding a candlestick and songbook as the music box played the tune "White Christmas."

I had placed it briefly on the coffee table, and when I turned back to it, Zack was shaking it in his chubby little hands, watching the snowflakes swirling around. Then it slipped through his fingers and crashed onto the hardwood floor, the glass splintering into tiny pieces. Zack wailed with tears, partly because the snow globe had broken, but mostly in response to the loud shriek that had escaped my lips.

I lifted him out of the wreckage and noticed that the snowman had broken loose from the base. It was far smaller than it had appeared in the glass globe—as if it had been miniaturized. I scooped it up, rinsed it in the kitchen sink, and handed it to him. He stopped crying.

For many months after, the snowman was his constant companion wherever he went. At night, he'd line the snowman up on his nightstand alongside Batman and Superman action figures. And during the day, he stuffed it in his pocket and proudly showed it to anyone who would listen.

"See? It came out of the broken snow globe," he'd say.

As Zack grew into a young boy, I'd lost track of the snowman. I can't help but wonder what meaning it holds for him now. Perhaps it's a reminder of simpler times, but could he, too, be searching for hope that out of something broken, some good might emerge?

CHAPTER EIGHTEEN

They've found a body. Just off a sandy trail a mile and a half from Ben's car. No sign of foul play.

It's not Ben.

On the phone, Detective Dawson tells me the details, but I'm so relieved it's not Ben that the specifics of the discovery don't sink in. As long as they don't find Ben's body, I cling to the hope that he might still be alive.

I switch on the TV in the kitchen, and Channel Eleven's Kate Bradley is delivering her report live from Joshua Tree National Park. Wearing a teal sleeveless dress, she stands in front of a twisted, spiky Joshua tree that looks like it's straight out of a Dr. Seuss book. "With temperatures soaring over 112 degrees today, police found the body of seventy-six-year-old Leonard Vazira in Joshua Tree National Park. Police believe Vazira succumbed to exhaustion and dehydration from the record heat.

"His brother, Robert Vazira, said Leonard suffered from mild to moderate dementia but lived on his own in a remote area about a hundred miles away from where his body was found. Robert suspects his brother was on his way to visit him in Hayfield, California, when he got lost in the desert only twenty-five miles from his destination. He is not clear how Leonard arrived in Joshua Tree, as he has no car and his driver's license was revoked several years ago.

"But what makes this discovery so relevant today is the body's close proximity to the car of missing Aurora restaurant owner Ben Mayfield. Police are investigating possible connections, but so far have found no evidence the events are related."

Kate goes on to describe it as another tragedy of the extreme temperatures and a cautionary tale of going into the desert alone without water and adequate preparation.

When her report is over, I'm even more on edge. The coroner estimated the man was in the desert for less than two days before he died. How would Ben survive this blistering heat? Especially when all the blood in the car suggested he was seriously wounded.

I know Joshua Tree, and that part of the desert has dunes that peak and valley, and there are shrubs, bushes, cacti everywhere. It won't be easy to find him, no matter how many search-and-rescue teams and volunteers are out there.

And if they do find him, will he still be alive?

———

Everyone is certain Ben is dead. But they don't dare say it to me. Their eyes give it away—even if their smiles radiate false hope. I've asked Lauren, Rachel—all of them—to leave so that I can have a few moments where no one is asking me what I need or telling me things I cannot begin to process.

A heavy tiredness blankets me, as though someone has increased Earth's gravity by fifty percent, slowing every movement and thought. I feel myself succumb to the darkness. Deep in my fuzzy, exhausted brain, I know that I cannot continue to cling to the hope that Ben will walk in the door any minute. I haul my heavy body upstairs to Zack's room and find him at his desk, hunched over his computer, writing a paper.

His teachers had given him extensions on his homework due dates, but he's immersed himself in the work, diving into assignments immediately instead of waiting until the last minute like he usually does.

He's a lot like me in this way. Escaping into work when the stress gets overwhelming. Finding comfort in the concrete and the certain.

I ruffle my fingers through his thick mop of hair that reminds me of Ben's when I first met him. "How're you holding up?"

He keeps his gaze fixed on the screen. "OK. I guess."

I tell him about the body they found in the desert, and he exhales sharply when he hears it's not his dad's.

I sit at the foot of his bed. "Can I ask you something about the hours before Dad went missing?"

"Yeah," he says, but his voice is filled with uncertainty.

"I saw on the security footage where Dad asked you to erase the DVR. And you helped him."

He's absolutely still for a moment, then swivels his chair to face me. "He made me swear not to tell you."

"Why?"

"He didn't say."

"And you didn't ask him why he was erasing it?"

"No. Why would I question *anything* when I was grounded? He just asked me where the delete button was and I showed him."

"Didn't you wonder why?"

He shakes his head. "It didn't seem strange or anything. He was like, 'Hey, show me how to erase the security-system DVR . . . but I want to surprise your mom, so don't tell her.'"

"He wanted to surprise *me*?"

He shrugs. "That's what he said . . ."

"Did you run a more powerful scrub utility after that? To erase it more thoroughly?"

He looks at me like I'm crazy. "Scrub utility? No. Why would I?"

"Well, someone did."

"I have no idea how to even run a scrub utility." His face softens. "Honest, Mom, I only did what Dad asked me to."

"Okay," I say and ruffle his hair once more, not entirely sure I believe him even though I want to.

I leave his room and head to my home office, then light a candle and shut off the lights. In the flicker of the candlelight, my breathing slows and my thoughts flow more easily. The darkness always makes me feel protected, like I do under the night sky.

Zack's descriptions of his last hours with Ben don't illuminate everything. He had no idea then that he wouldn't see his father again, so he hadn't paid attention to the details. It seems odd that Ben had casually asked him to delete the security-system hard drive under the guise of a surprise for me.

What was he hiding?

My questions are a way of distracting myself from the very real possibility that Ben is dead.

CHAPTER NINETEEN

Kate Bradley is standing on my doorstep later that evening. Instead of the dress or blazer and skirt she usually wears on TV, today she's dressed casually in a Breton black-and-white striped tee and black leggings. Her hair is pulled back in a loose braid.

"Can I talk to you for a moment?"

I look past her for Brad, the security guard, but don't see him anywhere. "How did you get past—"

"Brad's dealing with the Channel Four reporters, who're refusing to move their news van off your property. No doubt he'll be back up here any second and is going to physically remove me from this porch." She flashes a smile. "Unless you let me inside."

I place my hand on the door, ready to close it. "I'm not doing any interviews."

"The story about your husband being the prime suspect in Rebecca Stanton's murder is about to break," she says quickly. "I want to let you in on what we know so you can decide what to do."

What to do. I tighten my grip on the door. Should I pretend ignorance? "Who is Rebecca Stanton?" I imagine myself saying.

"Do you have any idea how bad your timing is?" I say. "My husband's car has been found in the desert. All evidence points to the real possibility that he's dead. You just reported on all this. And yet you're here to talk about his supposed connection with some *murder?*"

Her expression softens. "I know what they found in your home that links Ben to the murder. The timing might not be great, but don't *you* want to know?"

Of course I do. "What makes you an expert about anything to do with Ben?"

She looks over her shoulder and sees Brad heading up the driveway toward us. She speaks more quickly now. "I have an inside source at the FBI who's seen the evidence and knows the case. He spoke to me on the condition of remaining anonymous."

"Why would you tell me any of it?"

She lifts the corners of her mouth. "Isn't it obvious? I'm hoping you'll let me be the first to interview you. When you're ready to tell your side of the story."

"And if I don't let you interview me?"

"Time to move on, Kate," Brad interrupts. "You know reporters aren't allowed up here."

She looks at him but doesn't move. "Ten more seconds, Brad. Please." She turns back to me. "If I were in your shoes, I'd want to be interviewed by someone who's going to tell the whole story, not turn this into tabloid fare. But interview aside, don't you want to know what they found?"

I loosen my death grip on the door. "Brad, give me ten minutes with her."

"You sure?" he asks.

I nod. "I've got questions for *her*."

He eyes Kate. "If you're not back out here in ten minutes, I'm going to come in and extract you. Ten minutes."

She flashes him a smile. "Got it."

I let her inside and we head to the living room.

"Gorgeous tree. You do this?"

164

I shake my head. "Ben's creation."

She steps over to the tree. "Looks like he was a very handy guy."

"He *is* very handy," I correct her. *"Is."*

"I hear he's a good cook, too. That's why he's owned so many restaurants over the years."

"He's always been the kind of guy who could make a meal out of anything. When we were first married, he'd come home, pull out some olives, a brick of cheese, and Italian bread, then get to work making dinner with whatever else we had lying around the kitchen." I realize I'm describing the way things were years ago. A time I'm longing for.

"We're all hoping they'll find him soon," she says, running her fingers across the Santa on a Surfboard ornament. "Looks like someone collects Santa ornaments."

I suddenly realize that in the guise of casual banter between women, I've actually been letting her interview me. But I'm the one with the questions. "Tell me what evidence the FBI found in my house."

She lets go of the ornament. "My source says they found the murder weapon on your property. A gun that was registered to Rebecca Stanton. The FBI says Ben used Rebecca's own gun to kill her."

A wave of nausea overcomes me. The idea that Ben killed Rebecca is hard enough to grasp, but it's even more difficult to imagine that he took her gun and used it against her. I grab a bottle of water off the dining table and take a long swig. "What else?" My voice wobbles. "They took evidence out of here twice. What else did they find?"

She hesitates, looks down at her hands. "They found a photo of Rebecca that investigators say was taken from her apartment . . ."

Sweat breaks out on my brow and the nausea rolls in on a huge wave, threatening to overwhelm me. I gulp more water and feel it roil in my stomach. "A photo doesn't prove anything. Lots of people have photos of other people. It doesn't mean they murdered them."

"It proves that he had been in her apartment." She stops there, but I know what else she's thinking. It proves there was some kind of relationship between them. Why else does a man hold on to a woman's photo?

I close my eyes for a moment, gathering my thoughts.

"You okay?"

I turn to face her. "The FBI has a theory that my husband murdered Rebecca. But in science, all knowledge is tentative and provisional. The accepted theory of something is simply the best explanation for it *among all available alternatives at the time*. We know Ben was angry at Rebecca for breaking the deal, but that doesn't mean he killed her."

"Ben's fingerprints were found at her apartment. And there's an eyewitness who saw him leaving her apartment that morning. That's pretty strong evidence."

My voice is hoarse. "But I know my husband. And he's not a murderer."

"I know," she says quietly. "Everyone I interviewed about Ben says he's the nicest guy. Clever, creative, generous—everyone likes him. Well, except for the bartender at Paragon. He saw Ben with Rebecca, the night she was murdered. I guess he saw a different side of Ben."

I lower my hand from my face. I'm sure I must look like a sight to her: dark eyes flashing, pale skin. "What did he see?"

"He says Ben grabbed her arm, shouting something like 'I'm not letting you out of this deal.'"

I sink into the side chair, my thoughts jumbled. This is what Shane had told me about Ben. What I didn't want to believe. Confirmation that Ben had threatened Rebecca and had a motive to kill her. I gulp down some more water, waiting for the dizziness to subside.

"Can you tell me how to find the bartender so I can talk to him?"

She flips through her notebook. "His name is JJ Morten. But he's already been interviewed by police and FBI. What do you think you're going to find out from him that they couldn't?"

"They talked to him after they already suspected Ben murdered Rebecca, looking to corroborate what they thought they knew. I'm looking to understand everything that happened that night. Everything."

A ghost of a smile crosses her lips. "What you're asking is whether there was something more going on. Something they missed." She jots a note on a slip of paper and hands it to me. "Here's his number, but don't tell him you got it from me."

———

DAY SIX

"Give me your hand," Ben whispered.

I stretched out my hand and he turned it over, palm up.

"Now close your eyes."

I laughed. Shut my eyes.

"Okay, this is serious business," he said, but I heard the smile in his voice. "No peeking." He covered my eyes with his other hand.

He placed something in my palm. Round and wrapped in cellophane.

"Guess?"

I rolled it around in my hand. A lollipop. But that's not what he was asking me to guess. "Jupiter?"

"Nope. Hotter."

"Venus!" I shrieked and opened my eyes to see a yellowish-white lollipop decorated to look just like the cloud-covered planet.

Just after our tenth anniversary Ben discovered the "Big Bin of Sweets" at a nearby candy emporium. Every few weeks after that he sifted through the enormous bin searching for Planet Lollipops, clear candy with a heavenly body inside. They're rare—most times he couldn't find any despite burrowing through pounds of sweets—but he did it anyway, knowing I loved all the planet flavors, except Mercury, which tastes like burnt cotton candy. Tropical-punch-flavored Venus was my favorite back then and it still is, even though the candy tradition ended a few years ago.

Now, standing in my backyard, an hour before sunrise, the planet Venus shines bright in the sky. This is Venus as Morning Star. The ancient Greeks thought Venus was actually two separate objects, a star they observed at night and called Hesperus—star of the evening—and one they saw rising in the morning that they named Phosphorus, the bringer of light.

Beneath its light with the first sliver of the violet sunrise on the horizon, my own thinking is illuminated. Although I have slept little of the night, I have a clarity that I didn't have the day before. I have chosen to believe that Ben did not kill Rebecca Stanton. Even though there is rock-solid evidence that he did.

I know I've fallen victim to "disconfirmation bias"—when scientists expend disproportionate energy trying to debunk information we find uncomfortable. But I've chosen to question every assumption, to test each block of my understanding. Starting with a call to Paragon bartender JJ Morten.

I dial his number. I know it's nine in the morning in New York, and since JJ is a bartender, I don't expect him to pick up. I plan to leave a voice-mail message, yet a sleepy voice answers the phone.

"Hello?"

"JJ Morten?" I ask.

He sighs. "Yeah. Who's this?"

"My name is Sarah Mayfield. My husband is Ben Mayfield. Could I talk with you about what happened at Paragon the night Rebecca Stanton was murdered?"

His tone is gruff. "Yeah, no. It's early and I—" There's a long pause on the phone, and for a moment, I think he's hung up. Then I hear him draw in a deep breath. "Yeah, I don't—I told everything to FBI and police already."

"My husband is missing and—"

"I heard."

"I'm trying to piece together what happened to him."

"I have no way of knowing if you are who you say you are—"

"I am his wife. If it would help, I'll send you photos of our wedding. Or snapshots from the last fifteen years of our life together . . ."

Silence on the line.

"Would you answer just *one* question for me?" I say softly.

"One." His tone is resigned. I'm wearing him down.

"I've been hearing that my husband was drunk and maybe high on drugs, knocking things over, yelling at Rebecca. Is that what you saw that night?"

"Some of that is true."

"Which part?"

"That's *two* questions."

"Help me out here. Give me thirty more seconds of your time, then I'll leave you alone."

He sighs again. "Look, your husband seemed normal enough. Only had two drinks as far I remember, but the rest of what you say is true."

"What was Ben like when he was with Rebecca?"

"They didn't come in together," he said, misunderstanding the question. "Ben and his friend Shane were already at the bar when she showed up wearing a ginormous diamond engagement ring. Like four carats or something. Slaps her hand on the bar with that heavy rock on her finger and tells them she's getting married."

"Then what?"

"The next thing I know the three of them are shouting. It got so bad the manager had to come out and calm things down."

Anxiety rises in my throat. Ben was angry after Rebecca announced she was getting married. Maybe this was proof Ben *was* having an affair with her. Could jealousy and her business betrayal have spurred him to murder her later?

"Why do you think they got so mad?"

He's silent for a moment. "No idea. But every one of them was mad at the other two."

Every one of them was mad at the other two. That meant Ben was mad at both Rebecca and Shane.

I imagine Ben that night knowing that the Manhattan restaurant he'd been trying to land had slipped through his fingers. He must have been devastated. Furious at Shane for not saving the deal. Mad enough to murder Rebecca?

I glance at Venus as it fades away in the brightening sky and with it, my hope of gaining any proof that Ben did not murder Rebecca Stanton.

The proposal for the space telescope is due into NASA in a few days, and I head to my home office hoping I can focus long enough to analyze a sizable chunk of the data.

If our proposal is chosen, the telescope will scan the entire sky over the course of two years and catalog thousands of possible planets. The main goal is to find rocky planets with solid surfaces—planets that could show signs of life—but, as my own life unravels, I've lost touch with the project's importance.

Still, I force myself to focus on calculating a projection for the number of Earth-sized planets the telescope might discover in its two-year voyage. After several minutes, I have immersed myself so completely in the task that all the morning hours fly by and suddenly it is nearly one o'clock.

I've arranged to share my projections later that afternoon with my boss. As I hike across the campus to his office, I spot Aaron heading toward me. He's wearing glasses today, which have the expected effect of making him look studious but, oddly, more handsome.

"Hey, stranger," he says, breaking into a smile. He hugs me and we linger too long in the hug. "What brings you here?"

"I've completed my projection." I don't have to tell him what the projection is for. Aaron wants this space telescope to be approved almost as much as I do and has been working on the programming pipeline for processing massive amounts of data the telescope will collect.

"How's it looking?" he asks.

I breeze through my analysis. What will become a single chart in the proposal is the result of at least eighty hours of data crunching and forecasting. At first it feels odd to be talking about the work again, but it doesn't take long for me to settle back into it. And when Aaron nods at the challenges I've encountered in interpreting the data, I know he understands.

"Your detectability assumptions make sense to me," he says, leaving no doubt he appreciates the way I've attacked the problem. "Steven will like this."

"Let's hope you're right."

His blue eyes light up. "I am. Right, that is."

I meet his gaze, and then my mind flashes to kissing him outside the airport. I clear my throat. "Can I swing by later and get the DVR? If anyone found out you have it—"

"I've thought a lot about this, Sarah. I know what we're doing by hiding the DVR could land us—me—in serious trouble. But if this is the one way I can help you, I'm willing to do it."

His offer to help brings tears to my eyes, which I quickly whisk away. Many people are there for you when you rise to the top, but few are there for you when you hit rock bottom. "You've already done more than you should have for me. I can't let you keep putting yourself at risk."

"A friend of mine is sending me a data-recovery utility he just wrote that should unlock a chunk more data on the drive. Let me run that tonight and see what we can recover."

"You really shouldn't keep helping me like this."

Air rushes from my lungs. I try to deny my attraction to him but his warm smile draws me in. "I can't imagine doing anything else."

CHAPTER TWENTY

The story about Ben Mayfield killing Rebecca Stanton hits the national news an hour later. It's nonstop on every cable news channel, and there are countless posts about it popping up on social media and in my email. The *LA Times* and the *New York Times* are reporting it, of course. But there's a sensational quality to the story that has nearly every major news outlet covering it, too. "Crime of Passion," the *USA Today* headline reads.

I switch off the TV and toss my phone in a kitchen drawer, but I can still see the news images flashing in my mind. Rebecca's tanned face framed by flawless blonde hair. A few shots of Rebecca dancing in a shapely white dress at some club. Another photo of Ben and Rebecca with several sports stars at Paragon.

I look at her and feel plain in comparison. Then feel guilty because I'm actually jealous of a dead woman.

There's one photo of Ben, dressed in a black tux at the red-carpet grand opening of Aurora, standing next to an actor dressed in an outrageous superhero costume. Ben has one eyebrow cocked and a slight grin on his face, an expression that reads as flat-out adorable.

Even with the sound off, the story made sense: a beautiful woman and her gorgeous boyfriend quarreled about the sale of a trendy restaurant, and in an angry, alcohol-fueled moment, he killed her.

Except he isn't her boyfriend. He is my husband.

I call Steven Webster to share the news with him, and for the first time his voice sounds clipped. And nervous. "Let me talk to the higher-ups and figure out next steps." His words catch me off guard. Does "next steps" mean they might select someone less complicated to lead the space telescope project? It won't be difficult to find plenty of astronomers whose husbands aren't murder suspects or entangled in a sensational news story.

The doorbell pulls me out of my thoughts, but I don't answer it. I'm guessing it's one of the increasing number of reporters who are camped on the parkway, hoping for an interview. They'd become bolder, and a few had made it past Brad to my doorstep before he escorted them off the property. Rachel is also keeping watch through the front window.

"It's getting crazy out there," she sings under her breath, then heads to the front door to peek through the peephole.

I hear shouting outside and a voice I recognize as Brad's. "Okay to open up."

Rachel opens the door, and Shane is standing next to Brad on the doorstep.

"Lot of people trying to get to your front door today," Brad says. "But I knew you'd want me to let this guy through."

"Thanks, Brad."

Shane's dressed casually today—blue jeans and a checkered blue shirt—and carrying a large shopping bag.

He wraps me in a warm hug. "I tried calling—"

"Tossed my phone in the drawer."

"Can't blame you." He has a worried look on his face, and he's more pale than usual.

"The news I've been hearing about Ben is . . . forget that. What can I do?"

"Not much," I say. "Unless you have a way to wake me up from this nightmare."

He follows me into the living room. Rachel pads behind him and switches on the Christmas tree lights, filling the gloomy room with warmth.

"I brought some cookies for you and Zack," he says, lifting a box out of his paper bag. "Well, mostly for Zack."

"He'll like that," I say, accepting the gift.

Rachel takes the cookie box from me and heads to the kitchen to stow it alongside at least a dozen cakes and baked goods lining the kitchen counter. I think we almost have enough to open a bakery.

"This has been in the works for a while, but I've just made partner—chief investment officer—at the firm. Which means that Diane finally gets her wish and we're moving to London. We'll both be working on the same continent for a change."

"That's wonderful," I say, but my tone is flat.

"Look, with everything that's happened, I'm not here to celebrate . . ."

I wave my hand at him as though it's not an issue. But I'm having a hard time connecting with his happiness, or anything happy. Right now it feels like all the happiness and joy has been doled out to everyone else, and none of it has been left for me or Zack.

"Diane found us a great flat in London. You'll have to come visit." His face is glowing. "But I feel like I'm deserting you when you need us most. Before we take off in a few days, I want to figure out what I can do to help you and Zack."

He's talking about our family as though Ben is dead. And everything points to the fact that he is. But I still can't form a plan around a life like that, even though I had discussed divorce a little over a week ago. What does a life without Ben look like? Feel like. I can't imagine my future. I hope I'll get to go back to work on the new space telescope, of course. But even that's not certain. Zack will finish another three years of high school and head off to college. But suddenly there's a black hole where there once was a family.

His voice softens. "I've heard they're calling off the search for Ben."

I nod. Detective Dawson had told me about the sheriff's decision to end the search, and it had been all over the news today. Hundreds of trained rescuers and volunteers had searched for miles in the scorching heat of Joshua Tree and had not turned up anything to indicate Ben might still be alive.

I'm tired of answering questions. Not even sure I can process the answers anymore. But I have my own questions. "Did Rebecca and Ben have more than just a business relationship?"

He hesitates, looks at his hands. "I don't know why you're—"

"You have to tell me, Shane."

He looks up, a sober expression on his face. "Look, I don't know for sure, Sarah. There were . . . sparks between them. But I don't know anything more than that."

"Even if it's true that they were having an affair, I can't yet accept that he killed her. I know there is evidence. The murder weapon found in our backyard. An eyewitness who saw Ben leave her apartment in the morning. Fingerprints. There's even a motive with the business deal gone sour. But I can't accept what's been clearly laid out in front of me."

"I can't . . . I can't entirely wrap my head around what happened after I left, either. But I accept the proof. I have to. What's holding you back from accepting the evidence? That's not like you."

I look at him a moment. I hadn't told anyone—not even Rachel—about my suspicions, but it feels like I can confide in him. "Something about the way the murder weapon was found in the backyard seems . . . off to me. It was buried just an inch or two beneath the surface. As if someone *wanted* it to be found. If Ben was trying to hide the evidence, why wouldn't he make it harder to find?"

"We can't know his state of mind when he did it . . ."

"And there's something else that doesn't add up. The night Ben hid the murder weapon, he used a high-powered light to blind the security camera in the backyard so it wouldn't see or record anything. Why would he do that when all he'd have to do is stop the cameras from recording?"

Shock registers on his face. "You have security-camera footage? I thought you said it had been erased."

"I've recovered recordings of the hours and days before Ben disappeared. On one of the clips we can clearly see someone blinding the camera that's pointed right at where the murder weapon was found."

He furrows his brow. "Can you see who it is?"

"Not yet. But I'm recovering more and more of the data. And soon, I'll be able to figure out who was there that night and what they were doing. And everything else that happened in the days before Ben went missing."

"Want my honest opinion? All this looking at the past is probably a waste of your time. As hard as it is, you need to accept the evidence and start taking the next steps in your life."

I shake my head, suddenly feeling brave. "No astronomer, no scientist, just accepts the evidence. The best scientists are those who understand the limitations of the evidence. It's our job to challenge it. The most important discoveries are made when we question evidence and consider new possibilities."

CHAPTER TWENTY-ONE

It's nearly midnight and I'm sitting on the patio, telescope trained on the skies. I'm still not ready to go back inside. It seems like everything that is uncertain and disturbing exists somewhere else on this planet, while here underneath the moon and stars—this is where it's safe. Where things make sense.

Off in the northwest, I see the blue-white star Vega. Located only twenty-five light-years away, it is one of the brightest stars in the night sky.

I fell in love with Ben under this star.

We'd taken a weekend adventure to the Anza-Borrego Desert southeast of Los Angeles, one of a dozen certified International Dark Sky Parks dedicated to preserving night-sky visibility by enforcing low-lighting ordinances. Ben and I had been inseparable for six months, and this was our first overnight trip together.

Under a starry vault on a warm summer's night in June, we had gazed at the majestic swath of the Milky Way arching over the twinkling stars high above the Borrego Valley. We stared in awe of the sweeping view of the cosmos, knowing that we were seeing stars as they once were eons ago, perhaps as long as the beginning of time itself.

In the translucent light, I grabbed his hand and led him seventy yards through thick, knee-high grass to give him the best view of the Summer Triangle, an asterism—or pattern—of three brilliant stars, with Vega reigning at its apex.

Deep in the desert here, the stars seemed almost within reach, and without the moon in the sky, we could see the vast desert around us by starlight.

"Vega is the brightest star in the asterism," I said, pointing out each of the stars. "Over to her left is Deneb, and to her lower right is Altair. And the Milky Way passes right through them all."

As we breathed in the expansive view of the Milky Way, I told him the legend written in the stars. "Vega, the daughter of a king, falls in love with a shepherd named Altair. When Vega's father finds out, he forbids her to see him, but when he realizes nothing will stop the two lovers, he convinces the gods to place the two in the sky, where they're forever separated by the Celestial River represented by the Milky Way. But even though they can't be together, their love burns brighter than any star in the sky."

We stood there in silent amazement, and then I handed him a set of binoculars to reel in the gossamer beauty of it all, to see the haunting nebulae and star clusters straight from a midsummer night's dream. As he scanned the Milky Way and the Summer Triangle, his other hand holding mine, I felt powerfully alive, part of something glittering and gauzy.

"Beautiful, right?" I whispered.

He handed me the binoculars. My breath caught in my throat as I waited for him to speak. "The brightest star here isn't Vega. It's you, Sarah." He smiled in the incandescent light. "I think I've fallen in love with you . . ."

With Vega shining high above our heads, he wrapped me in his arms and I sensed our future laid out before us.

Back in my garden, the clouds journey across the sky, shuttering my view of Vega. It'll be several more months until summer comes and I can see her again in the Summer Triangle.

The Summer Triangle.

Is that what Ben was saying on the voice mail? Not summer angle, but Summer Triangle?

My mind races. Was it possible that Ben was telling me—in a kind of private code—where he was headed?

Could he have once been planning to go to the desert cabin we stayed in beneath the Summer Triangle?

———

I can't concentrate. I keep walking from room to room as if I expect to find the answers there.

I find the voice-mail recording of Ben's call the night of the shooting and listen to it again. There are many gaps, but Ben *could* be saying "Summer Triangle."

I wander into our bedroom, stare at Ben's athletic shoes still waiting by the closet door. I consider telling Detective Dawson about the Summer Triangle, but I doubt it's relevant anymore now that Ben is by all accounts dead.

A tear escapes my eye. Ben had left me a message. All this time, I'd been angry that he didn't tell me about the poisoning, the gun, or the million dollars in the bank account. But in the moments after he was shot, he had called me to say two important words: Summer Triangle.

Two words that would've given me hope if I'd heard them then. They were proof of his plan to escape from whoever was after him— Gary Stanton?—by going to the cabin we'd stayed in to experience the Summer Triangle.

Our cabin had been billed by the owner as "secluded" but was so remote that we had to drive on a narrow, rough dirt road for nearly three miles before reaching it. And it was so well hidden by stately Coulter pines and mounds of ribbonwood chaparral that we passed by it several times before spotting it.

The cabin didn't have running water, but there was a well about a half mile away, a twice-daily hike that had made Ben and me feel like true desert pioneers. We spent days exploring that remote region of the Anza-Borrego, climbing the lofty summit of Combs Peak and looking out toward some of Southern California's highest mountains, then gazing on the Salton Sea below. Although the cabin lacked any modern amenities—running water, electricity, Wi-Fi—it made up for it with amazing views, charming nooks for reading and napping, and a sturdy wraparound deck for stargazing.

We'd gathered massive pine cones and wood for our nightly fires in the stone fireplace, christened the cabin the Summer Triangle Haven—which Ben scrawled with his always-handy Sharpie on a piece of wood—and vowed to return there every year.

Though we only went once more.

And clearly Ben never made it to our haven. His car, splattered with bloody evidence of a severe injury, was found in Joshua Tree, a two-hour drive away.

Ben is dead.

The tears well up from somewhere deep inside. They're rough and bitter from waiting so long to come out, and they spill from my eyes, sliding down my cheeks in thick droplets.

"Are you crying?" I hear my sister whisper from behind. She wraps me in a hug. "Don't cry."

CHAPTER
TWENTY-TWO

DAY SEVEN

My phone is chiming. Insistent. A text, not a call.

I open my eyes and glance at the clock: 3:28. In the morning. In the darkened room, I grope around on my nightstand for the phone, then realize it's not there.

The chiming continues.

My head is heavy as I lift it off my pillow and make my way downstairs to find the phone.

I stumble into the kitchen, where moonlight streams through the window. The phone chimes again, so I sift through the piles of unopened mail on the countertop and find it beneath the property tax bill. In my haze, I don't remember leaving it there.

The bright screen makes my eyes water: *G188 AB BA1*

The phone number isn't in my contacts, so the caller ID says "Unknown." It's an area code I don't recognize.

Then a second text: *ABG 01X0*

The phone chimes again, startling me. A third text swoops across the screen: *0B ABG E1C8L. 6HFG ZB91*

For a moment, I wonder if someone sent a text to the wrong number, but then my brain wakes up to the idea of a code. But from whom? I don't dare hope that it's from Ben.

I flip on the overhead lights and grab a pen. My first clue is that there are numbers in the code, which means that the sender has included the numbers zero through nine in the cipher key. That makes it harder.

I try several simple substitution ciphers, ones that are the most common, but none of them turn up any real words.

I attempt blunt force, trying all shift possibilities one by one. The letter *A* is *B*, the letter *A* is *C*, and so on. My eyes are blurry and my hand is cramped by the time I finally stumble on the twenty-four-letter shift possibility.

The first word decodes: *TELL*

My hand trembles as I decipher the second word: *NO*

Then the third: *ONE*

TELL NO ONE

My breath is caught in my throat. The words swim in front of my eyes as I decode the next line:

NOT DEAD

My hand races across the paper as I unravel the last line:

DO NOT REPLY. JUST COME.

"Come where?" I say out loud. The words are breathy and my voice doesn't sound like my own.

"The Summer Triangle?" I wonder. "Joshua Tree? Where, Ben?"

I pace the kitchen floor. I don't dare allow myself to feel the joy that's welling up inside. Ready to burst.

Ben is not dead.

"Wait, just wait. Think. Think, Sarah." My voice sounds strange, like I've become a lunatic. *Calm down.*

I feel the blood rocketing through my veins. Then anger.

Why did he wait so long to tell me he was alive? Why did he put me through a week of agony?

Another chime:

QR PN QS A 00U SS OT J

It takes a bit to decode this one because it's a string of numbers.

34 20 35 N 117 55 16 W

Coordinates. Even with the markings for degrees, minutes, and seconds missing, I recognize this immediately as geographic coordinates. I plug them into the maps app on my phone and see where it is. It's not the Summer Triangle. Or Joshua Tree.

It's Buckhorn Campground in the Angeles National Forest. I type the location into Google and see that it's a well-known campground located about an hour from here. But it's closed for winter, and to reach it, I'll have to make my way along roads that twist and wind through the mountains. At night.

LBH XE1 5A 0XA31E. 3B ABJ

I scan the message and consider searching for an online code breaker but figure it'll take me longer to find my laptop than it will to decrypt this one.

YOU ARE IN DANGER. GO NOW.

I can't just leave. What about Rachel? Zack?

As if the sender—is it Ben?—could read my mind, another text zips across the screen:

4XI1 EXZ418 GX71 MXZ7 GB F2

The decoding comes more easily now.

HAVE RACHEL TAKE ZACK TO SF

I throw a few phone batteries in my backpack, my glasses, an extra pair of sunglasses, and a bottle of water. I don't know what to prepare for.

Ben's message says "tell no one," but I must tell Rachel. How else will I convince her to take Zack to San Francisco?

I rush into her room and jostle her awake.

"Rachel, I got a text from Ben. He's not dead. He's asking me to meet him. I have to go. Now. And you have to leave with Zack. Now."

"What?" She rubs the sleep from her eyes.

I thrust the phone in her face. Her jaw slackens.

"He sent it in *code*?" Rachel had always admired our encoded exchanges. For his thirtieth birthday, she'd even written him an entire birthday card in code, shifting every letter by eight.

"One of the simple Julius Caesar ciphers we've used before. He probably sent it in code so I'll know for certain it's from him. And he probably guesses police and FBI are monitoring my text messages."

Her eyes widen. "This is crazy."

"You have to get going. *We* have to get going."

Her voice is groggy. "There aren't flights to San Francisco at four in the morning."

I know what she's thinking. That I've come unhinged. And maybe I have. My heart is pounding so hard that I can hear it beating in my ears.

"I know," I say, slowing down. "But pack your things so you can try to get on an early flight. I'm going to get Zack ready."

"Wait. Where is he? Where is Ben?"

I stop and draw a deep breath. "He says to tell no one."

"Where is he?"

"A campground in the Angeles National Forest."

Her face flushes bright red. "It can't be true . . ."

"What can't be?"

"That Ben is alive and hiding in some campground in Angeles National Forest. You saw the photos of his car in the desert. All the blood. There's no way he—"

She's right. It's impossible.

"And why does he say you shouldn't reply? What would happen if you did?"

I'm usually the one who's calm, measured. Logical. But right now, she is. I try to think of a reason why I shouldn't reply.

"The FBI is monitoring all my communications. As long as I don't reply, this just looks like a spammy text some drunk person might have sent me. That's what the FBI might think. But if I reply, they'll immediately know there's some kind of communicating going on."

"But why wouldn't Ben want police to know where he is?"

"Because he's a murder suspect, Rachel."

As if to underscore my message, the grandfather clock downstairs chimes, startling us. We wait for it to finish its song, gathering our thoughts.

"How can you be sure this is really from Ben? Can you trace the number?"

"Doubt it. His phone broke in the shooting, remember? This is probably one of those prepaid cell phones."

"Then you can't be sure it's him, Sarah. You have to reply. That way, you can force whoever it is to prove he's Ben."

I'm not sure. If this is Ben, he must have a reason for asking me not to reply. What if replying puts him in some kind of danger?

Rachel lowers her voice. "And how does he know that I'm here with you?"

A chill rushes up my spine. I don't have an answer for that, either, and that bothers me. "Maybe he's just assuming . . . I mean, of course you'd be here."

But now uncertainty creeps into my veins.

Rachel takes my hand and squeezes it. "Ben is dead, Sarah. Whoever this is, it isn't him."

I don't want to accept her reasoning. Even though it's far more rational than my own. I decide to reply to the text with a question that only Ben would know. And in a code that no one but Ben could break.

I sit on the edge of Rachel's bed and type.

nuqDaq poH tuj bI'reS triangle?

———

My question is simple, but it's not encoded in a Julius Caesar cipher. It's in Klingon. My Klingon vocabulary isn't strong anymore, and I doubt Ben's is, either, but he'll certainly be able to figure out this phrase.

Where is Summer Triangle?

If it's Ben on the receiving end, he'll remember that *nuqDaq* means "where is." That's beginner-level Klingon. And even if he can't remember the long phrase for summer—*poH tuj bI'reS*—he'll certainly put the phrase in the context of the one English word "triangle" and figure out what I'm asking.

While I await an answer, I wake Zack and tell him what's happening. I know Ben has said to tell no one, but Zack will never get on a plane to San Francisco unless I explain. In his sleep stupor, I'm not sure he understands the details of what I'm saying, but there's no doubt he senses the urgency. He hugs me tight. "Dad is alive?"

I look into his deep brown eyes. "Yes. I'm going to find him."

"Why can't I go with you?"

"Dad wants you to go to San Francisco with Aunt Rachel."

"But why?"

I don't have an answer. "I'm sure he has a good reason."

"But how's it safer for you to go alone? Into the mountains?"

I've never been a particularly good driver in the mountains. I usually grip the steering wheel too tightly, certain that a pothole or rock will send the car hurtling over the edge. In the Angeles National Forest, there are spans of twisty highway without guardrails, and at that elevation, there can be snow or slick roads this time of year.

"I'll ask Brad to go with me."

That answer doesn't do much to lessen the panic in his eyes. "When am I coming back? Are you bringing Dad home with you?"

I wrap him in a big hug. "I don't know. But I'll text or call as soon as I do."

While he starts to toss some clothes into a small suitcase, I glance at my phone. No answer from Ben.

———

Forty-five minutes later I'm hurtling in the dark toward Angeles National Forest. The sun won't rise for another two hours, and outside of the sweep of my headlights, I'm surrounded by slate-gray mountains.

Sweat blooms along my hairline even though it's a cool sixty-four degrees. I glance at Brad in the passenger seat. His body is muscle on muscle, and he has the look of a sword-wielding deity, even though his muscles were likely earned in an air-conditioned gym. He hasn't said a single word this entire trip, and there's no doubt he's hyperfocused, scanning in front of and behind us, his hand gripping what looks like a high-powered rifle.

Still, I feel vulnerable. In danger.

I told Brad that I would drive. I need to, I had said. I want something to burn off the adrenaline that rips through my veins.

But as we leave the foothills and get a few miles into the narrow, winding Angeles Crest Highway through the mountains, I realize this is a mistake. Between the hairpin turns and chunks of rock and stone strewn in the roadway from the recent rains, my nerves are already shot.

Ben had said to tell no one, but in the space of less than an hour, I've already told three people. I think I'm doing the safe thing, but as I drive in the darkness, I have the shivery feeling that I've just put every-one around me in even greater danger.

Rachel and Zack have taken a taxi to the airport, and she has been texting every fifteen minutes to let me know that the trip is uneventful. Still, I can't stop the anxious roiling in my chest. I can barely focus on the road ahead.

Ben is alive.

Somehow he survived the shooting, escaped from the car in Joshua Tree, and made it all the way to Buckhorn Campground.

It seems impossible.

An edge of fear thickens my voice. "Still no answer?"

Brad glances at my phone and shakes his head.

"Maybe he can't answer," I say. "Maybe he doesn't have a way . . ."

On Brad's lap is the cipher key I've written in case Ben writes back in the Julius Caesar cipher code instead of Klingon. Why hasn't he replied? Would he really expect—assume—I'd drive high into the mountains at night without proof the texts were from him?

Even though that's exactly what I'm doing.

Brad shifts in his seat, and out of the corner of my eye the rifle on his lap glints in the white light from the dashboard. He has brought enough ammunition and firearms to withstand a riot.

Did Ben think the code itself was enough proof?

I think back to the meteorite necklace he had left for me under the Christmas tree. In code he had written I'M SORRY and signed it with his nickname, BENJI. Why didn't he sign his name this time?

As we reach the thirty-eight-mile marker, nausea burns at the back of my throat. Nerve pain shoots down my back as though my body is literally trying to sound an alarm.

We need to go back.

If it's Ben who's texting me, he would have responded by now. I know him. Even if he didn't know how to answer the question in

Klingon, he would've typed *something* in Klingon. *Hlja'* meaning "yes," or *nuqjatlh* meaning "what did you say."

I wrench the steering wheel into a tight U-turn, and for a long moment, the headlights pierce the darkness over the canyon below. I hear my tires crunch on the graveled shoulder. Then I hit the accelerator and head back down the mountain.

CHAPTER
TWENTY-THREE

My computer is gone. Not just the laptop, but every single external hard drive I own—all fourteen of them, each one labeled with their specific data contents. The thieves have also ripped the Blu-ray and DVR from the cabinet in the living room and snapped up the old laptop I kept in the kitchen.

One of the police officers dusting for fingerprints in the kitchen the next morning tells me it looks like teenagers are responsible. Even though I know he's wrong, I can see why he'd think that. The robbers took Zack's gaming keyboard and headphones along with his PlayStation and a dozen games. They got careless in the kitchen, leaving open cans of soda on the counter and spilling a jar of jellybeans.

Detective Dawson shakes his head as he snaps a photo of the jellybeans. "Nope, not kids. These thieves are pro. They tripped the alarm, took everything, and were out of here before police arrived fifteen minutes later." He turned to fix a pair of steely brown eyes on me. "The texts were just a diversion to get you out of the house. What do you think they were looking for?"

"Maybe CIT research?" I say convincingly. But I know that whoever broke in wants the security-system DVR yet had no idea that it was safely hidden in Aaron's office.

How did anyone know about it?

I mentioned it to Shane, of course, but he had no reason to want access to it. And then there were Zack's friends, who knew we were recording all activity at the house. Still, it didn't seem likely that his friends would cook up an elaborate scheme to lure us out of the house with fake texts in code just so they could get to whatever might be on the DVR.

Which left Ben's partners. Richard Jenkins. I remember how he glared at the security camera after he threatened Ben. Had the cameras captured something more that incriminated him?

Then there was the very real possibility that someone completely unknown to me—the intruders who've been coming onto the property at various times since the night before Ben disappeared—could be responsible.

But what I really want to know is what police found at Buckhorn Campground. At least a dozen officers had descended on it at dawn, scouring every square foot for any sign that Ben was there. Or had been.

But as the hours tick by and lunchtime nears with no sign of Ben, I know he never was at Buckhorn Campground. Most likely whoever was behind the texts wasn't there, either, but instead waited nearby for me to leave the house so that they could break in to steal the security-system DVR.

I think through all the clips we've recovered. *What is on that DVR that someone doesn't want anyone to find out?*

Through the kitchen window, I watch Detective Dawson talking on the phone as he stands in the middle of the garden by the lilac tree. Overnight, it seems, it has exploded in pure white blooms. I can't hear what he's saying, but the way his jaw is clenched I suspect it isn't good news. He must feel me watching him because he looks up and meets my gaze. He shakes his head.

Ben is not there.

It's not a surprise, but it's a shock to my body. I feel the room spin for a second, and my hands tingle with anxiety.

Ben is not alive.

The detective steps in the back door, places his phone back in the holster on his belt. "This time of year there aren't many people coming or going up there except a few regulars. No sign of Ben, and no one saw anything or anyone unusual."

"I understand." My voice is pitched too high.

His tone is suddenly sharp, surprising me. "It's a good thing he wasn't there because let me tell you, you just about got yourself into a huge mess. Ben is an official murder suspect, and helping him evade law enforcement is a felony."

"I wasn't . . . I just thought . . ."

My voice trails off. I'm not sure what I thought. Or if I was even thinking at all when I headed up into the mountains to find Ben. It seems as though I acted upon the vapors of hope, not reason.

The human brain is a marvel, its one hundred billion neurons forming an estimated five hundred trillion synapses yet powered by less than twenty watts. But we know more about the workings of the cosmos than we do about how our brain makes decisions. Right now I am proof of that.

I'd wanted so much for Ben to be alive—to be on the other end of those texts—that even in the face of overwhelming evidence that proved he wasn't, I still risked my life to search for him.

"Look," he says, his voice softening, "I know this is rough for you. I've told the FBI it was an honest mistake. And I think they've accepted that."

Something about the way he says it doesn't ring true. The FBI has accepted that I made *an honest mistake*? With shocking clarity I realize why.

"You're certain Ben is dead. That's the reason you're letting me off the hook, isn't it?"

He draws a big breath, exhales slowly. "We haven't reached any conclusions yet."

My voice shakes. "He may be a murder suspect, but none of you actually think he's still alive. You think someone made sure of it."

"It does appear that way . . . but we don't have concrete evidence yet. We're continuing to investigate Rebecca's father, Gary Stanton. He just made the investigation more difficult by leaving the country."

"Leaving the country?"

"That's what he does once he feels the heat of our investigations. Takes off for Italy or Spain. Sometimes Argentina."

"This is a long way of saying that you don't expect to find Ben alive."

He presses his lips together and looks at the ground. When he glances back up at me, his expression is grim. "It's an ongoing investigation, Sarah. We can't—"

"You're sure he's dead," I say softly. "Just say it."

He's silent for a long moment, and the only sound is the steady hum of the dishwasher. When he finally speaks, his voice is strained, full of regret. "I don't think we're ever going to find him alive."

———

"Hi, I'm Ben," he shouted over haunting electronic music I recognized as one of Depeche Mode's latest hits.

"Sarah," I shouted back from a dark corner of the club. While everyone else has dressed for the party, I was still wearing what I'd worn to work that day: dark pants and a blazer.

It was after midnight and the air was thick with heat and possibility. Colored lights pulsated around the dance floor and the party. Anything could and was happening.

Ben was dressed for the event, wearing a blue henley, which emphasized his muscled shoulders, and dark jeans. "What brings someone like you to a place like this, Sarah?"

I smiled at the cliché line. "I know the owner."

His lips twitched into an adorable, lazy grin. "You know the owner? What's he like?"

"Handsome. Smart. Sweet. Nothing like you at all."

He stepped forward, his hands grazing my hips. "*I* can be smart. Sweet. Anything you want."

"*Anything* I want?"

"Anything." As he leaned in to kiss me, I breathed in the scent of him. Old Spice. He gently pressed me against the wall behind me and I felt the length of him against me.

Two leggy brunettes in tight dresses brushed past, laughing as they headed to the packed dance floor. They stared at us, clearly confused about why the club owner was hitting on a girl who clearly hadn't dressed for the party.

They had no idea I was his wife of six months. That this superhot club, set up in a warehouse in a hip but gritty part of downtown LA, was Ben's first venture into running a restaurant/club.

"Let's get out of here," Ben whispered in my ear.

We'd done this before, pretending we were strangers at a party or a formal event at Caltech, where I was finishing my PhD. Sometimes our eyes would meet across the room and we'd slowly approach each other, acting as though we were meeting for the first time. Other times, he'd try to flirt with me and I'd pretend to resist his charms. Almost always, we ended up leaving the party early, rushing home, loving each other until we were breathless.

———

My sister is bringing me a fresh quinoa salad she prepared using herbs she picked from the garden and organic quinoa and vegetables she bought at the gourmet food store a few blocks away. I'm suspicious of the grainy salad at first, but find it sweeter and juicier than it looks.

She and Zack had made it all the way to the airport before I texted them to return, explaining that the whole thing was a hoax. And when I shared with them that there was no sign Ben had been in Buckhorn Campground, Zack sat by my side for nearly an hour, completely distraught, his face bloated from crying. Rachel hadn't said much, keeping her thoughts to herself.

"Quinoa is best when it's grown above twelve thousand feet," she says as if she's fascinated with the subject, but I know she's stalling. She's tensing her shoulders, a sure sign she wants to say something but is holding back.

"Your avocado tree needed some pruning . . . so I took care of that." Her voice is breathy, strained. "I gave it more water, too."

"Thank you . . ."

There's an awkward silence in the room as she watches me eat. I see her chest rise and fall rapidly as she sits across from me at the dining table. Whatever she wants to tell me is clearly troubling her.

"Can I tell you something?" Her voice is heavy with emotion. "The FBI has really strong evidence against Ben. It's all over the news. They've found his fingerprints at the scene. The murder weapon was found in your backyard. He had a photo of her somewhere in this house. And an eyewitness saw him leaving her apartment the morning of the murder. He had a motive."

I put my fork down and rein in my anger. "Why are you telling me what I already know?"

"Because I think you're in denial." She says it with authority, as though she's analyzed all my thoughts and feelings and reached a startling conclusion.

"What I don't know is what happened to Ben after that. And nei-ther do you. They haven't found Ben's body."

"And they won't. Gary Stanton will make sure they don't."

"We don't know with certainty that Gary killed Ben."

She turns her back to me and looks out the window. "You were like this when we were kids. Hoping Dad was going to come back. Every week you were sure it would happen. He'd write something funny in a birthday card and that was your proof. Or Mom would be in a good mood and you were sure that meant Dad was coming home. Remember that?"

My throat aches but I don't let her know how much her words hurt me. "I *was* wrong about Dad coming back. But I'm not twelve anymore. I'm a scientist, for Chrissake. I *live* in a world of concrete data and evidence. Do you really think in the face of all this proof I'm sitting *in denial* about what happened to Ben?"

"Actually, I do." Her voice has an edge to it. "Because there's some-thing you need to remember, Sarah. Even if he is alive, he wouldn't be coming back to any life the two of you had before. He's a murder suspect."

I sigh and push my chair away from the table. "Do you think I don't know that? Is this your way of saying 'I told you so' about Ben?"

Her face reddens. She smooths a wrinkle on the tablecloth. "I never thought he was right for you. His family founded one of the biggest department stores in Chicago. While our parents were . . . schoolteach-ers in Missouri. He wanted different things than you did. You always had your head in the stars, and he was talking about restaurants and co-ventures with movie stars."

"Twenty-three-year-old Ben was like that . . . but that's not the kind of husband or father he became."

She opens her mouth to say something, then closes it. She tilts her head. "C'mon, Sarah. You stopped talking about him the last year or so.

You'd tell me about the latest exoplanet discovery, the Kuiper belt, or whatever. Or what Zack did in school. But you didn't talk about Ben."

"That happens sometimes when you've been married a long time. You'd know that if you and Carl stuck it out for longer than three years."

Her eyes water. Carl was abusive and a cheater. It's hardly a fair comparison. I know I've hurt her, even though I didn't mean to. "That was a low blow," she says, almost under her breath.

"Sorry," I say, and reach out to touch her arm.

She grips my hand and looks me straight in the eye. "You've got to accept what's happened to Ben."

My voice breaks. "What makes you think I haven't?"

"Look how easily you were lured into believing those coded texts were from Ben. You drove halfway up the mountain *hoping* they were from him."

I let go of her hand and push the plate away. My voice shoots to the ceiling. "So what do you think I should be doing? Planning his funeral? Cleaning out his closet? What?"

She shakes her head. "I think you've got to accept that Ben is . . . not alive," she says, avoiding the word "dead." "And begin making plans."

———

Aaron is reeling. His face has turned bright crimson as though he's been in the hot sun all day, even though we are sitting in the air-conditioned cool of his office.

I'm telling him about the coded texts and the break-in. How all of my computer equipment—every single hard drive—had been stolen. He sits across from me, and as my story unfolds, I can see he is thinking, wondering if anyone knows he's been holding the security DVR all this time. Evaluating if he is at risk. Curious what's on the DVR that someone wants so badly they conned me into leaving my house, then broke in to steal it.

He tells me about the new utility he's run, which recovered nearly three hours of camera footage, then our conversation inevitably wanders to the space telescope proposal.

If science is the way the universe works, then math, and in particular scientific computer programming, is the language we scientists speak. That's because the human eye is a great tool, but it can't possibly process millions of images, searching for interesting objects in the stars. Instead, Aaron and I teach computers to grind through huge volumes of pixels, then we use our human brains to interpret the results. The biggest discoveries today are the result of exquisite, finely tuned computer programs.

Was this the root of my attraction to Aaron? His ability to speak my "language" and my admiration for his programming talents? And perhaps part of my fascination with him was that when we combined our efforts—his computer programming and my analysis—we gained remarkable new insights about our universe.

We'd made the greatest discoveries of our lives together. A few years ago it was a series of Earth-like planets orbiting a dwarf star only forty light-years away. This year it's the Trojan asteroid hidden in Earth's orbit unseen by humans ever before. Perhaps in a few years it would be discoveries made with the new space telescope.

But even as we linger to talk about the space telescope's mercury-cadmium-telluride detectors that will be capable of operating in the supercold environment of space, I know that whatever heat sparked between us is over. It has to be.

What we'd done could've jeopardized everything. If they ever found out about my momentary indiscretion, the higher-ups at CIT would certainly not approve, especially when I'm competing against presumably "less complicated" men for the top job overseeing the space telescope mission. Women had come a long way since the Rocket Girls who worked as "computers" in the fifties, but there are still unspoken rules of conduct for female bosses. Affairs aren't on the list.

And it wasn't just my work that would be compromised, Aaron's would, too. Even someone with rare talent like Aaron might find himself locked out of key assignments because of whispers of what happened between us.

Aaron crosses the room and unlocks the drawer in his desk, which has been harboring the DVR.

"I ran the utility my friend wrote and was able to recover another three hours of data," he says. "I . . . didn't watch any of it, but it's on this flash drive in a folder that I named Final Recovery."

I rise and take the DVR and flash drive from him. "I don't know how to thank you for everything . . . ," I say, letting my voice drift.

"You don't have to thank me. I'd do anything to help you."

I meet his warm gaze. "I'm sorry for bringing you into all this." I'm apologizing for more than that and I think he knows it.

But even as he smiles at me, I see his eyes cloud over.

He knows he's watching me go.

I make the decision to go as if I imagine it will be easy. As if it is simply a kind of research I am abandoning. An investigation that has gone awry that I am putting back on course.

CHAPTER
TWENTY-FOUR

A yellow moon is just cresting the horizon, and the first constellation I see in the night sky is Gemini. I point it out to Zack, but of course he's already spotted it. We've stargazed together since he was two—we'd spread blankets out on the lawn well past his bedtime and peer through binoculars while feasting on popcorn and M&Ms.

Tonight we are trying to regain our bearings—lounging on the back lawn together, high-powered binoculars in hand, scanning the skies for stars and calling out the constellations. Now he's taller than I am, with Ben's sturdy jawline and thick hair, but not even popcorn and M&Ms can soothe the ache of our loss.

At least we have the illusion of safety, as Brad is a few yards away, leaving only periodically to patrol the grounds. A month ago I would not have imagined that I'd be stargazing with Zack. He'd rejected our ritual, along with other things from his childhood, on his way to figuring out his young-adult self. But tonight I sense that the stars settle him in the familiar. When he calls out the constellations, I hear a slight lift in his voice—a tiny bit of joy—that I haven't heard in a long while.

In so many ways, we had become strangers over the last year or so. But here beneath the glittery stars—watching their movements and their own life cycles of nearly incomprehensible scale—we are reunited.

"Remember when we used to play dot-to-dot with the constellations?" I ask.

Zack keeps his binoculars trained on the sky. "Yeah . . . and, here we go, there's the Big Dipper," he says, his lips lifting in the beginnings of a smile. "And yes, Mom, I know that the Big Dipper *isn't* a constellation. It's an *asterism* that's part of the constellation Ursa Major."

I look at him and smile. Proud.

"Also known as the Big Bear constellation," he continues.

Then my eyes meet his in the starlight, and for a moment he is no longer a young teen struggling to find his way in the world, but again my little boy, his brown eyes wide with wonder.

I reach out to hug him, and he hugs me back. And doesn't let go. Then suddenly I'm holding him, just like I once used to, and the tears spill out of my eyes.

"See, I've been listening," he says softly.

I stroke his hair. What is to become of us without Ben? How will either of us ever make sense of what happened to him? I don't dare think death, even though everyone else is, because the concept feels too heavy and final.

Moments later, he lets go and points back to the stars. "Remember when I named my hamsters Mizar and Alcor after the stars in the Big Dipper?"

I smile. "We were all impressed. Especially your kindergarten teacher."

My eyes follow his hand across the sky as he traces the Big Dipper, an asterism I've seen thousands of times. With six second-magnitude stars, the constellation is bright enough to see no matter where you are north of the Equator.

Then it hits me. The Big Dipper's familiarity can fool us. If we aim a high-powered telescope at it we'll see that there are not just seven stars we all recognize, but thousands of stars in the space between those stars . . . and at least a dozen galaxies, including the huge and beautiful Pinwheel Galaxy.

"There's a lot more going on out there than what our eyes see," I say.

He looks at me and squirms. I think he's worried that this is going to turn into some kind of spiritual talk about losing his father. But neither of us is ready for that.

Instead, I wonder if I've been accepting the facts of Ben's disappearance but ignoring what might be beyond them. I've failed to search for answers my eyes cannot see. The facts, like the stars we can see, command our attention with their bright lights. They also blind us to what else might be there.

"If we're going to understand what happened to your dad, we have to look beyond what we can see," I say, "and search in the space between."

PART TWO

CHAPTER
TWENTY-FIVE

BEN

His body is shaking. Hard. Every thirty seconds or so. Like a jackhammer is stuck in his chest.

It's pitch-black. He blinks. For a moment, it feels as though he's gone blind. Not even a speck of light anywhere.

His eyes are bleary and crusted over with what, he isn't sure. He pulls down his lower lid to force it open.

His tongue is thick, caked to the bottom of his mouth.

He pulls the blanket tighter to his body, but it's not enough. The room is icy cold and yet he's burning up.

His shirt, the sheets, are soaked.

How long has he been lying here asleep? How long since Leonard left? A day perhaps. Or maybe three?

His body shakes again. This time it lasts for nearly thirty seconds.

Please let me make it until morning.

How many hours could it be until sunrise? Four? Six? It's so black outside the window that it's impossible to tell.

His lips are parched, cracked so badly that they burn when he licks them. He reaches for the paper cup on the nightstand next to his bed. Or at least he thinks it was there before.

He anticipates the feel of water on his dry tongue, his raw throat. Anxious for it to soothe his burning insides.

But his teeth are chattering so hard that his hand shakes and he knocks over the cup. The room is quiet, so still, he thinks he can hear it flutter through the air as it falls to the wood-plank floor.

He tries to move, to reach for it in the darkness, but searing pain rips like a knife through his left leg. The muscles in his back seem frozen, unmovable. He is stuck in this position, like a dead bug, pinned on his back. Wet.

He feels the sharp draft coming from the window. The cabin was built for summer, not winter, and there are gaps between the hand-sawn windows and its frames.

Gaps that are freezing the life out of him.

There is firewood. And matches. But he cannot imagine how he will get his body across the room, much less complete the mechanics of starting a fire. He tries to imagine the exact sequence he will need to follow to do that. Sit up. Bend his legs. Put weight on his leg. Crawl to the fireplace. It's what, six feet?

Impossible. He reaches down and touches his fingers to his left thigh, knowing what he'll find. Hard, dried blood. Sharp bolts of throbbing pain as though his skin and muscles are being ripped open by a monster within.

It's good that it's dark. He can't see how bad it is.

CHAPTER
TWENTY-SIX

Aaron's recovery utility has unscrambled at least three more hours of video. Some of it's mundane—shots of the front porch at night, lit only by the warm glow of the outside lanterns, and a long clip of the backyard, capturing a flock of goldfinches that played in the birdbath one early morning. The clips are a kind of time travel, a glimpse into my life and home in the past from angles I would otherwise never see.

The house appears to go through a metamorphosis during the late night and early morning hours. Beautiful, yet eerie. I wonder why it's easier to admire the world when I'm watching it through a lens.

Using a laptop that Rachel loaned me, I click through endless ordinary clips of Zack returning home from school, the gardener mowing the front lawn, and Zack raiding the refrigerator late at night. Then I stumble on a shot of Ben walking through the front door on Monday, the day before he disappeared.

He's dressed in a simple white T-shirt and blue jeans. He tosses his keys into the green bowl on the foyer table, then places something next to it. The camera is too far away to see what it is.

At first I think it's a flash drive because it's small and black. I enlarge the photo on the computer, but when the image becomes too grainy, I zoom back a little and see what it is. A velvet jewelry box.

Why is Ben carrying around a jewelry box, and what happened to it since then?

My mind takes one of those detours, and I wonder if the box belonged to Rebecca. I replay the clip and home in on Ben's face. It's only five seconds, so it's hard to discern much, but he doesn't look suspicious or nervous. He appears . . . happy. Or perhaps it only seems that way because of the delicate afternoon light playing through the foyer windows.

Another clip was shot on Saturday afternoon, an hour after I left for the airport. Ben is on the front porch, his back to the camera, and he's talking with Shane.

"I've thought about what you asked me to do," Shane says. His face is puffy, and there are dark circles under his eyes. "And I did it. No one ever has to know."

No one ever has to know.

What did Ben ask Shane to do just hours after Rebecca Stanton was murdered?

———

"Hi, Sarah?" Shane sounds hopeful. I can guess what news he's anticipating I'll share, and I'm disappointed to let him down. "I'm in a meeting with a client. Everything okay?"

"There's something important I have to ask you," I say. "Do you have a minute?"

"Of course." His voice is strained. I hear footsteps on concrete, like he's walking out of his meeting.

My mouth suddenly goes dry. "I'm looking through the home-security recordings, and there's a clip on the Saturday afternoon before

Ben went missing where you tell Ben that you took care of something he asked you to do. Then you say, 'No one has to know.' What was that about?"

There's a long silence on the phone. "I have no idea. Are you sure it's the Saturday *before* he went missing and not some other conversation earlier?"

"The time stamp says Saturday afternoon. The day after you both returned from New York. The day Rebecca Stanton was murdered."

"I remember coming over then. I guess you had already left for DC, maybe? Ben had asked me to rework some of the numbers for the Paragon deal, and I did."

"That's odd, don't you think?" I ask. "I mean, if Ben killed Rebecca Stanton—as the FBI said he did—early that morning, why would he ask you that afternoon to rework the numbers to resurrect the deal with her?"

"I hadn't thought of that." He draws a deep breath. "How are you even looking through the security recordings? I thought they had been erased?"

"I've finally figured out how to recover the data. All of it."

"Why, though?" He switches his tone to sympathetic. "Do you really think you're going to get a different answer about Ben by looking through that security footage than what the police and FBI have already discovered?"

I run my fingers through my hair, trying to get this discussion back on track. "Look, all I'm asking is what you did for him that 'no one has to know.' Are you sure it was about reworking the numbers? You look kind of upset in the video."

"I was a bit hungover, that's all. The whole conversation was just finance talk, Sarah."

Finance talk. His tone is annoyed, making it clear that he thinks I'm wasting my time, focusing on all the wrong things. My frustration mounts. I sense that he's not being honest with me, but I don't know if he's covering for Ben or if something else transpired between them that he won't talk about.

"I can't imagine what *finance talk* would have you saying, 'No one has to know.'"

"Ben had asked me to rework the numbers, and he didn't want me to share them with anyone yet. That's all it was."

CHAPTER TWENTY-SEVEN

BEN

He wonders if he imagined him. Leonard. Was he a hallucination of his fever-soaked delirium, or did the tall, wiry man with tufts of white hair actually exist?

He runs the memory through his mind, but it weighs as much as any of his troubled dreams.

"Get help," he'd told Leonard. "Take my car and drive to the nearest phone. Call my wife."

He remembers scrawling her number on a scrap of dirty paper, sweat pouring from his brow, stinging his eyes and smudging the ink. But where did he get the paper? The pen? Was that proof that it was a dream?

He hadn't had the ability to explore the cabin but knew from his previous visits that there was no pen or paper or telephone or lights. Or heat, except whatever fire he might start in the fireplace. He shivers in the cold.

After he pressed his way through an unlocked window, the room had spun like he was stuck on a forever merry-go-round. He'd circled around and around and around until he drifted off. Then some unknown quantity of liquid time had passed and he opened his eyes. Leonard was standing over him.

"Your car door is open," he'd said.

Afternoon sunlight made the shadows appear longer, sharper. Made Leonard look tall and skinny with a tiny head. Impossible. He can't remember much else about his features, but he remembers the way he talked. Slowly. Or was that just how it seemed, sprawled on the floor, burning up with fever, with the taste of vomit in his mouth.

Then he remembers the way he says his "r" in "car." Like an accent, maybe? Or a speech impediment.

"Take my keys," he remembers telling him and thrusting his leaden arms in the air, pointing to somewhere in the room where he'd guessed the keys had fallen, as the room began to orbit around him. Spinning.

But did Leonard take his keys? Or was Leonard as real as the thirty-foot lizards, black as night, he'd seen at the mouth of a cave? Turning from side to side, like the keel of a canoe. Those were surely of a dream.

"Once I used to," he remembers Leonard saying. Once I used to what? He searches for the memory, but he cannot remember what happened before or after those words. Was that proof of a dream?

Water. That would prove that Leonard had been here. Not a dream. He remembers Leonard brought in buckets of water. Maybe it came from the well fed by a natural spring a few hundred yards down the trail. He thinks he remembers Leonard pouring several paper cups and lining them up in a perfect row on the nightstand.

He had a memory that Leonard gave him a handful of pills—"Leftover antibiotics," he'd said—and Ben had gulped them down.

If Leonard was real, there would be paper cups on the nightstand. Pills.

In the blackness of the night, he reaches out. Gingerly feels the air with his fingertips. Touches a paper cup. His body shakes with chills again, but this time he controls it. Bears down hard on the trembling and wills it to stop. He grasps the cup in his hand and brings it to his lips.

Water.

Then he remembers saying, "You know how to drive a car, Leonard?"

Leonard rubs his chin. "Once I used to."

Once I used to.

CHAPTER TWENTY-EIGHT

Ben is wearing a white button-down, untucked, and a pair of dark jeans. He's sitting on the couch in my office, and in this minute-long clip from the Final Recovery folder, I see myself walk over and stiffly sit beside him, my posture slumped as though I'm trying to make myself smaller. The words I say are so quiet that the microphone barely picks them up.

"I think we're broken . . ."

I seem relaxed, as though I've rehearsed it, even though I hadn't. As though I'm only telling him about the amount of caffeine I consumed in order to complete the NASA presentation by three that morning.

I seem certain about it, but inside I'm a bundle of nerves, riddled with uneasiness. Hoping he'll resist. Or protest. Make me change my mind.

He looks like someone has just knocked the wind out of him. There's confusion in his eyes, like maybe he thinks I'm kidding. Then it registers and his jaw slackens.

"What do you want to do?"

I didn't know how to answer because I never considered divorce. Until I did. I can't pinpoint when things shifted. A year ago, maybe. It would be easy if it were one thing—an argument, a fight, or an unreasonable decision he made—but there wasn't any one thing. Things were good, then okay. Then bad for so many months I didn't even notice we weren't limping along anymore. We were broken.

"Neither of us has been happy in a long time," I say.

The words seem to crush him, yet his voice is tender. "I know."

"When was the last time we spent any time together? Or we were happy when we did?"

He draws a deep breath. "It's been a while. But we're both at a place in our lives and careers where things are stressful . . . we're *building* things."

"And when we are together, we can't ever seem to agree anymore. Everything is a battle."

"Look, we're going through a rough patch with the problems with Zack and our crazy schedules—"

"And we argue about every single little thing. We can't agree on the big stuff or even the stupid things. Even the color of the pool tile."

"That was six months ago."

"We didn't talk for a week after."

"So this is about the color of tile in the pool."

"No. This is about everything."

After I say it, I realize it's unfair. It's not about *everything*. Even if it feels like it. The more I focused on how he stopped noticing me, the more I saw of it. I noticed the way he looked at me—as if he sometimes saw right past me. I felt him withdraw from my attempts at silly jokes. And he rarely got excited about the things that made my heart leap—he seemed so disinterested in the Trojan asteroid that I stopped talking about it, even though it monopolized most of my waking thoughts.

But was that the way he truly felt about me?

The doorbell rings, startling us both.

I rise. "That's the driver for the car taking me to the airport."

His blue eyes plead for understanding. "Wait, you can't tell me you're thinking about divorce and then just leave."

He was right, but I was too stubborn to admit it. "Let's talk about it when I'm back on Tuesday."

Ben reaches out and clasps my hand. "All I want is for us to be happy together again."

CHAPTER
TWENTY-NINE

BEN

A loud bang. Like the sound of a car backfiring. The first shot shatters the glass on the driver's side. His heart skips a beat. And then a few more.

He jolts awake and gasps for breath.

The first signs of sunlight peek through the slats of the wooden shades, piercing the darkness. He blinks against the harsh light. He's in the bed, but he cannot remember exactly how he got there.

In his dreams, the story unfolds differently each time. Sometimes a winged creature carries him off. Or his son is standing there on the freeway, still in diapers, grasping a worn blanket as cars weave around him, barely missing him. When he's asleep, it's as though his brain cannot make sense of what really happened and manufactures alternate and disturbing storylines. Only in the waking moments are the memories reliable.

He thinks he knows what happened. And there are no winged creatures, or Zack, or missing limbs.

Two shots—rapid-fire—through the driver's side. Glass penetrates his skin like icy bullets. Antonio slumps over the wheel. Blood spatters on the windshield, puddling on the gray carpets. Turning them black.

A breathy hiss then hot pain in his upper arm. But there is no time to feel.

The car careens then smashes into the wall, jolting him forward and slamming his head hard against the windshield. Why didn't the airbags go off?

He unbuckles his seat belt. Hurls open the door, but it feels like it moves in slow motion.

His phone falls out, crashing on the pavement. Dead. He spies Antonio's phone on the floorboard and seizes it.

No thoughts. Only the need to run.

Cars are honking. In the dark, he's lost his bearings. Where did the shots come from? He has no idea if he's running away from them.

Or straight to them.

He hurdles the guardrail and lands in the field. It feels warmer, safer to be in the open, away from the streetlights and the buzz of the freeway. In the thick, dry grass that hasn't been mowed in weeks.

He'd made it easier to shoot him, of course. Like shooting fish in a barrel. That thought makes him run faster than he ever did, his feet barely touching the ground, skimming through the stiff grass, bounding over the gully. He feels invincible.

A single shot grazes his left thigh. Sharp pain shoots through his entire body. He falls. Lies motionless, unable to will his body to move.

This can't be how it's going to end.

The smell of loamy earth, warmed by hours in the sun, rises up. Out of the corner of his eye, he spots a scraggly bush ablaze with purple flowers. Inch by inch, he drags himself through the tall grass to the bush. Its branches scrape his face and arms as he coils himself inside. Waiting.

His breath comes in heaves now. Hands shaking, he dials 911. Shouts at the dispatcher that he needs an ambulance. Babbles his location, but he's not so sure it's right. Which freeway on-ramp is it? No response. They can't hear him.

Then he's on the move, ignoring the blistering heat in his thigh, the sticky blood that soaks his pants. He pushes through the prickly acacia, dials her number.

No answer.

He hangs up and dials again. And tells her his plan.

CHAPTER THIRTY

I don't like how I looked on that clip with Ben. Rigid and inflexible. Frustrated. Is that who I'd become? What happened to the person who used to tease him in Klingon, who would bake his favorite chocolate-raspberry cake, and would snuggle with him on the couch watching really bad sci-fi movies?

I suspect there are more clips from the meeting in the office, but I can't watch them. They're a harsh reminder of what happened to us. What I'd become.

I close the laptop and gaze instead at the Perseid meteor shower photo that I'd taken from Ben's office. The photo captures that night with perfection—the way the stars blossomed above us like brilliant blue and white forget-me-nots. The buzzy, electric feeling of his hand on my skin. If I could pick a night to relive, it would be that one.

"Have I ever told you how happy I am to be with you?" I'd asked him as the meteors streaked across the sky in front of the creamy Milky Way. "How lucky I am to share my life with you?"

"Almost every day."

I laughed. "Actually, I don't really say it every—"

"You don't need to. I know it."

"How do you know it?"

"When you pick up my favorite coffee beans at the store even though you hate coffee. Or the way you laugh—sometimes snorting unattractively, I might add—at my really terrible jokes."

That's when I realize the combination for the safe. It's not our anniversary date, one of our birth dates, or even Zack's birth date. It's the date Ben wanted to make sure I'd always remember.

"I want to remember this night forever," he had said. "Years from now, when we're both really, really old, I will make sure you remember it, too."

"How are you going to do that?" I said, wrapping my arms around his waist.

"I have my ways," he said slyly, then kissed me as the Perseid meteor shower rained above us.

The answer was hiding in plain sight. My hands tremble as I turn the dial: 08-07-05. The date he wanted me to remember forever.

I grasp the safe's cool steel handle and pull down. Without a sound, the heavy door glides open.

Inside, there are the expected documents, and only one set seems unfamiliar: the seven-million-dollar life insurance policy. I remember signing the application, but I hadn't paid attention to how substantial the benefit was.

The second shelf houses boxes of jewelry from Ben's grandmother, including a fourteen-carat-gold charm bracelet with airplane, scissors, and Happy Birthday charms, each engraved with a date from her life. It's Ben's favorite, because his most treasured memories of his grandmother were of her wearing that bracelet all the time—while kneading her infamous rye bread or playing Broadway show tunes on her upright piano.

I set the charm bracelet back inside the safe and notice that nestled in the corner is a black velvet ring box that I don't recognize. I open the box and bring it into the light to see what it is.

An infinity ring.

It's a look-alike to the ring I lost the day Ben asked me to marry him. With one breathtaking exception. Instead of two diamonds encased in the infinity symbol, Ben had replaced them with blue zoisite.

Zoisite.

The gems appeared blue in the light from the fluorescent lamp. But zoisite has dramatic color shifts depending on lighting conditions, and this otherworldly stone can also appear violet or burgundy.

I'd been obsessed with the gem ever since a geologist friend at Caltech showed me a zoisite crystal that appeared muddy reddish-brown until he heated it to about 650 degrees Fahrenheit. Then it turned rich blue, purple, and violet. I was awestruck, and I'm pretty sure I went overboard talking with Ben about it, fascinated by this rare stone found only in the foothills of Mount Kilimanjaro, under geological conditions so rare that the chance of finding a similar gem anywhere else in the world is more than a million to one.

Tears sting the corners of my eyes. *Ben remembered how much I loved this stone.* He could have afforded diamonds or expensive jewels. But he'd chosen the one stone that held the most meaning for me.

Was this his answer to the discussion about our broken marriage? A way to bridge the gap between us and start again?

I close the jewelry box and hold it in my hand. Then my mind races to the black jewelry box I'd seen on the security footage. Is this the same one? Was this what he was hiding? Not a piece of jewelry for Rebecca Stanton, but something for *me*?

I head upstairs to my office and replay the five-second clip captured on Tuesday, the day Ben went missing. He walks in the front door and sets a small black box on the foyer table. It looks identical to the one I'm holding in my hand.

I play it a second time, and this time I zero in on Ben's face. He's smiling.

But like gazing at the stars, I'm looking into the past, glimpsing a moment in time. He had no idea that tragedy would unfold in the coming hours.

CHAPTER
THIRTY-ONE

BEN

The expensive bourbon shots had launched the room into a tight spin. This, he remembers. He may not recall all the events of the days since the shooting—how many has it been?—but he remembers that night in detail.

He rose and caught a glimpse of himself in the mirror behind the bar. He should've known better than to drink so much bourbon so fast. Especially on an important night like that one. At least his reflection looked confident and assured. Even if inside he felt like a horrid failure, returning to LA empty-handed after torturous months of negotiations. Everything he'd been building—everything he'd worked for—had evaporated. Six words had decided his fate: "I can't sell you the restaurant."

He was surprised by his white-hot anger and the blistering words that burst from his mouth. His chest was clamped in a vise, adrenaline rocketing through his body.

He'd been betrayed in business deals before, but this one scorched his confidence and detonated his dreams. It's what happens when you crave things too much. He had already imagined owning the restaurant, renovating the nineties-era bar, and bringing his signature style to the place. He'd told his investors he'd soon have restaurants in Los Angeles and Manhattan. It had a nice ring to it. And this one would be all his. His first time without partners to wrangle. No one to steal from him.

He spied her purse on the seat across from his. The seat where she'd told him she wasn't going to sign the deal. He'd seen her lips moving but could not believe what she was saying. Her high cheekbones seemed almost contorted as she spoke, her mouth wrenched into a tight, grim frown. He felt rage swell up inside him, a harsh bitter taste in his mouth.

The purse was smooth brown leather with a debossed butterfly pattern. No doubt expensive. She'd fled quickly, leaving it behind.

He picked up the purse, deciding. Should he give it to JJ the bartender for safekeeping? Or might he take it to her himself?

He decided he would take it to her apartment. Maybe he could use it to change her mind.

CHAPTER
THIRTY-TWO

"So would you call yourself a planet hunter?" Kate asks. It's evening and we're in my living room, sitting in the glow of the Christmas lights, and I hear myself laugh for the first time in many days.

"Yes, I am a planet hunter. But we're also finding other amazing stuff, too. Like superluminous galaxies that are three hundred *trillion* times the brightness of our sun. Plus thirty new comets between Jupiter and Mars. And we've seen literally millions of black holes."

"Very cool," she says. "Why didn't I think to become an astronomer?"

Ben's attorney, Stuart, had encouraged me to do the interview with Kate Bradley. "It'll make viewers have sympathy for you instead of just thinking of you as the wife of a murder suspect," he had said. "And if anyone still thinks you might somehow be involved in all this, it'll convince them otherwise."

I don't want any more attention as we're about to submit our two-hundred-million-dollar space telescope proposal. My CIT bosses are still evaluating whether I'll get to lead the mission, and it won't help if I'm on TV again, unless I'm talking about astronomy or undiscovered planets. That's why I told Kate I'd talk with her but she had to leave the cameras behind.

I keep hoping that I won't ever have to talk about this anymore. That I'll wake up from this nightmare and have Ben back. I long to hear him moving about the kitchen grinding coffee beans, to hear his voice telling me about the subzero temperatures he just survived on a trip to Chicago, or to see him bounding through the front door after his early morning run, out of breath but in high spirits.

I expect her to ask the usual reporter questions about Rebecca Stanton's murder, but instead, she asks about the work I'm doing to find planets that might support life, how Ben and I met, and the best places in the world to stargaze.

She seems sympathetic when she asks what it's like to experience your husband being missing one day and becoming a murder suspect the next. All of it has the effect of making me unwind a little, which I think is her intention. I know she wants me to agree to an on-camera interview with her. And I have said no each time she's asked. Three separate times. But I'm guessing she's hoping that if she can gain my trust, I might change my mind. Despite my initial resistance, her plan is working.

When she asks about the Trojan asteroid, she seals the deal. "I'm fascinated by the fact that we've been looking at the solar system for so long in so many ways and yet, still, discoveries like this are being made. And I'm curious, why has this been so elusive?"

I smile. "Like so many things in the universe, the answers might be hiding in plain sight or obscured by what we see in front of us," I tell her. "So many of the most remarkable discoveries are made when we look past the obvious, when we find ways around being blinded by light, and when we discover new ways to see in the dark."

"You make the stars sound fascinating. Is stargazing something you and Ben like to do together?"

"Our first date was under the stars."

"Tell me about your favorite place to stargaze together."

I like that she uses the present tense, even when no one else does. I don't know if it's deliberate, but it makes the conversation, and me, feel less somber.

I tell her about the Summer Triangle Haven and share with her how the stars seem to come alive before your eyes when you stand beneath their canopy in the Anza-Borrego Desert. We talk about how Ben proposed to me there, and I tell her that once she actually experiences the Milky Way arching high overhead she'll understand why it's probably one of the most beautiful places on Earth.

"Sounds like the perfect spot to interview you," she says.

"It's a long drive deep in the desert."

"I'd be happy to drive out to this magical place to do an interview. Just say the word."

After she leaves, I close the door behind her, filled with aching loss.

I want to experience the magic of the Summer Triangle Haven again, the place where Ben and I forged forever memories. I long to roam again in the spectacle of rock and cloud and sky and space that is the Anza-Borrego Desert wilderness.

My heart leaps in my throat at the thought of returning there. Maybe even for just one day?

A single day to relive my memories of being there with Ben.

To figure out the next steps in my life now that he's gone.

To begin the process of letting go.

———

"You have every right to be angry or sad or mad about what's happened to Ben," my sister is saying. "If I were in your shoes, I'd cry or maybe throw a tantrum . . . or even punch a wall." She lowers her voice to a tentative whisper. "But don't do this. Not this."

I'd told her I was heading to the Summer Triangle Haven. Without Zack. Without her.

It makes no sense to her because of course Ben is not there. Maybe he once intended to go there, but now he is dead. The FBI has called off the search for him.

"You can't go alone. Not with everything that's happened. Something bad could happen to you deep in the desert in the middle of nowhere."

My sister has always had the ability to picture vivid scenes that are unlikely to actually take place, but she's not entirely wrong about this one.

I have a plan. If I leave in the early morning hours before dawn and make certain that no one follows me, I'm probably safer at the remote cabins than I have been at home.

It's not just my physical safety she's worried about, though. It's my emotions she thinks will shatter if I return alone to the cabin where Ben proposed. She imagines I'll go there, finally realize that Ben is gone forever, and drown in grief. Again, she's not wrong.

Rachel's voice trembles. "At least let me go with you," she says, hands on her hips. "And if you want me to stay with Zack, then take Lauren. No running water or electricity. What *are* you thinking?"

"I'll have my phone. And enough backup batteries to light up the mountain for a week. I'll take five gallons of water. And a case of protein bars."

"It's three days before Christmas," she says, steadying her voice. "Why don't you wait until after Christmas before making this decision?"

"I'll be back in twenty-four hours. You'll see. Then we'll drink eggnog and eat Santa's cookies . . . like we did when we were kids."

She looks up at the ceiling as if her response might be written there. Then she stomps her foot. "I won't have it. It's hard enough on Zack to lose his dad but then his mom deserts him, days before Christmas, slipping away on some reckless mission that makes no sense to anyone. This isn't fair to him."

"He's fourteen, not five. If I leave sometime around five in the morning, I can get there in a few hours, just as the sun is rising. And I'll be back in less than twenty-four hours."

"You're not going to find him there, Sarah."

"I *know* that, Rachel."

Her voice is soft. "Then why go?"

"I think it will help me . . . figure out what to do next."

"You should ask police or FBI or the bodyguard to go with you."

I shake my head. "And do what? Ask them to hang out with me while I figure out what I'm going to do with my life? Look, if someone was trying to harm me, they already had plenty of opportunities all the times I drove to CIT or walked to the coffee shop."

"True, but remember what happened last time you left."

"Rachel, be logical. Whoever lured me out to Buckhorn Campground wasn't after me, you, or Zack. None of us ever was in real danger, even if they said we were. They were after something in the house."

"At least take *someone* with you."

"I won't be alone. Kate Bradley from Channel Eleven wants to interview me. I'll ask her to meet me there tomorrow afternoon."

That idea seems to bring her anxiety down. But only a notch. "If Mom or Dad were still alive, they'd say—"

"They'd say what? That I shouldn't go to the place my husband talked about in his very last telephone message to me? The place where we got engaged?"

Tears slip out of her eyes again. "Mom would say stay home and spend Christmas with your son. And with me. And you'd probably have listened to her."

I reach out and hold her hand. "I'll be back *before* Christmas and I'm going to be fine."

But even though I don't think I'll be in physical danger, I cannot imagine what it will be like to witness the Summer Triangle's greatest celestial treasures—the Orion Nebula, the Milky Way, and the Andromeda Galaxy—without Ben beside me.

CHAPTER
THIRTY-THREE

BEN

Where is she? How many days have passed since he left her the message about the Summer Triangle? Why hasn't she come?

He feels panic rising as he realizes he cannot remember all the details of the accident or what happened after. There are giant potholes in his memory, gaps that confound him. Had the bullets come from a car? Or from someone on foot? He touches his fingers to his throbbing temple and feels the lump where it hit the windshield. Bruised. Crusted blood.

At least the memories are starting to flow together. Before, he could only remember fragments of moments that happened after he called her and told her his plan. It was as if darkness descended on his brain in the place where the memories lived.

His legs are heavy, like they're filled with thick molasses, the kind his grandmother used to make in her kitchen in the heat of summer, the light breeze fluttering the lace curtains above her window, Ella Fitzgerald playing on the radio.

That's how his legs felt that night, too, as he lumbered across the open field, his left leg dragging behind him.

He was lucky. The gunshot missed an artery. Instead, it grazed his leg, slicing off a layer of skin and muscle. The tourniquet he made from the sleeve of his shirt had slowed the bleeding but not stopped it.

His ragged breath came in big gulps as he ran, eyes scanning the shadows, wondering if whoever shot him was still hunting him in the field. Or while he trembled and heaved in the purple-flowered bush, had they seen no movement and assumed he was dead?

He spotted a street a hundred yards or so ahead, a row of small houses with their porch lights glowing. They become his destination. The adrenaline pumping through his veins dulled the sharp pain stabbing his left thigh, so he kept running, finding a rhythm, evading the pain as he plunged through the darkness.

He thought of Sarah. He had an image of her as she was bearing down, bringing Zack into the world with one final push. Her face was bright pink and glistening with sweat, yet everything about her was lit from within, more beautiful than physical appearances ever could be. When he saw his son for the first time, he felt a wave of emotion so powerful it nearly knocked him off his feet. He felt life.

Before the doctors handed her the baby, he wrapped his arms around her and she linked her arms around his neck. Her eyes met his and time slowed. No words were uttered, but a million were said.

Love. Powerful love burst through him.

His memories of Sarah carried him as he plodded past the row of houses and slogged down each city block, with every step the world becoming hazier as if someone was putting a shower curtain before his eyes. Sarah's high, trilled laugh when we pulled the Santa out of the wedding-gift box. Sarah heaving telescopes into the back of the car on one of their many stargazing jaunts. Sarah's lips, the warmth of her body against his, intoxicating him as they made love in Santa Barbara.

Then he recognized the streets. Aurora was not far.

It was only a mile—a distance he could normally run in under nine minutes—but it took another twenty to reach his car in the Aurora parking lot.

His lungs had turned to stone. Drenched in sweat, he rested his head on the steering wheel, pressed the ignition, and heard the familiar hum of the engine. The air conditioning blasted cold air on his face, but he couldn't muster the energy to turn it down. He glanced at the wound, deep and jagged, blood gushing down his leg.

His mind raced to decide what to do. He'd told her he was headed to the Summer Triangle Haven. But that was before he realized how much the bullet had ravaged his thigh. Maybe he should drive to the police station or hospital instead. Or call Travis and get another bodyguard?

One thing he knew with absolute certainty. He could not go home and put his family in danger. They would be safer if he stayed away for the night.

As he glimpsed the pale moon rising in the evening sky, the plan made sense. He'd head to the Summer Triangle Haven. Rest up. In the morning, he'd formulate a strategy and put a new plan in action.

He glanced at his leg. Maybe it wasn't as bad as it looked.

CHAPTER
THIRTY-FOUR

Dark clouds have formed on the horizon, but there's a light-gray chunk of the sky that illuminates my way into the desert. As that lighter section narrows with each passing mile, my anxiety begins to grow. I try to find comfort in the warm lights from the dashboard, the nearly full tank of gas, and the car full of food, batteries, Rachel's laptop, and medical supplies.

Rachel and Zack had helped pack the car as though I might be headed into the Amazon: antibiotics, medicines for altitude sickness, two first-aid kits, and seemingly every antiseptic known to man. At the last minute, they'd thrown in some serious mosquito repellent and antimalarial pills, even though I'm more likely to encounter scorpions in the desert—for which we had packed no remedy.

I don't know what kind of emergencies they thought I'd encounter on the highways and byways that will take me to the Summer Triangle Haven, but stuffing the car with everything I might need for any possible situation seems to persuade them to accept my journey.

Still, I wasn't taking any chances. When Rachel was busy filling up several water bottles, I'd slipped the gun out of its hiding place in the telescope case, loaded it, and placed it in the console between the front seats. I'd also called Kate Bradley, suggesting that she meet me at the cabin in late afternoon for an interview, a redundancy measure in case anything goes wrong while I'm there.

After all this preparation, it's the darkening skies that are troubling me.

An hour into the drive a bright light flashes across the sky. The low-hanging clouds rip open and, without warning, dump a massive amount of rain. I know from experience these desert storms don't last for very long, but that doesn't stop my mind from imagining my car spinning out on the rain-slicked road with no help available for miles.

I clutch the wheel tighter, and as I hurtle in the dark toward the cabin, it feels surreal to me that only a week ago I was returning home to my family after celebrating the biggest discovery of my career. I was one of the first humans in the world to "see" an asteroid that's been hiding in our orbit for thousands of years. And now I'm alone in a torrential desert storm on the way to a location deep in the Anza-Borrego Desert, trying to come to grips with the reality that my now dead husband was also a murderer.

As my windshield wipers struggle to keep up with the deluge and the wind, I feel like I'm being pulled back as much as I'm pushing forward. I know that I must accept the evidence that Ben killed Rebecca Stanton, but I can't reconcile that with what I know he did for me in the days after her murder.

Somehow he'd bought and decorated the most beautiful of Christmas trees, a tradition stretching back to my childhood that he knew always made me happy. He'd rekindled our ritual of saying "I'm sorry" in the most unusual way, by etching the words—in code, no less—on a meteorite as old as our planet. He'd even scoured the rafters of the house in what must have felt like a futile search for the long-lost Wedding Santa, an icon of our early years of marriage. And he improved on my lost infinity engagement ring with a stone he knew was so rare and unique that I'd never stopped thinking about it.

The memories of our best moments come flooding back, and I feel a lump swell in my throat. I fight the urge to cry. None of the moments he'd helped me remember were particularly big or grandiose. They might seem insignificant to others, but they were small moments made big because we'd made them—we'd built them—together.

I wonder if he too was searching for a better way to be together. If all of this was his way of creating a new start, a blending of powerful old memories with new possibilities.

As the last bit of gray shrinks into the black skies, I realize I'll never really know.

Thick tears fall from my eyes and roll down my face, echoing the raindrops on the window.

CHAPTER THIRTY-FIVE

BEN

If only he hadn't pressed the doorbell. If he hadn't, he wouldn't be caked in blood and sweat or alone in a cabin with no food or water or contact with the outside world. He would not have been poisoned. Shot.

He remembers the sleek feel of the stainless-steel button outside of one of the most notable apartment building addresses in Manhattan. Pressing it firmly.

No answer.

Then he craned his neck to find the number somewhere on the brick facade. This was the 400 block of Madison Avenue, right? It was barely five in the morning, and in his intoxicated state he wasn't sure. But he hoped he hadn't pressed the wrong doorbell and some irate neighbor was now heading down with a baseball bat. Or worse.

He cupped his hands around his eyes and peered through the brass-and-glass front door at the expansive lobby dominated by a crystal chandelier orb. Where was the doorman? In a white-glove apartment building like this, there was always one round-the-clock.

He knew she was angry. Probably spooked by his threats. She had good reason to ignore his insistent ring.

Suddenly the front door burst open and a woman with trendy lavender hair and two rambunctious French bulldog puppies on leashes sprang out.

"Morning," she grumbled as the dogs took off down the stairs, dragging her behind.

He grabbed the ornate brass door handle before it shut behind her.

"Hello?" he called into the empty lobby.

He rode the elevator to the penthouse floor, and when he stepped out, his shoes sank into white plush carpeting. The sweet scent of lilies from the over-the-top hallway floral display wafted through the air.

The door to her apartment was cracked open a little. Enough to signal that he was welcome to come in.

He stepped inside and took in the breathtaking view of the midtown and city skylines, still glittering against the nighttime sky.

He called out her name. No answer.

He placed the purse on the white granite kitchen counter, then noticed two wineglasses and a bottle of red. 1985 Cheval Blanc. Expensive. An invitation? A peace offering?

He called out her name again. Then lifted the wineglasses, wondering if she expected him to bring them to her.

A Montblanc chronograph watch lay next to the bottle, as if it had been casually left there, even though he suspected she'd staged it. Where had he seen it before?

The wine bottle was light. Half-empty. He picked it up and headed to her bedroom door.

CHAPTER
THIRTY-SIX

Headlights in my rearview mirror. I don't know how long they've been there, unnoticed by me. A few miles. Maybe longer.

The lights hang back about a mile, far enough that they appear to be just tiny starlike dots in my mirror. But they are keeping pace with me.

The car disappears for a moment, then crests the small hill behind me. The headlights are back.

A twinge of fear ignites in my belly. There is nothing—no street lights or homes—on this stretch of the road, and the dim lights I can see are in the distance, set back far from the road.

I press down on the accelerator, bumping up my speed another ten miles an hour and with it, my heart rate.

I place my hand on the loaded gun, feeling brave. I've watched enough YouTube videos on how this particular Glock works that I thoroughly understand the mechanics, even if I've never actually pulled the trigger.

The car behind me appears to keep pace with my uptick in speed. I try to imagine a reason for someone to be on this deserted byway into the desert just before dawn but none come to me.

I glance down at my phone. No signal.

Damn.

From the GPS map in the car, it doesn't look like there are any markers of civilization—gas stations, truck stops, etc.—anytime soon, so I start scanning to find a place where I can do an easy U-turn. That way I can head in the opposite direction for a mile or two and see if they keep following me.

When I spot the dirt road on my right, I wrench the car in a tight turn, and pull a wide U, my tires spinning on the sandy dirt road before locking in on the pavement again.

As I head back down the road toward the headlights, I'm hoping I'll see that the occupants of the car are an elderly couple or a family with a bunch of kids sleeping in the back seat. I imagine the relief of that discovery, knowing I'm not being followed after all. Then reality sinks in. Given how dark it is, I probably won't be able to make out exactly who's in the car.

I think about how Ben and his bodyguard had been shot while riding in an SUV. Was I in similar danger here?

It's too late to turn back.

My breathing is shallow as the headlights get closer. Then just as the distance between us closes to less than five hundred feet, the car makes a sudden right turn down a two-lane road.

I can't see the passengers or even make out silhouettes. All I can see are the red taillights barreling down the dirt road.

CHAPTER THIRTY-SEVEN

BEN

He breaks into a smile as he sits up for the first time. Swings his legs over the side of the bed and places his feet on the floor.

He pushes himself up. Searing hot pain shoots through his thigh as he stands for the first time. Stiff. Wobbly.

In the moonlight that streams through the slats of the wooden blinds, he examines the white pills Leonard had lined up on the nightstand. The letter C is imprinted on one side and the number 94 on the other. Leonard had just referred to it as "leftover antibiotics." Whatever they are, they're most certainly the reason his fever has subsided and the throbbing pain has dropped a notch or two.

He swallows another pill and drains the water from the cup. This is the last of it. He'd also eaten the final dry morsel of the granola bars yesterday.

He takes ten shaky steps to the bathroom, each one easier than the first.

He has a plan to get water. It's come to him over the last few nights. He's even dreamed parts of it. Maybe it's possible. Or maybe, like dreams, it only seems achievable.

At sunrise, he'll walk the half mile to the well. One thousand steps, which he can count off in groups of fifty or a hundred.

Surely he can do a thousand steps.

There's a campground about a mile—as the crow flies—from the well. He knows he won't be able to reach it, but if he can break a shard from the mirror on the bathroom wall, he could catch the sun's rays and flash for help. Someone might notice.

But Christmas is coming soon. Or at least he thinks so. Will anyone be at this remote campground this time of year?

Then he hears it. Twigs crackling outside his window. He'd heard the sound of small animals rummaging in the leaves outside his window before. But this sounds bigger. Deliberate.

He draws a quick breath and listens. Silence.

Two more loud snaps.

Does he dare hope it's someone outside who can help him?

Or is it someone who wants to do him harm?

He glances at the moon through the blinds and can't think of a legit reason anyone would be walking around these remote cabins in the middle of the night.

He takes a step, a shuffle really, toward the window but just as he reaches it, he hears a flurry of twigs breaking and the sound of whatever it is scuttling in the leaves and racing away.

CHAPTER
THIRTY-EIGHT

The Summer Triangle cabins are actually named the Mescal Bajada, after a nearby mountain range and an enormous ranch that was located there years ago. They're no-frills—one room with a fireplace and bathroom—and you can't reserve them. Show up with cash, and if a cabin is available and the owner happens to be around, he'll hand over the keys.

As the sun rises over the hills, I spot a campground and know I'm getting close to the Mescal Bajada. The campground is mostly empty this morning save for a few hardcore hikers whose tents and travel trailers dot the otherwise deserted area. My uneasiness grows as I pull off onto a narrow dusty road that meanders around boulders and through the tamarisk trees until it will eventually reach the Summer Triangle cabins. With each passing mile, images flash through my head, memories of being here with Ben.

I roll down a window and inhale the smell of the desert—this time of year when the sweet wildflowers aren't in bloom, the air has a dry, smoky scent. It stirs memories of our first night together in the desert, the heat of his body next to mine, as the wide sweep of the Milky Way arched over us and the velvety black sky studded with stars from horizon to horizon swirled around us.

On that moonless night with clear skies, I'd pointed out a few constellations, including Cygnus, with its gaping black hole at the swan's heart. Then I showed him Orion and the place where, just off the hunter's knee, we'd discovered the Witch Head Nebula, a giant nursery where baby stars are born.

"Amazing, right? You have a favorite?" I asked, leaning into him.

"I'm terrible at choices like this," he said, laughing. "I mean, you're asking me to choose between a star nursery and a ginormous black hole. Which would *you* choose?"

I don't hesitate. "Easy. Star nursery. Think of all the new stars that no one's ever seen before."

"Well, if I had to choose a favorite anything out here," he said, waving his hand from Cygnus in one swath of the sky to Orion in the other, "I wouldn't choose any of these."

I looked at him, surprised at his indifference to the mysteries unfolding above us.

He turns to look at me, and a warm desert wind blows past us, ruffling our hair. "I'd choose you."

CHAPTER
THIRTY-NINE

I must be dreaming.

As the sun breaks through the clouds, I crunch through the leaves beneath the tall tamarisk trees until I spot the Summer Triangle cabins hidden behind mounds of gray and golden ribbonwood chaparral.

Ben is standing on the front step of one of them. Leaning against the wooden rail.

Or at least it appears to be him.

I drop the water bottle I'm carrying and hear it thud on the ground.

My heart rate spikes as I try to figure out what I'm seeing. The man's pants are torn into cutoffs and he's wearing a sleeveless shirt. He's looking toward the trailhead, and from a distance his profile looks like Ben, only slimmer.

Is it Ben? Or is my imagination spinning out of control?

I pick up my water bottle and take a few small steps, trying to get a glimpse from another angle; the man's figure is silhouetted against the rising sun.

He turns his head slightly and then I have no doubt it's him. I'd know that face anywhere. The hard line of his jaw, the wave of his hair.

Emotions come flooding back all at once. Surprise. Relief. An over-whelming sense that what I'm seeing—what I'm experiencing—isn't real.

I open my mouth to say his name, but no sounds come out. I swal-low hard and try again. "Ben!"

He turns to look at me, and my stomach does a joyous flip.

"Sarah?" he calls out. Even from a distance I see a smile light up his face.

I run as fast as my legs will carry me through the sand and leaves, then scurry up the stairs of the cabin and throw my arms around him, holding him tight. He pulls me in hard, engulfing me in his arms.

"Promise me this isn't just a . . . dream," he says, caressing my hair.

I pull back and look at him. He's sporting a week-old beard and there's a purple-and-black bruise on his forehead. His normally tanned skin is pale and lined but even so, he is achingly handsome.

My voice is full of emotion. "I've missed you."

Then he folds me back in his arms, his lips grazing my cheek, and suddenly I feel like I'm twenty-two years old again, traveling back in time to our first visit to this cabin. I feel warm and safe in his arms even though I'm not sure why I need safety in a beautiful place like this.

"How did you . . . how are you alive?"

He doesn't answer. Instead, he cups my face in his hands and looks at me as if he's memorizing every detail. Then his blue eyes meet mine and I don't need words or an explanation for what he's been through. I can feel it, all the struggle and fear. And pain.

"You're here," he whispers.

So many questions are racing through my mind, but I'm lost in one single sensation: I had forgotten what it feels like to be held by him. Not just the physical sensation of my body touching his. I'd forgotten what it felt like to love him. And to feel it back.

His eyes shine with tears. "Zack is okay? You're both safe?"

For days now, I've wondered if I'd ever hear his voice again. But here it is. Warm and steady.

"We're fine."

His eyes fall on the meteorite necklace I'm wearing, and his lips lift into the beginnings of a smile. "You opened your Christmas present early."

"It's your best present yet."

He moves a lock of hair from my face. "Wait until you see what else I have for you."

I pretend not to know about the infinity ring. In that moment I'm also pretending that he's not a murder suspect. But one thing that isn't pretend, the thing that surprises me, is the depth of my feelings for him. Standing here, I feel a spark ignite between us, a rush of adrenaline as if I were meeting him for the first time.

"I'm sorry for putting you through all this." He runs his fingers through mussed hair. That's when I notice that the sleeves of his black cotton shirt have been ripped off. "It was a mistake coming here. I thought by hiding out for a day or two, I'd be protecting you and Zack. I had no idea I'd end up sick and stranded without food or water. How long . . . how long have I been here?"

"Over a week."

He closes his eyes and lets that sink in. "A week?" He slowly lowers himself to a sitting position on the wooden steps. "How can a week have passed already?"

I sit beside him and hand him my water. He unscrews the cap and gulps down the entire bottle in under twenty seconds. That's when I get a good look at the blood-soaked cloth on his left thigh and the open wound on his upper arm.

I have so many questions, but I don't know where to start, so I ask the one that scares me the most. "Did you kill Rebecca Stanton? Is that why you came here to hide?"

He looks at me, his eyes seemingly bluer than ever. "I did not kill Rebecca Stanton."

———

All the evidence points to Ben murdering Rebecca. The fingerprints. An eyewitness. The murder weapon buried in our backyard. And yet in this very moment, I believe he didn't do it.

What is wrong with me? Have I fallen victim to believing something because I want it to be true, even if the evidence says otherwise?

For a long moment, I sit with him, my hand clasped in his, and pretend the events of the past week were of a waking dream. But I can't keep my questions in check for very long.

"If you didn't kill Rebecca, then who did?" I ask finally.

"I have no idea. But I know how it looks. It *looks* like I did it. And then I went missing . . ."

I draw a deep breath. "Everyone . . . everyone thinks you're dead, Ben. They found your car abandoned in Joshua Tree."

His face crumples. He tells me about how Leonard found him sprawled on the cabin floor. About giving Leonard the keys to the car and asking him to get help. How Leonard never returned.

"The sheriff found Leonard's body in Joshua Tree. Not far from the car," I tell him.

"Joshua Tree? That's so far from here . . ."

"They think he got disoriented in the heat. Apparently he had dementia."

"Dementia." He closes his eyes as if to shut out the news. His voice is low and troubled. "He saved my life. Brought me food and water. Medicine. Took care of me that first delirious day . . ."

He shifts his body on the steps and winces. I study his thigh, red and swollen, covered in a blood-stained fabric that looks like it came from his shirt.

"Let's get you to a hospital and have a doctor take a look at that."

He swallows hard. "Someone is after me, Sarah. And it looks like they'll stop at nothing to get me. We have to think this through. It's not safe for me to be out in the open, even at a hospital. It's not even safe for you to be with me."

I scan the wound on his upper arm. It's not nearly as severe as his thigh but still swollen and scabbed over. "You can't stay hidden forever. You need medical help."

"What I really need is something to eat."

"Of course." I wonder why I didn't think of that first. I race back to the car and grab a handful of granola bars, a couple of large water bottles, and a first-aid kit. He devours a bar like it's a five-star meal and downs the bottle of water.

While I remove the dressing on his thigh and try my hand at cleaning around the six-inch black scab that snakes down his leg, he starts on another granola bar and tells me how he'd been shot while riding in the SUV with Antonio, about hiding in the field by the freeway, then making his way to his car parked at Aurora. He talks about searching in the dark for the Summer Triangle cabins, then climbing through an open window and falling in a heap on the floor.

"In hindsight? It was a mistake," he says, opening another bottle of water. "But I thought it was the best way to keep you and Zack safe from whoever was after me."

I have so many questions, but I can't stop thinking that the smart thing to do is set them aside and get him medical help. I have no idea where the nearest hospital or clinic is, but judging how deep we are in the desert, it has to be at least an hour away. Shouldn't we get going that direction? I wrap a fresh bandage around his thigh. "I think we should get someone to look at this."

Ben puts his hand on mine. "Am I a suspect in Rebecca's murder?"

I don't answer right away, trying to gauge the best way to tell him that he's the prime suspect. The only suspect. I can imagine what a harsh blow it'll be after spending the past week fighting for his life.

"They found the murder weapon, the gun, buried in our backyard by the lilac tree."

Shock registers on his face. "In *our* backyard? That's impossible."

"And somewhere in our house, they found a photo of Rebecca that had been taken from her apartment."

"A photo of Rebecca?"

My voice is calm, but I'm on edge. "How did they get there?"

I see the alarm in his eyes. "*Someone is trying to make it look like I did it.* But I didn't kill Rebecca. I know why my fingerprints are in the apartment and why there's an eyewitness who saw me leaving the apartment that morning. Because I had been in Rebecca's apartment that morning, returning her purse. And when I left, the woman across the hall greeted me. But I did not kill Rebecca. And if the gun that killed her was found in our backyard, then someone planted it there."

He opens another bottle of water and takes a long slug. Seeing him like this tears at my insides.

"And I never had a photo of Rebecca. So that had to be planted, too," he says quietly.

His eyes meet mine and he knows the silent question I'm asking, even though I don't say it aloud. "No, Sarah, Rebecca and I weren't—nothing ever happened between us."

Then a sick feeling starts in my stomach and spreads throughout my body. I'm not sure I believe him. "Then why did you erase all the video from our security system? I saw the footage where you asked Zack to help you delete everything."

His face falls. "You think I erased that drive because I was hiding evidence that I killed Rebecca?" he whispers, incredulous.

I look away, noticing the way the rising sun is beginning to cast long shadows through the trees. "Why else would you erase it?"

I'm afraid of his answer. Because I suspect he doesn't have one. And then I'll know that I've been wrong to believe him about Rebecca. That maybe he is a murderer after all. And then what will I do?

"I *did* ask Zack to help me erase the data. There was something I didn't want you to see on that security footage. But it had nothing to do with Rebecca or her murder."

"What didn't you want me to see?"

He's silent, and when he finally speaks, his tone is quiet and tentative. "After you suggested divorce, I didn't know what to do with myself. I was in shock and anxious, my whole life was spiraling out of control. I couldn't imagine living without you, Sarah. I still can't. I couldn't find my way out of it until I had the idea to get you something that would remind you of what we once were. And what we could be again. I wanted to give you physical proof of what our future could be."

His words swirl around, enchanting me. "So I bought you a new infinity ring—like the one we lost somewhere here in the desert sixteen years ago—only this time I had it set with that stone you were always talking about, zoisite.

"The jeweler who made the ring came over to the house, and I realized my whole exchange with him was captured by the security cameras. I knew you'd be checking on Zack by scanning through the footage, so I asked him to show me how to erase it."

He takes my hand in his and something rises within me. A feeling of possibility. For the first time in a long time, I could imagine our future, and it might be better than it is now.

"I wanted the ring to be a surprise. So you'd come back to me."

CHAPTER
FORTY

I'm in awe of the man I thought I knew completely. After so many years together, I thought I knew all he was capable of. Yet here with the tamarisk trees swaying in the gentle wind, I see him in a new, unexpected light. He is a man who was willing to go into hiding so that he could keep Zack and me safe from whoever was targeting our family. He's tougher than I thought, surviving a serious injury and a harrowing week in the wilderness. And he's a man determined to win me back.

Even though he's not holding the ring, I feel him give it to me. As if he's actually placing it on my finger. And like the moment we both stood beneath the Summer Triangle asterism, I feel infinity yawn in front of us.

He brushes my cheek with the back of his hand. "Will you come back to me, Sarah?"

It feels as though I'm seeing him for the first time. I anticipate his kiss, but it doesn't come. He's searching my face, looking for something more.

"You still have doubts about me."

He's right. The ring and all he's been saying is drawing me back to him, but I can't get past the big question: Is he a murderer?

His face clouds over. "How can I prove to you I didn't do it?"

I'm not sure what to tell him. There are so many missing pieces to the puzzle that I don't know where to start.

"Let's start with how the gun was found in our backyard. If you didn't put it there, how did it get there?"

The hard line of his jaw twitches. "Someone definitely wants to make it look like I killed Rebecca. But I wonder if the gun was planted Monday night. I heard someone in the backyard, and the neighbor's dogs were barking like crazy, so I called 911. By the time police arrived, no one was there."

"Wait." My pulse quickens. "I recovered a clip from that night where someone blinds the camera in the backyard with a really bright light. You can't see who it is because they're in silhouette, but they're blinding the camera that overlooks the garden where the gun was found."

"Someone *was* back there," he whispers. "Do you have it? The security footage from that night?"

I tell him how someone lured me out of the house by pretending to be him, then broke in and ransacked the place, hunting for the hard drive. When I finish, his face is as white as powder.

"They texted you in code? *Our* code? Then stole the security footage?"

I shake my head. "Yes to the code. But no to getting the footage. They stole every piece of electronics we own, but I had hidden the drive at work."

He lifts his gaze. "There's something on that DVR that someone doesn't want us to see. But what is it?"

We're both silent for a long moment, listening to the bluebirds calling out to the sun. The only other sound is the wind rustling the trees.

"I brought a copy of the footage. Let me get it and show you what I recovered," I say, rising.

He rises as well, favoring his left leg. He takes both of my hands in his, and there's a spark in his eye I hadn't seen in a very long time. "I don't know what's going to happen tomorrow or the next day. Or what truth we're going to uncover. But I want you to know, you're the only thing that matters to me."

He leans in and I'm sure he's going to kiss me this time, but instead he plants a soft, lingering kiss on my forehead.

There's a spring in my step as I head back to the car. The question of whether Ben killed Rebecca still hovers around me, but I feel unexpected joy at being with him again and knowing how he feels about me. Are my feelings blinding me from the truth?

I pull the laptop out of the trunk, and as I'm about to close it, I see movement—a slight blur—in the mounds of golden chaparral across the road. I freeze, holding my breath while scanning the area, hoping the motion came from a jackrabbit or even a roadrunner.

I fix my gaze on a sprawling indigo bush fifty yards away. A chill races up my spine. I have the feeling someone is watching me.

———

The gun feels heavy in my hands as I lift it out of the console. I hold it firmly, my mouth locked in a rigid line, trying to look determined and confident, even though inside I'm on the edge of terrified. I hold the gun casually by my side, as if it's as natural to be holding a Glock as it is to be carrying a telescope.

If it's a roadrunner on the other side of those bushes, I'm going to feel ridiculous. But if it's a person, I want to signal that I'm not an easy target. I walk swiftly back to the cabin, turning around and walking backward, at once terrified that I'm going to see someone in the bushes and equally frightened that I won't.

Ben's eyes widen when he spots the gun in my hand. "Let's go inside and I'll explain," I say under my breath.

He slowly pushes himself up to a standing position, then hobbles to the door. I follow him inside and swiftly lock the door then scan through the window for activity. But the area around us is quiet and serene, and the only movement is the birds flitting through the air and the trees swaying in the gentle wind as the sun hangs high in the sky.

Ben stands beside me and I know he sees what I see. Beauty. Most people assume the desert is lifeless and forbidding, with razor-sharp plants and hostile, sandy areas not meant for humans. But this part of the Anza-Borrego Desert hides many secrets that Ben and I had discovered together—secluded watering holes, sightings of bighorn sheep and golden eagles, and places of such austere beauty that they border on the mystical.

"I thought I saw movement in the chaparral across the road," I say once I catch my breath. "Could have been a roadrunner, but . . . I feel like it might have been something—or someone—else."

"We can't be too careful," he says, then closes the blinds. "I heard some noises outside the cabin last night. Sounded like a large animal. Or a person. Did you tell anyone you were coming here?"

"Just Rachel and Zack. And later in the afternoon, I'm meeting a reporter from Channel Eleven."

I look around the rustic cabin—the rumpled sheets, stained with blood, on the bed by the window, a nightstand littered with paper cups. How had Ben survived a week here alone?

He takes the gun from me. "I bought this when I was released from the hospital. Sometime after you left on that Saturday, someone tried to poison me."

"Matt told me."

He turns the gun over in his hand. "After that, and then the backyard break-in, I figured the gun was the only way to keep us all safe. Did you see the deposit in your Indiana bank account?"

"A million dollars, Ben. Why?"

"I know I went overboard on that, but Sarah, I panicked. After I was poisoned, I worried about someone trying to do it again—but succeeding this time—so I transferred money from my trust account. For you and Zack. In case I didn't make it."

What he thought were just practical plans actually make my heart soar. While thinking his life was in serious danger, while readying for a trial against his partners, Ben's first instinct was to make sure Zack and I were safe.

Ben slowly settles into the worn leather couch by the fireplace, rubbing his sore leg. "Show me what you recovered."

I sit beside him and open the laptop, playing the footage from late Monday night when he was home. In the clip we can see a silhouette of someone blinding the camera with bright light.

I point at the action on the screen. "I think this is when they buried the gun by the lilac bush."

"Is there other footage that might show who's there?"

"Could be." I click on the Final Recovery folder Aaron created, where there are hours of clips I haven't reviewed yet. "But we'd have to look through lots of footage."

It's a daunting task and I doubt Ben has the energy or patience to do it, but he surprises me by clicking on a few. Some of the clips are brief—five seconds of the swimming pool, a boring clip of the liquor cabinet in my office, Zack making a grilled cheese sandwich in the kitchen. But one clip captures his attention. It's a shot of the living room as he and Zack work on the Christmas tree, laughing as they toss tinsel on the branches while "Please Come Home for Christmas" plays in the background.

He plays it again, and this time his eyes shimmer with tears. "Look at the life we've made together, Sarah. Look at our son," he whispers. "Sometimes we forget to really pay attention to how lucky we are . . ."

I reach for his hand and hold it. "Quite a masterpiece tree you guys made." I'm aware of how close we're sitting, how our thighs touch, and how natural and exciting that feels.

"I don't know if you noticed, but I mastered the physics on the tree base this year. Thor himself couldn't pull that tree over."

I smile through the beginning of tears. Then when I look at him, he's leaning over the laptop, a puzzled expression on his face. "This doesn't seem right," he says quietly, then plays the clip. It's a twenty-second clip taken in the foyer. Shane comes in the front door and disarms the alarm. The time stamp reads Tuesday at 9:15 p.m.

"I gave Shane the alarm code a couple of weeks ago so he could drop off a bunch of file boxes related to the Paragon purchase during the day, when neither of us were home. But the time code says this happened Tuesday, the night Antonio and I were shot. That can't be right."

"He's not carrying any boxes, so maybe he actually came back again Tuesday night?"

He runs his hands through his hair. "Why would Shane come into our house four days after Rebecca called the deal off? Is it possible the time code is wrong?"

———

The time discrepancy on the clip is troubling both of us. Does this mean the data is unreliable, or was Shane actually in our home the night Ben was shot? If he was, why was he there and why hadn't he mentioned it to me?

Ben's face has turned white with distress, and it's clear his mind is whirling, trying to process it all as his body is fighting to recover. I can see fatigue in his red-rimmed eyes, but he's trying to power through it.

"Let's call him and ask why he was there Tuesday night." I pull out my phone to make the call, but before I can dial, Ben stops me.

"Who do police think shot at me and Antonio? Do they have any suspects?"

"They're investigating Rebecca's father, Gary Stanton."

His face falls. "God, I hope that's not true, Sarah. He was at a meeting I had with Rebecca once, and he's got a way about him . . . well, he's the scariest man I ever met. If he's the one after me . . . I'm a dead man."

His dark tone takes me by surprise. Ben has never been one for hyperbole or melodrama. He's surprisingly calm in tense situations, but Gary Stanton definitely has him rattled.

"The FBI says he's left the country, so maybe we're . . . safe?"

He shakes his head. "Gary doesn't do the dirty work himself. Shane says he has people who carry out whatever he wants done."

"How would Shane know?"

"Shane grew up down the street from the Stanton family on Long Island. That's how I met Rebecca—Shane introduced me to his childhood friend. He told me to keep a distance from the rest of the family—and whoever Gary's 'helper' guys were—but he swore Rebecca was above all that."

"Maybe a 'helper guy' shot at you and Antonio." It's not lost on me that we're talking about "helper guys" and killers as if it's an everyday thing. "If we can find out his name, we could get the FBI to look into it."

Ben looks skeptical. It seems impossible that we'll ever figure out who's behind all this. Whoever it is has been too fast and nimble. And far too determined. "I'm betting the FBI already knows who Gary's guys are."

I take out my phone and search for Shane's number in my contacts. "You're probably right, but let's see if we can get the name from Shane so we can pass it along. And let's find out why he was in our house that night."

I'm grasping at straws and I know it. But I also know that we have to keep moving or the fear that's growing inside is going to paralyze me.

I click on Shane's number in my phone. Moments later I get a recorded message: *The number you've reached is no longer in service. Please check the number and dial again.*

"Strange. He called me from this number a few days ago."

"Maybe try him at work?"

"What's the name of his company again?"

"Ingenious Capital Management in Pasadena."

I look up Ingenious on my phone and find it easily. They're apparently one of the leading investment companies specializing in real estate, hospitality, and media investment.

The receptionist answers with a posh British accent.

"Shane Russo, please," I say.

There's a long pause on the line, then he asks me to spell the last name, then the first name.

"I'm sorry," he says. "We don't have anyone by that name here."

"Would he be in the London office, then? He said he was just promoted to partner and is transferring there."

I hear a flurry of keystrokes. Then resignation in his voice. "I've checked the database and there's no one by the name of Shane Russo in any of our operations. And no new partners have been named in the last five years."

I thank him and hang up. "Are you sure the company was named Ingenious?" I ask Ben.

He looks puzzled. "Positive. There's a lot I don't remember about the last week or so, but I'm sure about Ingenious. That's the company he said was going to back my offer to buy Paragon. It's not something I'd forget."

"I recovered a clip where Shane tells you he 'took care of it' and 'no one has to know.' What did he take care of for you?"

"It's complicated." Ben closes his eyes and rests his head on the back of the couch. "And you're not going to like hearing it."

"What is it?"

He blows out a breath. "The morning I went to Rebecca's apartment to return her purse, I noticed a Montblanc chronograph watch alongside the wine bottle and wineglasses on the counter. It's got a very distinctive look to it and I thought I'd seen it somewhere before. So when I was on my way to the airport the next morning, I called Shane and told him that I dropped off Rebecca's purse, but I didn't find her anywhere in the apartment. That's when I realized the watch belonged to him. I remembered him wearing it the night before. And that meant he and Rebecca were . . . back together."

"*Back together?* But he and Diane . . ."

He sucks in a harsh breath. "He'd been having an on-again, off-again affair with Rebecca for years. When we started the deal for Paragon, he'd promised me it was over between them. But when I realized it was *his* watch at her apartment early in the morning, I called him out on it. I told him he had to knock it off with Rebecca because his affair was going to blow up the deal I was trying to resurrect."

"Was the watch his?"

"He denied it. Told me there are lots of guys with watches like that. But I remembered his had a big scratch on the crystal, just like this one did. I told him not to bullshit me anymore, I knew the watch was his. And if he didn't stop screwing around with Rebecca, I was going to tell Diane and cut him out of the deal, if there ever was one."

"What did he say?"

"At first he was really calm. He begged me to keep his secret. Said I owed it to him after all the years we'd been friends. When I told him I *wasn't* going to keep his secret, he told me to eff off and hung up on me."

"So when he told you on Saturday he 'took care of it,' he meant . . ."

"He meant that he broke it off with Rebecca." He thinks about that for a moment. "But that's kind of impossible, right? Because by then Rebecca was already dead."

CHAPTER
FORTY-ONE

How well did we know Shane Russo? He'd come back into our lives nine months ago, but it'd been nearly two decades since we'd all been in college together. He'd told us that he was an executive in finance earning millions. And we'd believed him.

"Did he even live on Acacia like he said he did?" I ask. "I mean, we never went there because they were always in the midst of renovation."

"Or he said they were."

There's no Wi-Fi, so I use my phone to search up one of those sites that allows you to type in a homeowner's name and see what properties they own. When I type in "Shane Russo," it returns "0 properties."

I look up the address where they supposedly live on Acacia in Brentwood, and the current homeowners since its purchase ten years ago are listed as Andrew and Kelly Moore.

Was anything Shane Russo told us about himself true?

When I finally ask the question we're both thinking, my voice sounds distant, hollow. "Could Shane have killed Rebecca?"

Ben sucks in a deep breath before he speaks. "We know he was in her apartment that night. And he was the last person to see her alive." His tone is raw, uneven. "And earlier that night when she came in wearing that engagement ring, he wasn't just jealous. He was furious. And stoned out of his mind . . ."

Everything starts to come into focus. It feels like looking through a telescope and adjusting the lens until an indistinguishable blob in the sky sharpens so you see what it actually is. "So for the moment, let's go with the theory that Shane killed Rebecca. In a fit of anger or rage, maybe. Or it could've been an accident. We don't know. And when you confronted him about the watch the next day—"

"That was the only evidence connecting him to her murder. And *I* was the only one that knew it was his. All I had to do was tell police and he'd become the prime suspect." His voice is a raspy whisper. "So that's why he poisoned me. Because if I told anyone about his watch being at the crime scene, he'd lose—"

"Everything," I say, finishing his sentence. "But how could he poison you? Travis says there's no way the poison could've gotten into your lunch at the Parkway Bistro that afternoon."

He lifts a water bottle off the floor and stares at it as he turns it in his hands, as if the answers might be written there. "If Shane is behind it, then it didn't happen at the Parkway Bistro. Maybe it happened when Shane came over Saturday afternoon. He brought me a drink—a hangover cure from some nearby juice place. It's the kind of stuff he was always bringing me, so I didn't think anything of it. Only this one had charcoal and some other crap in it so it tasted horrible."

"Which covered up the bitter taste of the belladonna."

His voice is weary, exhausted. "And when the poisoning didn't work, he sent someone to . . . make sure I could never tell police what I knew about the night Rebecca was murdered. If we're right, then Rebecca's father, Gary Stanton, might not be behind any of this. All of this is Shane's doing. He's the one who poisoned me, who hired people to kill me, who planted the murder weapon . . ."

Dazed by Shane's betrayal, I feel a sudden rush of nausea. It's hard to grasp that someone who murdered Rebecca and then tried to kill Ben was ever our friend.

But what sickens me most is all his visits after Ben went missing. Under the guise of our friendship, he came with food and comforting words, but in truth he'd only been there to get information about Ben's whereabouts and the security-system recordings. And to tell me lies about Ben.

Ben looks crushed. "What are we saying? This is *Shane* we're talking about. In college, he was almost like a brother to me. All those hours we spent together, figuring out which restaurants to buy, hammering out business plans, crossing the country checking them out, hanging out over a few beers. I had no idea . . ."

I pull up Shane's profile photo on Facebook. He's standing by the Bridge of Sighs in Venice, dressed in a bright-white polo and tan slacks, with his hands in the air. His broad smile says he has the whole world in his hands. Yet when I look at his brown eyes, I think I can sense that he's hiding a secret. Is it simply because I know that he is?

And there's something else. A distinctive watch on his wrist. I zoom in on the photo and point it out to Ben.

He nods and closes his eyes, as if willing all of this to go away. When he finally speaks, there's a quality to his voice that I can't pinpoint. Sadness. Betrayal. "All we really know about him was what he told us. Remember how he went on and on about how much money he was spending to redo his five-million-dollar house? Over a million, right?"

"And he was always talking about all the places he was going. Prague last month. And the month before, Dubai."

"And what about that African safari he went on last spring where he said he hung out with that James Bond actor, what's his name?"

"Daniel Craig. He was pretending to be someone he *wanted* to be. A rich, successful businessman . . . a partner in a major international investment firm. But none of that was true."

We sit there for a long moment, the weight of our discovery stifling us both. My head is swimming, trying to come up with a plan. What to do next. Then I'm suddenly aware that Ben is looking at me.

"You know what I'm thinking?" he asks, meeting my gaze.

"That we're *really* bad at choosing our friends?" I say, trying to lighten the mood.

"That too," he says, smiling. "I was thinking that while you and I have been figuring all this out, I realize how smart and practical and beautiful you are. How lucky I am to create a life with you."

His eyes search my face. I'm not used to compliments, especially from Ben, so I'm taken by surprise. And momentarily speechless.

"After everything I've been through, I can't take anything for granted," he continues. "So if it's okay with you, I'm not going to keep quiet when I notice things I love about you."

Notice things I love about you.

My heart leaps at what he says. I can't seem to catch my breath. Then my eyes meet his, but I don't know how to respond. Everything around us—even my fear—fades away, and suddenly it feels like we're the only two people in the world, discovering each other for the first time. He drops his gaze to my lips, and I'm sure this time he's going to kiss me.

He leans in, but his lips linger on mine for only a moment.

"I'm happy you're here," he says, his voice caressing me. I inhale a short breath, surprised at the effect that the brief kiss has on me.

I close my eyes for a few fluttery heartbeats, then lean in to kiss him again, allowing myself to dissolve into the feelings this kiss awakens in me until reality inevitably comes roaring back.

———

A few minutes later, Ben is back at the window, scanning the area around the cabin.

"We should get you to a hospital," I say, noticing the blood seeping through the new bandage I'd applied.

"So they can fix me up and then arrest me? We need *proof* that Shane framed me. We don't have that."

"Maybe there's something more on the footage?"

As he sits back down beside me, I zip through more clips, starting with ones dated the night Ben was shot. Tuesday night. There's so much footage to review that we start watching them at double speed, which is mind-numbing after a while. Long minutes later, I finally find a clip of Zack arriving home around nine thirty, just like he said he did. He unlocks the door, tilts his head to the side with a confused expression, and looks at the alarm box.

A chill races through me. I explain to Ben how Zack had set the alarm that night, but when he came home it was off. "That makes sense now. Shane had disarmed it using the security code you gave him. But when Zack came home, he *was still in the house.* That explains the footprints in the tub in the guest bathroom. Once Zack got home, leaving through the bathroom window was the only way Shane could get out undetected."

I scan through several other clips from Tuesday night where nothing interesting is happening, until I finally find one that sends another cold blast up my spine.

In this thirty-second clip, Shane enters our bedroom, crosses the room, opens the door to Ben's closet, then quickly places something in the pocket of one of Ben's sport jackets. I rewind the action and but whatever he places in the pocket is small and it's hard to tell what it is.

Ben leans forward and his eyes widen. "Are we seeing this right?"

"It could be the photo the FBI says was taken from Rebecca's apartment. I mean, what else could it be?" I sit up straight. "There's something not right about this. Shane *knew* we had a security-camera system.

He knew the cameras were recording round-the-clock. Why would he walk around the house with the lights on and plant evidence? That seems like the stupidest thing he could do."

I scan through the clips from that evening at double speed until I see Shane again. This time he's walking through the doorway of my office and heading to my desk. The clip shuts off.

"Unless . . . ," I say. "Unless he knew he was going to erase it all anyway. Remember when you and Zack erased the security system? Well, that internal delete function does a crappy job of deleting the data. But when I tried to recover it later, it was obvious that someone had run a more powerful scrub utility to wipe the drive clean. Maybe *that's what Shane is doing in my office.*"

Ben rubs his face, his eyes heavy from the hurt and betrayal.

"When I told him I had recovered most of the data, he knew I'd find proof that he had planted the evidence. That's why he lured me out of the house by pretending to be you with our secret code. He needed to make sure no one ever saw what was on this DVR."

Ben is quiet for a long moment and when he speaks, his voice is strained. "Shane knew about our coded messages. Back in college, he was always teasing me about our secret code. Thought it was super geeky."

"It *is* super geeky," I say with pride. "But he didn't know Klingon, because when I texted back in Klingon, he didn't answer."

He turns to face me, renewed energy in his eyes. "Besides us, how many people in the world do you think *actually* know how to read and write in Klingon?"

I smile. "We might be surprised. I'll bet there are a lot of people like us."

"Not like us," he says softly. "No one is like us."

Our eyes do a little dance, then he wraps me in his arms and kisses me gently like he's discovering me for the first time. The second kiss is strong, as if he's afraid I might be a dream. That I might slip away. I feel the coarse heat of his beard and grow dizzy, dissolving into his smell. Something in my heart unfurls then, and the kiss—he—becomes my whole universe.

My phone chirps and a text flashes across the screen. I ignore it, lost in our slow, almost wondrous kiss, the world around us fading into oblivion. Then another text insists.

It's from Rachel, so I read it aloud: *Are you okay?!?*

Then another: *All is good here. Zack and I are heading out Christmas shopping. And then maybe gorge on the cookies we made. When will you be back?!*

Then another: *Shane came by early this morning. After your last conversation with him, he's really worried about you.*

Then another text swoops across the screen: *You are okay, right?!* This one is followed by a string of heart emojis.

Then finally: *I hope it's okay that I told him where you are.*

CHAPTER
FORTY-TWO

"If we're right about Shane . . ." I hear the tremor in my voice and it scares me even more.

"Let's get out of here," he says, finishing my sentence.

I grasp his hand, trying to hold on to the feeling, the intimacy, of the moment before. "You don't think he'd—"

"Come here himself? No way. But did he send someone? Probably. That could be why you thought you saw someone in the bushes."

"We should go." I hear the panic in my voice.

I help him off the couch and he leans some of his weight on my shoulder.

"Do you think you can make it to the car? It's down the road a bit."

He draws a deep breath. "No, but I'm sure as hell going to do it anyway."

I grab the gun and grip it tightly. Ben's able to walk/hobble easier than I expect, but getting down the five wooden steps is particularly hard on him, and it takes us a half minute to navigate them. "I'm holding things up, aren't I?"

"You're fine. Everything's fine." If I keep saying that, maybe it'll be true.

I place my hand on his back, and I'm aware of his body beneath my fingertips and the way his hand feels on my shoulder. It's at least two hundred feet through dirt and leaves, and he makes me laugh when he compares his walking skills to an alien on *Star Trek* who had trouble on Earth because her planet had very low gravity. I'm sure he has no idea the effect he has on me, but even in the worst of situations, Ben has an uncanny ability to make me smile and is the only person on the planet who can make my entire body laugh.

I'm aware of the wild pounding of my heart and our loud, heavy breaths as we race to the car, stopping and starting like two people in one of those potato-sack races. And I'm aware of his fingers, entwined in mine, a feeling that is at once familiar but is suddenly kindled with possibility. The warm sensation is the same, yet somehow I am changed.

But our smiles disappear the moment we reach the car.

All of the tires have been slashed.

———

My first instinct is to call 911 and get police here. Fast. As Ben leans against the car, holding the gun, I dial. With scorching fear in my voice, I tell the dispatcher my name, that my husband's been shot, and I've seen someone hiding in the bushes.

"What is their description?" she asks.

"I can't see. Hurry, please."

Giving her the location is pretty complicated. The cabins don't have addresses, of course, and they're only reachable by dirt roads that might have names or numbers, but I don't know them. I open the Compass app on my phone, and with a wobble in my voice, I read off the coordinates on the bottom of the screen.

She dispatches a patrol car but can't tell me exactly when they'll get here because the roads are slow going and one lane in places. When

I press her for a more definitive arrival time, she says firmly, "Ma'am, hang tight and get inside. We'll be there as soon as we can."

"Let's get back to the cabin," Ben says. He's been scanning the area, but the fact that he hasn't seen anything seems to be making him even more nervous.

Then a shot ruptures the silence, and a bullet whizzes past his head, barely missing him. My heart rate spikes and we both drop to the ground, ducking behind the car. Terror shoots through me like a jolt of electricity. I want to scream, but my throat is completely closed.

As the sound of the bullet blast echoes across the valley, Ben motions to a wide strip of land across the road near the indigo bushes. "Over there," he whispers.

Seconds tick by and our ears become hypersensitive, listening for the slightest movement.

We hear something—a click, or is it a twig snapping?—and freeze, straining to hear. My breathing is shallow, even my own exhale seems like it's too loud.

"Should we try to get away in the car?" I whisper.

He shakes his head. "Too many windows."

I scan the area for a safer place to hide—a boulder, a large tree, anything. *There is nowhere to go.*

Ben grabs my hand and squeezes it. Fear surges in his eyes. Then he whispers something I don't expect. "I got this."

He takes the gun from me, presses a quick kiss to my lips, then crawls to the rear of the car and slides on his stomach, peering around the back wheel. Time slows as he waits there, eyes trained across the road, and hands rigidly gripping the gun, his finger a fraction above the trigger. Watching.

"I see someone," he whispers.

A cold stone forms in my chest. It could be at least another thirty minutes before police arrive. With trembling hands, I dial 911 again and whisper into the receiver.

"This is Sarah Mayfield again. I called a few minutes ago." I draw a deep breath and try to slow the trembling in my chest. "There's now an active shooter here."

She asks a series of questions, but they come at me like white noise. My heart is pounding so hard in my ears that, even though the dispatcher has a commanding voice, I can barely hear her.

As if I'm watching in slow motion, I see Ben pull the trigger. The shot shatters the silence and is quickly returned by whoever is across the road. But their shot is a little off target, a few feet from the car.

A line of sweat snakes down the side of Ben's face. "Need to keep them where they are until police can get here," he whispers.

How long can he keep this up?

There's no way to know if there's more than one gunman or how much ammunition they have. But the relative accuracy of their shots makes me think they have some serious skills that Ben, who's never shot a gun, cannot match.

Then I hear the rumbling of a car engine and the crunch of tires on the dirt road. Is it too much to hope that police have arrived?

I crane my neck to see what's coming up the road. This area is so remote that the last time we were here, we didn't see a single vehicle for three entire days.

I squint into the bright light and see it's a white van and there are no flashing lights. My stomach drops. Is it Shane?

Then the van comes into better view. It's the Channel Eleven news van.

———

It heads up the road toward us, its cheery, multicolored Channel Eleven logo looking completely out of place, given the situation.

Kate Bradley is several hours early for my interview with her.

My hands fumble to find her number in my contacts and I press it. She answers on the first ring.

"I know I'm early but which cabin—"

"Stay back! There's a shooter here," I interrupt. "We're behind the blue car on the road ahead of you."

"Okay," she says so calmly that I'm sure she hasn't heard me. "Josh, call 911," she says to someone in the van. "Sarah, we're going to pull up behind you and you're going to jump in the van."

"It's not safe. He's already shot at us once."

"Okay." Her voice is steady, as though I've just told her where to park, not that she's in the line of fire. "We're coming anyway. Be ready."

Ben turns his head to look at me, trying to understand who I'm talking to. "Channel Eleven," I whisper. "They're going to help."

The news van pulls up and the side door opens.

"Let's go," I whisper, then scurry through the dry leaves and sand to the van door. Prickly heat races up my neck as I scramble inside, then turn to help Ben.

He's not there.

I crane my neck out the door and see he's still on his stomach, peering around the back wheel of our car, aiming the gun across the road. But more to the right than he was before.

"Ben," I say, but the sound barely escapes my throat.

He doesn't move. *Why isn't he getting into the van?*

"Ben," I try again.

Suddenly he pulls on the trigger, and another shot echoes across the desert floor. Then, using his elbows to propel him, he crawls army-style with surprising speed toward the door.

"Stay down," he calls out to me.

Two more shots ring out, but I can't tell where they're coming from or where they're headed.

When he reaches the van, I stretch out my arms to help him in, certain his injured leg will make the eighteen-inch climb near impossible. But in one swift move, Ben pushes up and lifts himself into the van.

As the driver slams the accelerator to the floor, I fling the door shut. We hear another gunshot blast behind us, but the van keeps gaining speed as we race down the road.

———

The buzzing panic makes it hard to concentrate. My hands are tingling and my fingers have gone numb with anxiety. I focus on taking two long, deep breaths.

The Channel Eleven driver, a twentysomething with curly blond hair, is talking quickly on the phone as he steers us around rocks and dips in the bumpy, winding road. I think he's talking to 911 because he's describing what just happened to us.

"Thank you," I say to Kate.

But she's not looking at me; she's looking at Ben. Her voice is incredulous. "Ben . . . Mayfield?"

He nods and turns his head to look through the back window. "Are we being followed?"

"So far, no," Kate says, checking her side view mirror. "The only car we saw on the way up here was about a half mile back. If that's your gunman's car, he's got a long sprint ahead of him before he can follow us."

Kate doesn't take her eyes off of Ben. And the gun in his hand. "You both are going to explain what happened back there in a minute. But do you mind, um, unloading the gun?"

Though she sounds easygoing, I know this isn't a casual request. The way she's looking at him, it's clear she doesn't see Ben Mayfield, my husband, but instead the man who murdered Rebecca Stanton.

She holds out her hand.

Ben unloads the gun's magazine and hands it to her.

Her eyes fall to Ben's injured leg. "Looks like we should get you to a hospital. And get some help from the police."

Ben shakes his head. "No hospital or police. All they're going to see is that their prime suspect in Rebecca Stanton's murder is alive."

Kate frowns. "Actually, that's what I see, too. I helped you out back there, but I want to be clear—we won't be harboring a fugitive."

At those words, the driver stops talking to the 911 operator and whips his head around to look at Ben.

Ben meets Kate's gaze. "I didn't do it." There's a quiet confidence in his words that rises above the rumble of the wheels on the dirt road. The words swirl around me, and even if I didn't already have proof or evidence, I'd sense they were true.

Kate doesn't hide her surprise. Or her skepticism. "The FBI has proof you did. Fingerprints. Eyewitness. Murder weapon found on your property."

My voice is breathy, on edge. "We've got proof that the evidence was planted. And we know who did it."

CHAPTER
FORTY-THREE

FBI agents Elizabeth Elliott and Samuel Nelson look like they're seeing a ghost. Whatever training they've been through to ensure they always appear unflappable and composed is failing them because their eyes widen and their mouths gape as if they can't believe what they're seeing.

Ben sits on the couch across from them in the living room, the lights from the Christmas tree playing across his face. He's showered and even though it's a chilly late afternoon, he's wearing shorts and a T-shirt so that he can show them the places where the bullets grazed his arm and thigh.

Next to him is Zack, who hasn't taken his eyes off Ben since he came into the room. It's as if he thinks that if he blinks, Ben might somehow disappear again. He's leaning his shoulder against Ben's, the beginnings of a smile lighting up his face.

Ben speaks slowly, explaining everything he remembers from the night Rebecca was murdered. He tells them about discovering Shane's watch in the apartment.

Elizabeth nods. She discloses to us that the watch was evidence the FBI found but never announced publicly. The fact that he knows about it is either going to incriminate him or help exonerate him.

I pull up a Facebook photo of Shane wearing that iconic watch. It doesn't prove the watch in Rebecca's apartment was Shane's, but I can tell from their supportive nods that they see where this is heading.

Ben is calm when he describes how he confronted Shane about the watch and threatened to tell his wife about the ongoing affair. But his voice shakes when he reveals how Shane later arrived with a drink that he suspects was laced with belladonna.

Then his face turns white as parchment as he recalls the harrowing night he was shot and his decision to hide out. He details the moment he realized he'd made a big mistake and the fear that overwhelmed him when he realized he was alone in the desert, seriously injured, without a car or any way to get help.

All of that seems to have the effect of laying out a compelling story for the FBI agents, but I can see that they are dubious. All of us, even scientists, are skeptical when we're confronted with a discovery that changes everything we thought we knew.

I bring out the clips from the DVR and explain how the drive had been erased but I'd used various utilities to recover the data. Then I show them what happened the night Ben went missing. The clip of the backyard security camera being blinded by bright light clearly intrigues them because they ask me to play it several times. But when Samuel sees Shane enter our bedroom and place something in Ben's sport coat, even he can't stop himself from saying what we're all thinking.

"Incredible," he whispers. "That's exactly where we found Rebecca Stanton's photo."

Elizabeth has a theory of her own: perhaps it was Shane who had called the FBI to report seeing the Stanton murder weapon in our backyard. The man provided enough detailed information about the gun that the FBI was able to get a search warrant because his description matched what the FBI already knew about the murder weapon.

He claimed to be our gardener, but the FBI was unable to track him down from the information he provided.

"We can see why Shane would think he needed to frame you for Rebecca's murder," Samuel says. "Because you were the only person who knew he'd been in her apartment that night."

"And once he failed to get rid of you," Elizabeth continues, "he knew the only way to save himself was to make it look like you did it."

They have a lot of questions after that. How did Shane get into our house? How did the DVR get erased? How had I recovered the clips?

We take turns answering each of them, and as Ben tells how Shane has known the Stanton family since childhood, my eyes briefly catch his across the room. Even under the intense and unrelenting scrutiny of the FBI's questions, I feel a jolt of electricity every time I look at him.

"I wouldn't be here talking to either of you today if it weren't for Sarah," Ben tells the agents. "I owe it all to her."

My eyes meet his and a soft smile sweeps across his face. I look into his eyes, always my favorite part of him, and all the things we've experienced together, created together, rush over me.

As unscientific as it sounds, something shifts in the atmosphere—a spark of some kind—and suddenly I am changed, it seems. Exhilarated.

That's when I realize I'm no longer the Trojan asteroid—orbiting around him yet unseen. I'm no longer invisible.

He's spotted me with his telescope. And he's chosen me.

CHAPTER
FORTY-FOUR

It's Christmas morning and I've hidden the Wedding Santa in a place so difficult I'm sure Ben will never find it. It's deep in the tree, accessible only if he moves aside a bulky wooden Planet Earth and a goofy ornament of a Christmas Elf in a rowboat fishing with a candy cane. And for the first time, I've slung a silky bag over Santa's shoulder, filled with a surprise for Ben.

But he has no trouble finding the Wedding Santa, extracting it from the tree in under two minutes. "Found it!" He holds it up in triumph.

He digs into Santa's bag and pulls out seven vintage DVDs. With an expression of complete confusion, he flips through them. "Seven sci-fi movies," he says slowly. "Really bad, bordering on terrible . . . maybe worst-ever-made sci-fi movies."

He looks at me, hoping for an explanation, but all I do is nod at him, as if to say, "Figure it out."

He scans through the stack again, then notices that I've highlighted, in neon yellow, the first letter of each title. "*Invasion of the Saucer Men, Mars Invaders, Space Master B-7 . . .*"

He speeds through the stack, skimming the titles. "*Outer Space Strangers . . . Red Planet Mars . . . Riders to Neptune . . . Year of the Space Creatures.*"

His eyes light up as he realizes what they spell out.

Our gazes lock. "I'm sorry," I say softly. "I was wrong about us. We are not broken. Let's begin again."

He leans in for a kiss, smelling of Old Spice. I feel a rush as his hands move up my body to cup my face.

My cell phone dings, alerting me to a text. I ignore it, losing myself in his kiss, which has grown from gentle to hot in 3.14 seconds.

When my phone dings again, I reluctantly break off the kiss and glance at the screen.

"It's Detective Dawson," I say. "He's out front."

Ben heads to the door and even though he only opens it briefly to let in the detective, flashes go off and there's an immediate hubbub of reporters shouting questions from the street. He closes the door swiftly and locks it, hushing the sounds.

"Ben Mayfield," he says, extending his hand.

Detective Dawson stares at him. No doubt he already knew that Ben was alive, but that doesn't seem to make it any less shocking to come face-to-face with him.

"Detective James . . . Dawson, LAPD," he says, stumbling through his introduction. "A lot of reporters out there," he says, making small talk, but it's obvious that he's flustered, probably still absorbing the reality that Ben is standing in front of him. "You'd think this would've died down already."

After her help in the Anza-Borrego, we'd given the first interview to Kate Bradley, but now that Ben was no longer a suspect in Rebecca Stanton's murder, a new wave of reporters, vans, TV cameras, and people holding microphones camped out on our street, hoping to catch a glimpse—or a sound bite—from Ben. It only got worse when word leaked out that Ben and his Aurora partners had settled the lawsuit for an undisclosed sum. That sent another rush of reporters to our already choked street.

To the delight of my CIT bosses, some of the reporters—and not just the science journals—wrote about the Trojan asteroid discovery. And the ones who really did their research reported on the proposal for the new space telescope that CIT had just submitted with my name attached as principal investigator.

Detective Dawson turns to face Ben. "We've found the man who shot at you two in the Anza-Borrego. He tried to flee the scene, but the police officers responding to your 911 call were able to apprehend him."

"Who is he?"

He looks at his notepad. "His name is Kevin Gates. He's been part of the Stanton family operation for years, but that's not who he was working for. He was hired by Shane Russo. He also confessed to shooting you and Antonio Spear."

Although it's not a surprise, my skin still pricks with goosebumps hearing the proof that Shane had hired someone to kill Ben.

"Where is Shane?" Ben asks. "Have you found him?"

"He's not living in Brentwood, as he said he did. We found his apartment in Highland Park—that's where his car was registered, too. But he took off. And left his wife behind."

"Diane?"

"Yeah," he says. "She's pretty shaken up. Said Shane just left in the middle of the night and hasn't come back. Claims she didn't know anything about Rebecca Stanton, except that she was a childhood friend of Shane's."

The detective draws a deep breath. "The FBI has a whole team looking for him. And we'll keep looking until we find him."

"What about us? Are we still in danger?" I ask.

"Can't say for sure, but now that it's all over the news that Shane's the prime suspect in Rebecca's murder, he's got no real motivation to keep you quiet anymore."

True to form, the detective steps over to the Christmas tree and twists a Diamond Icicle between his fingers. "You know, it always struck me as kind of remarkable that with all the things happening to you, you still found time to decorate the tree like this." He lifts a cardboard snowman ornament Zack made in second grade. "Not just a few ornaments here and there . . . your family's story is up on this tree." He glances at Ben. "What made you do this in the middle of . . . everything?"

"The tree helped remind me what was important," Ben says, his eyes meeting mine across the room. "And I hoped it would help me win back something I'd lost."

———

The laws of physics work across our solar system, our galaxy, perhaps across the universe and time itself. We see Newton's law of gravity at work when we track the orbits of asteroids, comets, and planets. Light in our solar system shows the same chemical signature that we find in the most distant objects in the universe.

The fact that we see these physical laws in play throughout the cosmos makes the universe a simple, understandable place.

The human heart is not so easily understood. Sometimes what we're seeking is right in front of us, even if we can't see it. Sometimes we have to look beyond what's concrete and measurable and trust in what's unknowable.

Tonight the heavens are putting on a dazzling light show as Ben and I stand beneath a starry, glittery sky in the Anza-Borrego. It's a new moon, ushering in new beginnings, so the moon is invisible tonight. After shining brightly for two weeks, it seems to have vanished. But although we cannot see it, we know it's there, orbiting around as it has for millions of years.

Across the sky, I point my finger from the ladle of the Big Dipper to the North Star. It's an ordinary star, one we've both seen a thousand times, but tonight it seems to burn brighter in the inky-black sky.

"The light from the North Star began its voyage 680 years ago," I say. "Can you imagine that? The light we're seeing began its journey centuries before Galileo. Before Newton. Before even *Star Trek*."

Ben doesn't answer. Or laugh. Then I notice that he's not looking at the sky at all. He seems lost in thought, his eyes scanning the desert horizon.

"What's wrong? Do you see something?"

He shakes his head. I search his eyes, looking for a clue to what's on his mind.

"I was thinking about the time we came here. I proposed and gave you the infinity ring. Then we lost it."

I nod, not sure what he's getting at.

"Remember how we looked everywhere around here?" He sweeps his hand across the desert landscape. "And we ended up in that field of hedgehog cactus over there for what seemed like hours."

I laugh. "Only it was the wrong field of cactus, remember? And we both ended up covered in cactus barbs."

"All down our backs, too. Remember what happened after that?"

"No. Not really."

"We were so set on finding that infinity ring that we split up, figuring we could cover more ground that way."

"Only both of us got seriously lost," I say, remembering. "And it took us forever to find our way back."

There's a lightness in his eyes when he looks at me. "Proof that we're better together." He brings out a black velvet ring box from his pocket, and even though I already know what's inside, I feel a jolt of anticipation. As if it were only yesterday, I remember the gentle look in his eyes as he placed that ring on my finger and we both dreamed of the life we'd make together. We could not have envisioned the challenges of the next fifteen years, but neither could we imagine how our love would burn brighter.

He flips open the box and lifts out the infinity ring, its zoisite gemstones radiating a bright blue in the starlight.

"Come back to me, Sarah," he whispers. "We're better together."

ACKNOWLEDGMENTS

There is magic in the night sky. When I was ten, my parents took us camping in Southern Illinois, and I remember stepping out of my tent in the middle of the night and seeing the stars blazing high above me against an inky-blue sky. The longer I stared at the sparkling white dots rising above the towering oak trees, the more I noticed thousands and thousands of stars that had been invisible to me at home. As the Milky Way arched above me, I remember feeling a deep wonder and awe—a sense that I was connected to a world far more grand and mysterious than I had ever imagined.

My love for the stars has followed me into my adult life, where I've been an executive producer of an astronomy series for kids, *Ready Jet Go!*. While working on the series, I began to see that there is a profound connection between all we are discovering in the realm of the stars, and the universe of emotions within ourselves.

To me, the stars offer an ideal backdrop for a story about rediscovering a love that's been right in front of us all along. In the universe, as in love, so many of our most important discoveries are made when we look past what seems to be true, when we find ways around our blind spots, and when we discover new ways to see through the darkness into the light.

This novel would not have been possible without the patience and love from the stars in my life: my husband, Paul, and our children Ben,

Jake, and Lauren. I'm also forever thankful to friends who provided creative havens beneath the stars while I wrote this novel: Steve Monas and Maggie Megaw in beautiful Cape Cod and author Kes Trester at the glorious beach. And to Lake Union Publishing editor Christopher Werner, Krista Stroever, Laura Whittemore, and the entire editorial team—thank you for bringing out the best in this story and making it shine.

A special thank you to friend and astronomer Amy Mainzer at NASA's Jet Propulsion Laboratory, whose insights about our planet and the universe always fascinate me, and who showed me that art and science are truly complementary—both are seeking to observe and understand the world around us.

ABOUT THE AUTHOR

Dete Meserve is the award-winning, bestselling author of *Good Sam* and *Perfectly Good Crime*. When she's not writing, she is a film and television producer in Los Angeles and a partner and CEO of Wind Dancer Films. One of the series she's producing is *Ready Jet Go!*, an award-winning astronomy and earth science series watched by millions of kids and families on PBS and around the globe. Her grandmother worked at NASA's Manned Spacecraft Center (now Johnson Space Center) during the Mercury, Gemini, and Apollo missions. Meserve lives in Los Angeles with her husband and three children—and a very good cat that rules them all.